I0638779

Hit n Run

'Hit n Run' tells the story of what can happen when lives collide. An accident has spiralling consequences that change the life of the victim and everyone around him forever. This insightful book shows the world through the eyes of the two people closest to the victim, his wife and his friend. It is about how they face the moral and immoral dilemmas that life throws at them.

Simon and Jenny Coleridge are young, married and comfortable. Then, in a split second, their world shifts. Simon's accident doesn't just change him physically, it changes his relationships. Extrovert Simon's passion for exercise is challenged by life in a wheel chair. Sweet, quiet Jenny too has to face up to life-changing decisions as well as the trauma of trying to cope. What was it that Sir Walter Scott said? "Oh what a tangled web we weave, when first we practice to deceive."

PLEASE NOTE - CONTAINS ADULT CONTENT

First published in Great Britain in 2014 by U P Publications Ltd
145-157 St. John Street, LONDON EC1V 4PW

Cover design copyright © U P Publications 2014

Copyright © Brian F. Orgill 2014

Brian Orgill has asserted his moral rights

A CIP Catalogue record of this book is available from the British Library

Paper Back Edition
ISBN 978-1908135568

Kindle Edition
ISBN 978-1908135575

FIRST PAPERBACK EDITION

Published by U P Publications –
Printed in England by The Lightning Source Group

www.uppbooks.com
www.BrianOrgill.com

Hit n Run

Brian Orgill

2014
U P Publications Ltd

**This book is dedicated
to my wife Ann.**

Thank you for everything.

Laurie

1

Christ, slow down y' sod... I could only think it. Not a prayer of even gasping it out, never mind shouting it. Slap, slap went my running partner's hundred-quid Nikes, clearly audible in the warm evening air. I was also aware of the sound of my own cheap trainers, as my breath dragged at my tortured lungs. For the last few miles, somehow I had managed to hang on. Why the bloody hell was I doing this…again? Soon we'd be at the bottom of the hill. The soddin' hill! I can't do this... *Oh yes you bloody-well can,* I thought. The slap-slap was really beginning to irritate me. I could taste blood, my insides were burning, and my lungs were gasping for air, but he just ran: so smoothly. Slap, slap, bloody slap.

We were getting close to the bottom of the hill. The soddin' rotten HILL. It's not really that long, but it's so bloody steep. About halfway up I sensed 'the gap' opening up. He turned his head slightly. He was bloody smirking. I know he was …the bastard! The thought made me grit my teeth. The gap was opening up now. My lungs were just about bursting, I could still taste blood, and my legs had 'gone'.

"Bugger it... Oh bugger it!" I wheezed, and then he was away - like a bloody gazelle. My hero! Well that's what he'd like me to think. Why should I think it would be any different this time?

It's always the bloody same. He's just too good! He's so much better than me. He ran for the school, for Christ's sake. He's run at county level. Okay it was a few years ago. Even so! He's in a different class. I slowed to a walk. Gasping, still struggling to draw breath into my lungs. I looked up the hill into the fading light. He was almost there. As he reached the top – the very top – he turned slowly, retraced his steps and said, "You lazy bugger! ...Bloody 'ell, Laurie, you were almost there... Almost soddin' there man!"

We both stood for a few moments, taking in great big breaths of exquisite oxygen. Bent forward, hands on hips, heads slowly coming up, looking at each other. He started to grin – I didn't!

"What? ...What?" he said smugly.

"Get stuffed. Sod off!" I replied, but I couldn't stop a weak smile improving, just ever so slightly, the way I felt. Even though we turned back now, down the HILL for the last half-mile, back to Simon's luxurious bungalow with its luxurious shower, I would still feel knackered until we got to the warmth and comfort of *The Feathers*, and a glorious pint of Boddingtons' bitter.

2

Let me tell you a little bit about Simon and Jenny Coleridge …although I suppose it's only good manners to introduce myself first. I'm Laurence, Laurence Breakspeare. The few friends I have usually call me Laurie. Of course there's the occasional reference to 'The Bard', such as, "To have a pint, or not to have a pint, that is the question". This usually comes from Melanie, the landlady of *The Feathers,* and a more apt name would be hard to find: Melons …if you get my drift. She's what you might call 'a big girl', in the bosom department. Oh, and sometimes it's, "Alas poor Laurie". You know …as in Hamlet's "Alas poor Yoric". Sometimes I wish my name *was* Shakespeare.

Where was I? Oh, yes …the Coleridges. Simon? Well, he's tall …and he has a lot of very dark wavy hair, and a beard of which he is extremely proud. Yes, tall, dark, and handsome …that truly sums up our Simon. I suppose I became an instant friend of his in secondary school. He came to my rescue one day, when he saved me from getting a good hiding from one of the school bullies: something to do with the fact that I wore 'goggles' and was therefore a four-eyed twat. As if I didn't know this already! Simon was a big lad even then – getting on for six foot. He sort of took me under his wing after that, and looked after me until we finished school. He never called me friend though. It was always 'old mate'. "Now then old mate" or "How's it hanging old mate?" he would ask, in his soft Merseyside accent. We lost touch immediately after leaving school.

Simon had done well for himself. He went to 'tech' to study electronics. He then worked as an electrician for a local firm until starting his own company at the age of twenty-five. He met Jenny when he was about twenty-three. She was nineteen. She's a qualified pharmacist, and works for a local chemist. As I have already mentioned, they live in a rather luxurious bungalow. This is situated in a very desirable area of the Wirral. What you might call 'leafy suburbia'. I, incidentally, live in a two-up, two-down, in Whitby. Not the 'Bram Stoker' Whitby on the east coast, the one near Ellsmere Port – sort of 'Lowryesque'.

Simon drives a dark blue B.M.W. 3 series – whatever that means! The '3 series' bit I mean. Simon refers to it as HIS car, or his 'BEEMA'. He recently bought Jenny a brand-new V.W. Polo for her birthday. The old Clio she'd had and loved for years, finally gave up the ghost. I, incidentally, have a two-tone (blue and rust) Focus to which I sometimes whisper encouraging endearments, and to which I sometimes give a less encouraging kick.

Alcohol plays a rather large part in Simon's life. He usually drinks lager. He has a penchant for 'Stella'. Jenny rarely drinks alcohol, other than the occasional glass of wine.

With regard to sex, Simon is very active. Or so he tells me! So is Jenny, so Simon tells me! Me? Oh, yes I enjoy the occasional pint of bitter, and I did actually enjoy the odd bit of sex myself once upon a time, but then my wife buggered off with another bloke.

You might be forgiven if you think that I am just a little bit envious of Simon's success, and his handsome visage. Moi, envious? Not a bit of it. Why should I be envious, when I get so much satisfaction helping to create 'Simon's Empire' by working for him? Yes, I work for him. Truth be told, I actually work with him, but somehow it still feels like I work for him. And strange as it may seem, whilst I'm no oil-painting, and I don't possess Simon's good-looks or outgoing personality, the envy that I do feel, lies in a very different direction.

Envy? Oh it's far worse than that! I'm actually bloody crackers about his wife …Jenny. Absolutely crackers about her! She doesn't know of course – nor does he. If he did, he'd probably kill me. Christ knows what he'd do if he was privy to the sexual fantasies that I have about her. Jenny is absolutely gorgeous. Slim, pert, with ash-blonde hair, and as I say, absolutely bloody gorgeous! And her voice is music to my ears: soft and sensually hushed.

3

Yippee, it's match day! Yes it's Saturday, and the REDS are at home. Anfield here we come. Simon's supported Liverpool since he was a lad. He dragged me along to a match a few years ago, and somehow now I don't seem to be able to get out of it. Sometimes I actually find myself quite enjoying it. We usually go by mini-bus, from *The Feathers*: seven or eight of us. Safety in numbers I always think.

Not that we've ever actually had any bother at a match, but you never know. Simon, if confronted, does have a rather unfortunate habit of saying exactly what he thinks. If he's angry or upset about anything, his language can be colourful to say the least. Liberally peppered with 'effin' this or 'effin' that. Of course, I never swear! As we entered *The Feathers* Simon slipped a £20 note into my hand and said, "Get 'em in Laurie, I'm bustin' f'r a piss."

A bloody twenty! I bet he didn't even know what he'd given me. Mind, he'd soon notice if I didn't give him the change. I pushed my way to the bar. Before I could open my mouth, "To have a pint or not to have a pint, that is the question." Melanie the landlady grinned cheerily.

"Ooh, yes please Melanie." My eyes went directly to her very generous, bosom. "I'll have a pint of Boddies." I said as suggestively as I could. She takes it all in good part, bless her. "And a pint of 'Stella' for his 'lordship'," I added.

"Will he manage in there, by himself, or should I just pop in and give him a hand?" Melanie asked cheekily, glancing over in the direction of the 'Gents'. Such a sweet girl: Girl? She must be getting on for, what …Fifty? Too late, anyway dear, here he comes: Mr Bloody Wonderful!

"Cheers," said Simon, taking the Stella and downing nearly half of it in one gulp.

"Come on you Reds," shouted one of our motley crew from the far side of the bar. The chant of "Liverpoool …Liverpoool" was taken up by the rest of our group. Simon looked at his watch, "That bus here yet?" Beep-beep. Right on cue! Anfield here we come. "Oh by the way, got my change?"

The mini-bus entered the tunnel. Simon never failed to say it. "Christ, I hate these chuffin' tunnels. They give me the soddin' creeps." It's good to know that at least one thing, unsettles the indefatigable Simon.

"Are we 'avin' one before we go in?" enquired one of the 'lads'. We all looked to Simon for guidance on this most pressing of questions.

"Just time for a 'quickie' ", our leader informed us.

The Ball, was absolutely heaving; a mass of excited football fans. "Who's round is it?" asked one of the 'lads'.

'One of the lads'! …Phil? I think it's Phil. I suddenly realised that I didn't really know any of them at all. Oh, I knew some of them by name. But what did I actually know about them? What did I want to know? Nothing really! It was my fault, not theirs. I'm what you might call an anti-social sod, a sad git, an all-round miserable bastard.

"Here get that down y' neck, an' cheer up y' miserable git." Simon said, as he passed over a pint of bitter. I made an effort to look keen and 'up' for the game.

"Who's ale is it?" I asked. A perfectly reasonable question, surely.

"It's yours, y' prat," muttered one of our lot.

"Come on lads, get um' necked, we don't want t' miss the kick off," said he who must be obeyed. He then quickly drained his glass.

We pushed and shoved our way to our seats. Sitting down at a football match just didn't feel right, but of course we at Anfield know exactly why we were sitting down. The Hillsborough disaster!

The referee eventually blew his whistle signalling the end of a rather boring 'first-half': Arsenal 1 Liverpool 0.

"That soddin' Lucas; he's bloody useless. My missus could 'ave scored from the chances 'e's 'ad," one of our lot opined – Tony, I think? Simon glances over towards him and said,

"Oh, ye' fickle-faced football fan."

"That's bloody brilliant, that Simon, I've never 'eard that before," said Tony sarcastically.

"Well, no Tony, not since the last match day anyway," I said irritably. "Are we going for a pint before the game? Are we going for a curry after? Can I kiss your arse, Simon?" I continued. Well, for Christ's sake! They all looked at me as though I have gone completely 'mental'.

"Oo, handbags at forty paces luv," said Simon in a very camp manner. "He'll be wearing a Red and White scarf next... Bovril all round, is it?"

We all nodded in agreement.

All in all, I have to admit, it was a cracking game, and the result, you had to agree, was fair. Naturally, as we drove back the whole game was analysed and dissected. Liverpool V Arsenal is always likely to be a 'cracker'.

"Suarez ON ... Van Persie ONE," said one wag.

"LUCAS...ONE! ...'e's chuffin' great, that Lucas," shouted Simon. 2-1 to the Reds. Great stuff! The obligatory after-match kebab, and then we can get off home. Oh, great, that's something to look forward to: just me and the telly, and an early night. No change there then.

The 'lads' were dropped-off as required, en-route back to *The Feathers*. As we arrived at the pub, Simon looked around from 'his' seat beside the driver, and asked, "What a' y' doin' this evening?"

For no reason that made any sense, I looked at my watch. "Telly I suppose."

"Bloody 'ell Laurence, is that the best y' can do on a Saturday night? Come on you sad git; let's sink a few. Make a night of it. You never know y' could finish off by givin' Big Melanie one."

Oh, you are such a wit Simon, I thought, but I didn't waste my breath saying anything. I paid the mini-bus driver, and then followed Simon into *The Feathers*. I was given a short but blessed respite, while Simon went the bar. When he returned he thrust a drink into my hand. "Seriously, Laurie you should lighten-up… Get a life, man. You're not the first to have his wife bugger off with another man y' know. Just look around in here …there must be something that y' fancy… What about her?" he gestured towards a young blonde woman. "Christ I'd like to give her one myself. Nice lookin'…good body …what more could you ask for?" asked the leering Simon.

"She might be married. Probably is," I said.

"What's that got to do with anything? You only want to shag her for Christ's sake."

Do I, I wondered? *No I don't …I want to shag your wife, Simon.* I felt shock at my thinking the word shag. Was I blushing? I didn't want to shag Jenny. Of course not! I wanted to make love to her – and her to me!

"Come on, drink up. It's your round and for Christ's sake cheer up. You've gor' a face like a slapped arse," Simon passed me his empty glass.

'Stella?' I asked.'

"Of course, what else?" He looked at me as though I

was stupid.

"Here you are,' I smiled affectedly, as I returned from the bar.

"Bloody hell, what's brought that on? Our Mel' bin feelin' y' knob, 'as she?"

"Yes, an' she wants me to stick it between 'er tits later on," I came back at him. Oh, such laddish banter. Such bon-vivant. Jenny, oh bloody 'ell Jenny!

Glancing at my watch I was surprised to see that it was almost nine-thirty. Yes …might as well make a night of it.

What's Jenny up to tonight? Out with the girls?" I asked, as innocently as I could. Simon almost choked on his lager. "Girls …what girls? No, she'll be watching the telly, or listening to some of her c-d's. Pavarotti, or she's into that Russell Watson now. You know Jenny, not one for goin' out a lot."

How often do you suggest, that you both go out together? How often do you actually treat your wife as she – that lovely desirable woman, deserves to be treated, you rotten sod? I thought angrily.

"Answer me that," I said out loud. The Boddies was obviously beginning to take effect.

"What was that? I didn't catch it," Simon asked, putting his hand to his ear.

"Nothing …it's nothing …I'm going to get off, Simon. I've had enough," I said, feigning a yawn. *And enough of you for one day, my old mate,* I thought moodily.

"What do you want to do? Get a taxi, or kip at ours?" Simon offered.

"I'll phone a taxi. You don't mind do you?" I asked.

Bloody mind?

Why should he mind?

As long as he gets his 'leg-over', and that's something I definitely don't want to listen to, his bloody moans and groans, of sexual passion.

Taxi it is then!

4

Thursday evening and another jogging session was almost over. Simon hates it when I say, "We've been joggin'."

"We go runnin', not bloody joggin'," he would remind me grumpily.

"Nearly there old mate," Simon said, his breathing coming easily. *Bang on bloody cue! Never bloody fails! 'You condescending chuff.'* The thought went through my mind as we approached Simon's bungalow. We stood for a moment in the driveway.

I actually felt better tonight. Much better! I honestly thought he had to dig deeper than usual before he 'dropped me' on the HILL. So now a pleasant relaxing shower, and for 'afters', QUIZ NIGHT at THE FEATHERS. Yippee! I could hardly contain myself. Selling three-pin plugs and endless metres of cable nearly every day, going jogging, sorry running, and now quiz-night… Oh what an exciting life I lead.

We pulled off our trainers before entering the

kitchen – Simon's thinking, not Jenny's. He's the fussy one. She was the first thing I looked for. She wasn't there, but I could hear music coming from the lounge. Was she watching the telly, or perhaps she was listening to her classical stuff?

"Here get this down y' neck," Simon took a couple of cans of isotonic drink from the fridge, and thrust one in my direction. I took a deep slurp from the can.

"Ah, that's better," I said gratefully, waiting more in hope than expectation, for him to say something like, "You did much better to-night Laurie."

Instead, he simply said, "Go on, you go first," nodding in the direction of the shower and sauna-unit, that they have had fitted in addition to the bathroom (as one does, on The Wirral).

I stripped off my running kit and entered the shower. Soon I was luxuriating in the warmth of the water and the steam. My mind started to drift.

I knew exactly where it was drifting to. I knew that I should stop it. But, I couldn't stop it.

I didn't want to stop it ...I'm sitting in the sauna.

It's very hot!

The light is quite dim.

The smell of pine is very sensual.

Naturally I'm naked – and alone, but of course not for long.

Jenny enters the sauna, wrapped in a short, white towel. She stands close, with her back to me and then she drops the towel. I catch my breath as my eyes gaze down the length of her lovely back and then linger on her gorgeous bottom. My hands reach out to touch it.

She turns and sits down opposite me.

Perspiration runs in rivulets down her body – down between her perfectly formed breasts: down her belly, and down to that special place that I struggle to name.

Why do I struggle to name it? Why hasn't someone thought of a nice name for it? I mean …Vagina! I suppose it's Latin …something to do with virgins. Pussie, is horrible. I could never think of Jenny's 'what's it' by that name. And I could never use the C-word! I suppose fanny is about the best. I gradually realise that she is looking at me. She's looking straight at my rather big, and very erect penis. Cock? Prick? Knob? Love Handle? John Thomas? Whatever …she's looking straight at it and smiling. "Is that all for me?" she whispers as she rises, and…

Suddenly there was a loud banging on the shower-room door.

"A' you going t' be much longer in there? I'm gaggin' for a pint," Simon shouted. The harshness of his voice made me jump. I felt rather ashamed. *A cold shower old lad …that's what you need, as my old schoolmaster might have said.* I did turn the temperature down, but not too cold. I looked down at my limp cock. Ah, well, no problem there then. "Christ, I thought you'd gone down the plughole mate. I hope it was only water you were splashing about," he added as I came out.

"Simon, don't be so crude. Take no notice of him Laurence. He's just a mucky beggar."

I looked over to see the lovely Jenny, as she came into the kitchen. I was praying that I wasn't blushing.

As Simon went to shower, she asked, "coffee Laurence?"

"Please Jenny." I nodded and smiled. As she turned, opened the cupboard then reached up for the jar, my hand reached out mentally, and my fingers ran gently down her back.

"Go through into the lounge Laurence. I'll bring the coffee through in a minute," she said in that wonderful sensual voice.

We sat across from each other in the deep easy chairs: drinking coffee, making small talk. *Take your time Simon ...take all night if y' like.* Even though I felt guilty – really, so very guilty, I couldn't stop wanting her ...loving her. Loving her? Bloody hell! Do I? Is that what I feel? Love?

"Laurence, do you ever feel that you are in a rut? Y' know, doing the same things day after day, week after week."

Jenny brought me back from my reverie.

"Sorry, what? Oh, right ...well yes," I floundered. "I suppose I do sometimes – like most people do. Don't you?"

She looked right into my eyes; right into them and said, "Oh, yes Laurence, I do. I really do!"

"Why don't you come with us ...to *The Feathers* for the quiz? I bet you'd enjoy it."

I wanted to see her smile again. But she didn't smile, as she said, "No, I don't think so. I wouldn't want to cramp Simon's style. Anyway, he thinks I'm a bit of a handicap as far as quizzes go."

Before I could disagree she continued, "Tell me

something Laurence …what is it that's so special about *The Feathers* anyway? I mean it's not exactly the smartest of pubs is it?"

Caught off guard, I answered thoughtfully, "Well …it's a proper pub, not one of these blinkin' modern theme pubs."

"Right: nothing to do with the landlady's double d's then?" said Jenny, with raised eyebrows, and just a hint of a smile.

Stifling any expression, I simply replied, "I couldn't possibly comment."

5

As I think I mentioned before, after leaving school Simon and I went our separate ways. I didn't see anything of him for several years. Then, one Saturday morning in the summer of 97, whilst I was walking into town, I spotted something that stopped me in my tracks. A small corner shop that had been boarded up for some months was now freshly painted and a sign over the window, said 'COLERIDGE ELECTRICS'.

I had heard something on the grapevine about Simon going to the 'tech' to study electronics, so of course this set me thinking. I crossed the street and walked in. A chap with a dark beard was sitting behind the counter, reading a magazine. It looked like a 'gentleman's magazine' if you know what I mean. It wasn't until he glanced up and spoke, that I was absolutely sure that it was him.

"Good morning sir. Can I help you?" he said, quickly putting the magazine away. Then, with surprise, "Chuffin' 'ell! Now then, it's Laurence, isn't it? Laurence Breakspeare. Chuffin' 'ell!"

I grinned, "That's right. How are you, Simon?"

We then spent the next half-hour or so exchanging stories, filling in the years since we had last seen each other.

"So, what are you doing with yourself these days?" he asked.

"Not a lot. Just going down to the job centre once a week, trying to keep out of the wife's way," I replied. Simon looked me up and down, then he went quiet for a few moments.

"So you're out of work? And are you actually looking for a job?" Before I could answer he continued. "What do you know about electrical goods?" Again as I started to open my mouth, he continued. "I mean, you can tell an electric kettle from a toaster can't you? You can tell a microwave from a fridge. That only leaves plugs, sockets, cable and a few other odds and sods." I still hadn't managed to get a word in. "Look, I couldn't pay you a great deal, but I can make it worth your while getting out of bed. As I've told you I'm only just starting out, and I'm already finding it a bit too much on my own. I need somebody: you need a job ...so what do you say?"

I simply said, "Okay you're on."

That was about eleven or twelve years ago. Two or three years later as the business grew, we moved into bigger premises. Then just over twelve months ago we moved into one of the units on a new industrial estate. As Simon said at the time, it was a bit of a gamble, but thankfully, up to now it seems to be paying off. Well it's paying Simon and Jenny! There I go again; the green-eyed monster rears his ugly head. Truth be told I'm not that bothered. I'm ticking over. Admittedly, Simon keeps saying that I need a good kick up the arse. He's probably right …but for the time being I'll carry on being the martyr. Bully for me!

Right now I'm waiting for the kettle to boil. You should just see it. The flex is taped up, and the lid's cracked. I've told Simon, if I get a shock from it, I'll sue him for every penny he's got. I was run off my feet earlier on, but it's quietened down now. He's out on a call, a Mrs Johnston. The microwave she purchased from us isn't working properly. No doubt Super Simon will sort it for her.

"Put the kettle on please, will you Laurie?" Simon said as he entered the office. Bloody hell! I nearly fainted from shock. Please! Will you? That's not like Simon.

"Did you manage fix it?" I asked, in all innocence.

"Please Laurence. A man of my experience! Of course I fixed it," he replied with good humour, "and I'll tell you something else …if she calls again, I'm sending you! Y' know, those big houses on Grasmere Road? Long drive! Brand new 'Jag'. I ring the bell – those old-fashioned 'Avon Calling' chimes – she opens the door, and she's in her dressing gown. Christ, she must have been sixty if she was a day. Straight away the alarm bells are ringing… Through here Simon, she says, leading me into the kitchen."

It was at this point in Simon's narrative, that I struggled to stop myself from bursting into laughter, at his attempt to paint the scene by use of the high-pitched tones of a female impersonator.

"You will have to forgive the dressing gown; I've just come out of the shower. Would you like a drink? Tea, coffee, or perhaps something a bit stronger? An' she's got that look on her face. You know what I mean. Christ I've not been in the house two bloody minutes. Bloody hell Laurie …I wouldn't touch her with yours …I say no thanks, and go straight over to the microwave. I check it over. It's working fine. *Oh, she says …silly me. I can't have read the instructions properly.* She puts the instruction manual on the table in front of me, stands opposite me and honest to Christ Laurie, her soddin' dressing gown is gapin' open. She's obviously done it on purpose. I can see one of her tits hangin' down. Bloody great saggy thing. Then quick as a flash, she's around beside me pretendin' to be lookin' at the book. I tell you, I'm out of there, quick as you like. If she rings again you can soddin' well go."

"Thanks, Simon you're all heart," I grinned.

"You're very welcome old mate. Anyway, your need is greater than mine."

That was not a really typical day at work. It's not normally as exciting as that. But, as they say, it pays the rent and for the odd pint.

6

"Right, it's time we were off. Go on, I'll lock up. I'll pick you up at seven," said Simon, rattling the warehouse keys.

"What?" I replied, puzzled.

"Wednesday! Squash night," he said, sighing almost sympathetically.

"Oh, I don't know Simon, I thought I might stop in to wash my hair," I said, rather camply.

"Come on, sod that Laurence. You know how much I rely on your support. And, I've not played this chap before. They reckon he's a bit on the good side. Then I'll let you give me a thrashing at darts later on."

"Chuffin' *let* me!" I retorted.

Even with the Simons of this world, there is usually something that you can 'top' them with. For me it's darts. Oh don't get me wrong I'm not brilliant, but I'm not bad either. I used to play for *The Anchor* in the pub league, a couple of years back. And I have to admit, it did make me feel good putting one over on the usually smug Simon.

It was one minute to seven when he knocked loudly on the front door.

"When are you gunna' get that soddin' bell fixed? You're a right bloody example for an electrician."

"How often do I have to say it? I'm not an electrician! You're the organ-grinder. I'm just the monkey," I said, climbing into the car. Or into the 'BEEMA' as Simon usually called it. It was a mucky night having gone dark early and it was drizzling, but it was nice and warm in the car: that expensive smell of leather: stereo playing some 'pop' station ...nice and comfortable. I thought of my old Focus. Was I envious? No, of course not – as if!

"Good luck," I said, as he headed for the changing room. He stuck his thumbs up, and I made my way to the spectator's gallery.

His opponent was a slightly built chap and a good bit younger by the look of him. They warmed up for about five minutes, showing nothing. No clues, no emotion, dead-pan faced. Let battle commence. I could soon see that all was not well for Simon. He hadn't lost a match for some time ...but it looked as though he could lose this one. The other guy was too quick. He was like greased lightning. 'He's too young for you Simon old lad.' I thought. Simon lost by three games to one. Even the game that he won was a very close call.

Simon was very quiet. He just smiled wryly. "You win some, you lose some," he said eventually.

"You were a bit unlucky," I offered.

"Bollocks Laurence. He was just younger and better than me. I'd better stick to the darts from now on."

"Oh, yes …right. We'll see about that," I said as we approach *The Feathers*.

We entered the 'tap-room.' As luck had it the darts board was free. Simon ordered the drinks while I wiped the chalk from the scoreboard, and took my Schofields from my jacket pocket. Simon borrowed a set of darts from behind the bar.

"301?" I asked.

"Yes if you like – whatever," he replied rather moodily.

I actually found myself feeling a bit sorry for him. Should I be a bit easy on him? After all, he had just been hammered at squash, and I had to work with the chuff tomorrow …no, bugger that, he never takes it easy on me when we're out running. Anyway, to be fair, he wouldn't want it that way. After a couple of games, "Like taking candy from a baby," I boasted.

"Okay don't rub it in. That's enough of that. Let's go through to the lounge."

I nodded in agreement, "You get a table, an' I'll get the drinks." Bloody hell; listen to me dishing out the orders. Just because he was having a bad night, don't go getting too big for your boots Laurence. If he's gor' a 'cob on' in the morning, you'll be the one to pay.

Well surprise, surprise! When I brought the drinks over, Simon was sitting at a table beside two young women. I sat down, smiled, and quietly said, "Good evening."

"This is Laurence. He prefers Laurie though, don't you Laurence? I'm not best pleased with our Laurence. He's just thrashed me at darts, haven't you Laurence? Don't say anything about the squash Laurence."

Simon gave me a meaningful look, before he continued. "Suffice to say ladies, my spirits are at a very low ebb. I'm in desperate need of some T.L.C. I wonder, whether either of you dear sweet things, could do anything thing to lift my spirits?" As he said this he put the back of his hand against his brow, and smiled a 'little boy lost' smile. That's my boy! He's back on form. You can't keep Simon down for long.

"Laurence, this is Karen." Simon smiled at a very attractive brunette, who I took to be about thirty. She was obviously the one he fancied. He gave me a, 'hands off', sort of look. "And this is Harriet," he added, gesturing towards the other woman, but looking directly at me.

"Good evening ladies," I said, without a great deal of enthusiasm. After a moment or two, I took a furtive look in Harriet's direction. A bit plain, I thought. I glanced again. Actually no she wasn't, she was really rather nice-looking: early to mid thirties? I took a drink from my glass, and took another glance: darkish, medium length hair, and not too much make-up. She had the sort of figure that caught one's attention. Not plump, but certainly not skinny. As Simon went off to the bar an uneasy silence descended.

Suddenly Harriet said, "Simon says you're unattached."

Caught off guard, I didn't say anything for a

moment or two. I just thanked Simon under my breath. I took yet another look at her. She really was rather nice. *What's this Laurie, you old sod, are you fancying a bit? Getting 'horny' eh,* I couldn't help but wonder to myself. "Unattached? Well yes, I suppose I am." I felt a bit out of my depth. It was Simon that did the flirting …not me.

He returned with the drinks and announced, "I'm going to get off when I've drunk this, if you want a lift, Laurence."

Harriet looked me straight in the eyes and said, "I can drop you off if you like Laurie. I've got my car outside."

She bit her lip in that sexy way women sometimes do in men's fantasies. Simon looked at me with raised eyebrows, waiting for me to decline the lady's offer courteously.

"Thank you, Harriet, that's most kind. If you're sure it's not out of your way." To the best of my knowledge, Harriet hadn't a clue where I lived. I looked at Simon. He looked shocked. I looked pleased! I might even have had a smirk on my face.

"You get in the front, Laurence. Drop me off first will you Harriet," Karen said, more as an instruction with that *it'll leave you two free, to do whatever,* tone in her voice.

Getting into the car, I looked at Harriet and said, "Is that okay? After all, you've only met me tonight."

She smiled and simply said, "Where exactly is it you live Laurie?"

"Just off the old Chester road – I can show you, if

you're sure you don't mind?"

As it happened, it wasn't really that far out of her way. Ten minutes or so later we were saying 'goodnight' to Karen. Another ten minutes and we were at my place. I cleared my throat, "Here we are. I'm not sure, but is this where I'm supposed to say …would you like to come in for a coffee or something?" Before she could reply, I went on, "Only, I'm in a bit of a mess. Typical bachelor I'm afraid."

Even though was dark in the car, I could just about see Harriet's smile as she said, "That's okay, I should get off. You know, work in the morning." Then there was that few seconds when neither of us spoke – not sure what to say.

Then …"Well it's been nice meeting you."

"Yes, it has." Another moment or two of silence, then somehow we were closer.

Then we were touching: arms going around each other. And then a brief kiss: lips barely making contact. Then the proper kiss.

Passionate?

No, not really passionate.

But it was a long kiss.

A nice kiss.

I enjoyed it anyway, and I think she did. Well something must have been right, because she said she would like to see me again. Then she gave me her telephone number. "Phone me," she said, with a smile. I climbed out of the car, and she drove off into the night.

I climbed into bed, and soon 'dropped-off', but not before enjoying a mental replay.

I actually kissed a woman tonight. *Kissed* a woman!

When did I last kiss a woman?

It would have been Molly, just before she 'buggered off' with that shit of a – what was he? Oh, yes, he played guitar in a group.

Well he's welcome to her. Stuff her!

I've got Harriet now! Suddenly, I remembered Jenny.

Christ I'm such an arse. Jenny! Oh, hell! …Hang on a minute. *She's married, to the bloke you work for, f' Christ's sake. You've met someone who is at least willing to see you again. And you do fancy her, don't you?* Yes I did; I couldn't deny that.

7

"Good morning, you randy old sod," Simon called, as soon as he came into the warehouse. "Did you get your end away? Was she gaggin' for it, eh ...you randy old git?" Even as I opened my mouth to answer, Simon blundered on. "Mind you, I'm bloody glad I didn't bother with that Karen one. Me and Jenny got it together last night, big time!" *Here we go, I thought...all the gory details*. "Three times Laurence. Three bloody times! Jesus, when she's in the mood she nearly soddin' cripples me."

Simon you big-headed shit, I don't want to soddin' know. I don't want to hear it, you big-headed sod. With these thoughts banging away in my head, I turned towards the office. "Shall I put the kettle on?" I said, doing my best to convey to him that I wasn't really interested in his sexual exploits. Especially not this morning.

We sat quietly, drinking our coffee.

"Well, did you?' he asked. "Give 'er one?"

"No, of course not. It wasn't like that. We just had a bit of a snog. I did get her telephone number though, so I might be seeing her again."

"Right, good for you old mate. You go for it," Simon nodded. "It's about bloody time."

A couple of evenings later I was sitting watching telly, when the phone rang. "Hello, it's Harriet. I'm just ringing to say how much I enjoyed the other evening."

"Oh, hi Harriet, yes it was very enjoyable." I floundered. "I was going to phone you tomorrow." Even as I said the words, I wondered if that was true.

"Were you? Honestly? It's alright if you've been having second thoughts. I will understand," she said quietly.

"No, honestly, I was going to ring." Another lie? "I really would like to see you again," I said. This time, I realised that I wasn't lying. Yes, I really would like to see her again.

"That's good, because I'd like to see you too. Are you doing anything on Saturday? Would you like to come over for your tea?"

I thought about it for a moment or two. The Reds would away to West Ham; so we wouldn't be going to the football. Sometimes on a Saturday I'd go jogging with Simon but how often do I get asked to tea by a young lady?

Simon will just have to jog on his own.

"Yes, that would be really nice. I'll bring some wine shall I? What do you like? Red or white?' I asked, trying to sound casual, as though I did this sort of thing all the time.

"Oh, anything ...perhaps white would be best. Will about six o'clock be okay? Then perhaps later, we could go out somewhere if you like. Maybe to a cinema," she suggested.

"Yes, sounds fine to me. See you at six on Saturday then," I said, waiting to see whether she would prolong the conversation.

But no, just, "Okay ...bye for now, Laurie," she said, but in the sort of way that made me want Saturday to come as quickly as possible.

I go into work most Saturday mornings, just 'til about twelve. His 'lordship' doesn't come in unless there is something urgent or pressing. This particular Saturday morning Simon did drop by.

"Just thought I'd collect the gear I need for that rewiring job over at Heswall on Monday. It'll give me a good early start." We got everything together, and loaded it into the boot of the B.M.W. "See you later then," he said.

I looked at him with a bemused expression. He just shook his head and said, "Runnin'? Our Saturday run? Honestly, your memory is getting' worse."

"Oh right ...runnin'! No, sorry I can't. I'm doing something," I stammered.

"Doing something!" he said, looking as if to say, what could you be doing that was more important, than coming out running with your best friend.

"Actually, I'm seeing Harriet. I'm going round to hers for tea." I couldn't help a rather self-satisfied smile. He seemed slightly taken aback.

"Bloody 'ell Laurence. 'avin' a shag is one thing, but goin' f' y' tea, that's well dodgy old mate. You want to be careful. She'll 'ave you washing the chuffin' pots afterwards."

"You're just bloody jealous," I grinned, wanting him to be.

"Bollocks! Jealous, when I've got Jenny? Anyway, I'm gunna' get off. See you on Monday then. Give 'er one for me," he said, as he walked out to the car. "An' don't forget, get there a few minutes late. Make her sweat. There's more than one way t' make a woman sweat Laurie old mate," he added with a lecherous grin.

I fidgeted my way through the afternoon. I couldn't settle to watch the telly; couldn't concentrate on anything at all. Truth was, I felt a bit nervous about going to Harriet's for tea. I even thought about crying off ...but I told myself not be so bloody stupid. I showered and changed. Three times, I changed my clothes. I finished up wearing jeans and a sweatshirt, after discarding a suit, with shirt and tie.

I was due to arrive at Harriet's at about six-o-clock. She lived about fifteen minutes' drive away. I was ready at four-thirty! It started to rain just as I was getting into the car. I pulled up outside Harriet's semi in Neston, at five-fifty. So much, for taking Simon's advice. It was still raining as I walked quickly to the front door. I was just about to ring the bell when the door opened.

"Come on in before you get wet through. What awful weather. Here, let me take your coat," she greeted me with a smile. "Come on through into the lounge." Then she gestured to me to sit in an easy chair.

She looked really lovely, and even though she wasn't exactly 'dressed up to the nines', I could see that she had made more of an effort than I had. I should have stuck with the suit, I thought to myself.

"You look lovely," I said, rather lamely. "I feel a bit scruffy now."

"Thank you Laurie. You're very kind. Anyway, don't be silly. You look very nice …very handsome! Tea will be about ten minutes. I hope you like pasta. I know you sportsmen need a lot of pasta. Your friend – Simon, was it? He was telling Karen and I, what a good runner you are, and how he struggles to keep up with you."

The meal was absolutely delicious. At one point, she started to pour a second glass of wine for me. I held my hand up to stop her. "Better not, got t' drive home."

"Oh, that's a shame." She paused. Then looking at the settee, said, "You're not working to-morrow, are you? Could you manage to sleep on there? I mean I don't want you to get the wrong idea, but it would be a shame if you couldn't have a few glasses of wine; especially as you brought it."

"Well yes, I think I could sleep on there …if you're sure."

Even as I was saying it, I couldn't help but wonder if that was where I would actually finish up sleeping.

As we washed the pots together, I thanked Harriet for a lovely meal. She peered through the curtains and said, "It's still raining. Are you bothered about the pictures, or would you rather stay in? We can watch television, or something. I've got some beer in the fridge. It is Boddingtons you like, isn't it?"

Was it my imagination? Or was I just hoping there was something in the way she said, *or something.* "Staying in sounds a good idea t' me …and yes Boddingtons is fine, thanks."

Pots washed and dried, Harriet said, "You go and sit down in the lounge. I'll just put these away. Turn the television on if you want."

I really started to feel that things were going the way they were supposed to do, when Harriet joined me on the settee. We had both had just enough alcohol to, shall I say, loosen our inhibitions. It seemed the most natural thing, as we embraced and kissed each other. Moments later, as my hand came from her back and quickly to one of her breasts, she took hold of my fingers and whispered, "I don't think either of us is really bothered about the telly, are we?"

She switched off the TV then, taking my hand, led me through the door towards the stairs. I could say that she led me screaming and kicking. Or I could say something laddish, such as, *I went up the stairs casually, three at a time,* but neither would be true. I did however experience a number of different feelings as we climbed those stairs. Nervousness, excitement, trepidation, and I'm fairly sure there could have been a fair bit of lust in there too.

I was doing okay until Harriet let go of my hand as she opened the bedroom door. She went to the far side of the bed, where she switched on a small bedside lamp. While I stood dithering, she, with her back to me quickly undressed. Glancing over her shoulder she said, "Are you going to stand there all night, or are you going to get into bed?"

Oh Lord, it had been so long. It was as though I had to force my legs to move. As I crossed the floor, I was vaguely aware of her naked body climbing into the bed and slipping beneath the bedclothes. I undressed quickly. My back turned towards her. Do I leave my underpants on, I wondered? Don't be such a prat, I thought, trying to slip them off as nonchalantly as possible. Then I was in bed. We were both in the bed! Both just lying there on our backs, looking at the ceiling in silence.

After a few moments I turned my head, and looked at her. She was smiling. "It's been a while, hasn't it?"

"Yes I'm afraid it has," I answered quietly.

"Don't worry, me too," she said. Then putting her arms around me, she gently pulled me towards her. Then we kissed, softly at first, then with more passion. My hand found her right breast. I squeezed and stroked it. I sort of twiddled the nipple between my finger and thumb. I felt it harden. Oh, I was so dexterous. Truthfully? No, I wasn't. She gently guided my head towards her other breast, and I put my mouth to it. I licked and sucked, and sucked and licked. Rather clumsily I'm afraid. She then took my hand, and firmly pushed it downwards to her belly. Low on her belly. Really low! Oh hell, here comes the tricky bit. I thought. And then suddenly, just to make things worse, more of Simon's advice came to mind. "Don't forget the 'clit' old mate. Don't neglect the old clit...oris. They never let you forget it if you do."

Here we go. I thought, as my hand started to gently probe between Harriet's legs. I really did try. As though sensing my awkwardness she put a hand on my shoulder, and gently pushed me until I was lying on my back. Was it my turn now? Her hand was suddenly between my thighs, and she started stroking my balls. Then she ...I can only say, *fondled* them. And then she was holding my cock. Oh Christ! Oh, my god! Her hand was, oh so slowly, oh so gently moving up and down it. I was on my way to heaven. Someone was quietly moaning. Was it me? Oh yes, it was definitely me. Then suddenly, she was kissing and licking my belly.

"Oh yes please... *Please*," I gasped. My body tensed. I wanted her to do it *so* much. And then she *was* doing it! But then, oh so quickly, Harriet lifted her head. She seemed to rummage around under the pillow for a second or two, and then I was aware of something rather strange happening, in the cock department. Quickly, she straddled me, and I felt myself make my 'grand entrance'.

"Agh!" I gasped.

Harriet started very slowly, just moving so slightly, her body erect, then arching backwards. It was then, that I realised what large breasts she had. They were wonderfully large. They were bouncing. They were swinging. I reached out, and took both of them in my hands. As she began to thrust harder and faster, her upper body now bent forward, those spectacularly wonderful breasts came to my mouth: first one, then the other. Her breasts were covered in sweat. Sweating? *'Horses sweat…men perspire…and women merely glow'*. Not Harriet! She was sweating! She was wet through. We both were. As she began to thrust harder and faster, her upper body now bent forwards, and those spectacularly wonderful breasts came to my mouth. One, then the other. By this time we were both going like the clappers. And then it happened! I just couldn't help it! I couldn't stop it! Fireworks in the head! Shooting stars! Oh Christ! "Agh, agh!"

I was vaguely aware of Harriet still thrusting and moaning, for some seconds after my own body had stilled. Then she gave a deep sigh. Satisfaction? Oh yes, please let it be satisfaction.

Isn't it amazing how very quiet and still everything is for a few minutes after sex. That awkward silence. What to say? In the past, you may well have reached for a cigarette. Harriet eventually whispered, "Laurence Breakspeare. You sex machine! That was one hell of shag. Bloody wonderful!"

I looked to see her smiling. I said a little *'thank you, God'* in my head. "I'm so pleased that madam is satisfied. Our aim is to please," I said, and couldn't help laughing.

"Oh, you did that alright *sexy,*" she said.

I was nearly purring with pride. *Me, sexy! Me, a sex machine!*

I put my arms around her and whispered, "Let's be honest, it was you… You were wonderful Harriet. I've never – well, had sex anything like that." We kissed again. Only, in a very gentle way now. Just before I drifted off to sleep, I was vaguely aware of Harriet getting out of bed. I heard the toilet flush. The next sound that I heard was that of Harriet's voice. "Come on lazy bones. Breakfast's ready."

8

As I dressed I looked around the bedroom. The scene of my conquest! I went to the bathroom and quickly rinsed my face. As I went down stairs I could hear the radio playing. Harriet was humming along to the music.

"Good morning," I said, feeling slightly embarrassed.

"Good morning Laurence. Did you sleep well?" She came to me, put her arms round me, and we kissed. "I hope you like a Sunday morning fry-up."

"Yes, that sounds great. Just what the doctor ordered," I said with a smile, as I sat down at the table. We ate our breakfast, and we made small-talk. Then inexplicably my mood changed. I took a quick glance at the clock. Twenty past eight! Christ! I usually have a lie-in on Sunday morning. I got up, kissed her, made some feeble excuse, and then promising to phone, I left. Why did I feel the need to get away so quickly? Last night had been brilliant. Bloody brilliant! So why now the anti-climax? All these thoughts were going through my head, as I drove steadily home.

I parked the car and entered my two-up, two-down. A feeling of melancholy came over me. Why? I put the kettle on. A cuppa would sort me out.

I realised that part of the problem was, that I was feeling guilty. You sleep with a woman – in my case for the first time in ages. You have great sex. She makes you breakfast, and then, with hardly a word, you clear off with, "I'll give you a ring." She must think I'm a real shit. I could phone. We could go out somewhere. I poured the tea, and looked over towards the phone. That's when I noticed there was a message on the answer-machine. I put my tea down and went over and pressed the button.

"Laurence, if you're there please pick up the phone. Please Laurence." It was Jenny's voice. She sounded extremely agitated. After a few seconds she continued. "Laurence I'm at the Arrowe Park Hospital in Birkenhead. There's been an accident. Simon has been knocked down. Please Laurence come as quick as you can. It's bad Laurence. Really bad!" I grabbed the car keys, glanced at the clock – ten to nine. I locked the house, jumped into the car and, thankfully it started first time! I can barely remember the journey to the hospital.

Jenny

9

I was working in a large pharmaceutical store in Birkenhead, when I first saw Simon. I was walking to the small café, where I usually took my lunch-break. He was just coming out of the technical college. He was the very epitome of tall, dark, and handsome. To me, he looked tall and so strikingly dark – very dark wavy hair, with a full beard. The strange thing was, at that time, I didn't like beards. I really quite disliked them but somehow, not on him ...and so handsome. My god, he was handsome!

The next day I passed the college at exactly the same time, but there was no sign of him. I felt so disappointed. I felt let down. It made me feel like a rather foolish schoolgirl. I was also surprised, by the strength of my desire to see him. It wasn't at all like me. I simply wasn't the kind of girl to go chasing after a man but I was there again the next day, looking for him and this time, he *was* there. He crossed the road, and purposefully walked straight towards me. "Oh my god, he's going to speak," I uttered under my breath. But he *didn't* speak. He smiled the most gorgeous smile imaginable, and then just carried on walking.

As I walked past the college the next day, there was no sign of him: disappointment again. I sat in the café sipping my cappuccino, and picking at my sandwich – the enjoyment of my lunch spoiled by the non-appearance of my mystery man.

"Excuse me, is that seat free?" said a wonderfully deep, sexy voice. Startled, I looked up from my cup. It was *him.* At first I simply stared at him. Eventually, I managed to convey that, yes, the seat was free. "Do you mind if I join you?" he asked, in *that* voice. My mouth was dry, as I struggled to speak coherently. Somehow I managed to say, "No …yes …please do."

That was almost fifteen years ago. Not only was Simon tall, dark and handsome, he was also very persuasive. Not that I took a lot of persuading. We started 'going out' with one another, almost immediately. Going to the cinema or a pop-concert was fine, but going to pubs didn't come easy to me. I had never found alcohol particularly attractive, but Simon did enjoy his 'pint', so quite a lot of our time together was spent in pubs. Of course, some of our time was spent in other ways. Sex in those early days, was something of a dilemma for me. I had been brought up to be a 'good girl'. I was extremely naive with regard to sex. I was nineteen and still a virgin. Not for long!

Simon had what he called a healthy sexual appetite. He was also a very athletic person. He did a lot of running. He competed at county level and I usually went along to support him. He played squash at least once a week. I would go along and support him at that also. Yes, Simon was …and still is, very competitive.

He lived in a bed-sit on the outskirts of town. I still lived at home with my parents. We had been going 'steady' for several months before I managed to coax Simon to meet them but we had been seeing one another for less than two weeks, when he managed to coax me into his bed. Initially, sex wasn't very satisfying for either of us. I wasn't very cooperative at first. My emotions confused me terribly.

Part of me was desperate to satisfy Simon, and to make him happy. I was so scared of losing him. Yet at the same time, I was torn with guilt. Even though Simon would use a condom, my lack of experience made me terrified of falling pregnant. Gradually, the sex became much better. That, I must admit, was not only due to Simon skill and patience, but also to the quite rapid increase in my own sexual appetite.

Simon worked for a small electrical retailer in Birkenhead. He attended college, with the express intention of getting the necessary qualifications to start up his own business. Within two years of the start of our relationship, he had achieved it. He opened his first shop in Ellesmere Port, just before his twenty-fifth birthday. In those early days, the business could have had an adverse affect on our relationship. Simon worked all the hours that God sends.

"Sorry, Jenny luv, I just can't afford t' turn it down," he'd say. How many times did I hear that? But thankfully, it has all been worth it. Because of Simon's hard work and business acumen, we now enjoy a very pleasant lifestyle. Oh I know that I'm thought by some to be, 'the little woman at home', but I can assure you, there's a bit more to me than that.

We had known each other for about five years, when suddenly out of the blue, Simon announced that it was, "About time that we got married". No romantic proposal. That isn't his way. The wedding however was wonderful. Nothing left to chance. No expense spared. My parents had always had their doubts about Simon. They considered him rather too 'laddish'.

"Just don't let him walk all over you my girl," was dad's advice. But on the day, they both looked as proud as punch. We honeymooned in Paris, for just one week.

"I daren't leave the business f' too long luv," said Simon, rather patronisingly.

The onerous duty of 'looking after things', was left to Laurence Breakspeare.

Laurence had worked for Simon for some time, and was very reliable. He was also Simon's best friend, so naturally he was his 'best-man' at the wedding. I had always found Laurence to be rather dull. In time I would have to revaluate my opinion of Laurence!

The only real low point of our lives was when I miscarried.

It was a terrible time for both of us and, unfortunately, the doctor explained that in his considered opinion conceiving, in the future, might be at the least problematic.

However, we are both young and healthy, and we haven't given up hope altogether. Who knows, what might happen one day? Now there's a question that tempts fate!

10

I stepped out of the shower, and wrapped a bath towel around myself. I went into the bedroom, stood in front of the full-length mirror and slowly let the towel drop. I scrutinized my reflection. Not bad! No, not too bad at all for your age, I thought. The only thing I don't really like about my body, are my boobs. I don't think they are really quite big enough. I did briefly think about having them enlarged. But I don't fancy risking any after effects. And anyway, Simon says I'm being silly. He says my boobs are just right. So that's okay then.

So what to wear? Jeans and blouse, or something a little bit more feminine? Simon was out running. He has suggested that we go out for a meal this evening. So yes, a dress I think. The little red number as Simon calls it. Some nice sexy undies with a 'sussie': a couple of glasses of wine with the meal, and who knows Simon? Play your cards right and you might just get lucky.

Just then I heard the front door bell. Had he gone

without his keys again? I slipped a dressing gown on, and crossed the entrance hall. I opened the door, and was just about to call him something like 'silly beggar', when I realised that two people were standing in the doorway. A man and a woman. They were both police officers.

"Mrs Coleridge? Mrs *Jennifer*. Coleridge?"

"Yes, that's right."

"Could we come inside for a few moments please Mrs Coleridge?" said the young man. I froze for a second or two. Then as I moved back into the house they followed, the young man beckoning towards the lounge and saying, "Perhaps you'd better sit down Mrs Coleridge."

I was now beginning to feel very frightened. "What is it? It's Simon, isn't it?"

I looked at them in fear as we all sat down.

"I'm afraid there's been an accident, Mrs Coleridge. Your husband as been knocked down. It would appear that a motor vehicle was involved. As the vehicle didn't stop, I'm afraid it looks very much like a 'hit 'n' run'."

The young policeman spoke very quietly. So quietly that I struggled to take in what he was telling me.

"Oh my god, no," I said, my hand going to my mouth.

The policewoman was quickly by my side, her arms around me. She knelt in front of me and looked me straight in the eyes and said, "Mrs Coleridge, we understand that your husband is alive, but you do need to get to the hospital as quickly as possible. If you can get dressed, we will drive you there."

Almost in a blind panic, I quickly dressed, locked the house and we all dashed to the police car.

"Where have they taken him?" I asked, nervously.

"Arrowe Park. It won't take long to get there," said the young woman.

My head was spinning, as I asked. "How badly hurt is he? Where was he? Who found him? Did he say anything?"

The young woman looked at me sympathetically and said, "We don't really know that much Mrs Coleridge. A chap was out walking his dog along Lyndale Avenue and he spotted Mr Coleridge lying in the road. As to whether he said anything, we've no idea."

As the police car pulled up outside the A&E department, I jumped out and dashed inside. By the time I had found the reception I realised that the young policewoman was still with me. She took over. "I believe you have a Mr Simon Coleridge – a road traffic accident brought in a short time ago. This lady is his wife."

The receptionist picked up a telephone, spoke briefly into the receiver, then said to me, "Please take a seat, Mrs Coleridge. Someone will be out to see you in a moment or two." I felt cold, as though I was somewhere else. Nothing felt real. Somehow the young policewoman managed to get me to sit down. Again she put her arm around me. I know that if she hadn't been there I would not have been able to cope.

After what seemed an age, we were approached by a small, balding bespectacled man in a white coat. "Mrs. Coleridge? I'm Dr. Jacobsen. I'm in charge of caring for your husband."

Before he could continue I grabbed his arm. "How is he? Please, please tell me. Oh, please say he's going to be alright." I was squeezing his arm and pleading with him. He gently eased my hand away. Then just as gently took my hand in his.

"Mr Coleridge is still in theatre. He'll be there for some time yet. We need to examine him thoroughly, to assess the full extent of his injuries." He paused for a moment, and I sensed his hold on my hand tighten slightly as he continued. He looked directly into my eyes and quietly said, "However Mrs Coleridge, there is something that I do have to tell you. Your husband's life is no longer in danger. The fact that he is a young man and is fit and healthy, has stood him in good stead to cope with the trauma of the accident …but I'm afraid his injuries are very severe. There is severe damage to his spine and pelvis. His spinal cord has been severed." He continued to look straight into my eyes. "I'm afraid to say, this means that it is extremely unlikely that he will ever be able to walk again."

He sighed very deeply. I just sat there looking at him in a state of utter shock. What was he saying? This was my Simon he was talking about. Not able to walk? Of course he can walk! I was vaguely aware of the doctor's voice. It sounded strangely muffled. "Mrs Coleridge I must go back the theatre now. As soon as your husband is transferred to a ward I will arrange for you to see him. He will need you to be strong." I sensed him let go of my hand, and then he was gone.

The young policewoman, who had been with me all

this time suddenly said, "Mrs Coleridge, someone will need to come and take a statement from your husband, as soon as he is well enough. We will also be talking to the chap who found Mr Coleridge. We'll do everything we can to find the driver of the car. Now, I'll see if I can get you a drink of tea. Then I'm afraid I'm going to have to go." A few minutes later I was sitting there totally alone, staring at the cup in my hand.

Slowly I started to focus my thoughts into some semblance of rationality. What time is it now? Nearly 7.20 pm. I had to contact Simon's parents. That would not be easy, as they had moved to France a few years ago. I would need to look up their telephone number when I get back home and my parents will need to be told. I'll phone them after I've been in touch with Simon's mum and dad, I thought. But I need someone here with me now. Laurence! Of course! I felt for my mobile phone, then realised that in my hurry I had forgotten it. I got up from the seat and crossed to the reception. "Could you tell me where the nearest telephone is please?" I asked.

Without looking up, the receptionist pointed a finger. I felt like screaming at her, "My husband is fighting for his life, and you can't even be bothered to lift your bloody head."

I dialled Laurence's number, but could only get the answer-machine. "Laurence, Laurence, if you're there please pick up the phone. Please Laurence. Laurence there's been an accident. Simon has been knocked down. Please Laurence come as quick as you can. It's bad. Really bad!"

The time passed so slowly. I just sat there, praying…worrying, and wondering why I hadn't cried?

"Where are you, Laurence?" I sighed. I looked at the clock for what seemed like the thousandth time. 9.40 pm. "Please help me. Dear God, someone please help me." Then suddenly the tears did come, and I sobbed.

11

I don't know how long I waited. Just sitting there. Then getting out of the chair, and pacing up and down. In my haste to get here, not only had I forgotten my phone, I had also forgotten my watch. That didn't stop me from looking at my wrist every few minutes. After what seemed ages, I was approached by a rather officious looking nurse.

"Mrs Coleridge?" she asked, as she sat down beside me. I just nodded. "Mr Coleridge is out of theatre now. We've put him into a private ward. I'm aware that Dr. Jacobsen has spoken to you, but there are one or two points I would like to go through with you, before you see your husband." She spoke calmly, with a reassuring smile. "Firstly, your husband is now out of danger, and he's as comfortable as can be expected. I believe Dr. Jacobsen has told you, that your husband has received a serious injury to his spine. Because of this he will be transferred later today, to the spinal unit at Southport Hospital. The good news however, is that there was no serious injury to the head. I know this may sound a strange question, but would you like to see him now?"

I just sat there looking at her. I felt as though I was fastened to the chair. Eventually I managed to say, "Yes please." She took my elbow, and gently helped me from the seat. Then as she led me along the corridor she said quietly, "I must just tell you my dear; Mr. Coleridge is still unconscious. That is purely because of the anaesthetic. And ...he is connected to several pieces of equipment. That's just to monitor his progress, nothing to worry about. He will be fine. It will just take time and lots of love and care."

She opened the ward door, and followed me in. Even though I had tried to prepare myself, seeing my husband lying there was such an awful shock. Even though the nurse had warned me. The machines: the I.V drip, the hi-tech bed with the sidebars, and the dim lighting. It was just as I had seen it in so many hospital dramas on the television. And yet strangely, Simon was so still – not really looking like someone terribly injured. Even as I tried to walk to his side, the nurse had to ease me into the chair by the side of the bed. I just looked at him. No words would come. My mouth was so dry. As I heard her voice, my eyes turned to meet hers. "I'll leave you alone with him for a while. If you need anything just ring that bell,' she said pointing. "Would you care for a cup of tea?"

"No thank you, I'll be fine, and thank you for being so kind. Oh, could you tell me the time?"

She looked at her wristwatch. "It's a quarter to nine

dear."

I rose from the chair, and went to Simon's side. I bent over him and carefully kissed his forehead. He didn't react. Not that I expected him to of course. His breathing was quiet and steady. There wasn't a mark on his face. Just the tubes taped to his nose and arms. His arms – his strong arms with the black hair – that were lying perfectly still on top of the bedclothes. There was no blood. No cuts. No bruises.

I took his hand in mine and whispered, "Simon it's me, Jenny. I'm here luv. Try not to worry. Everything is going to be alright. You're going to be fine. Can you hear me Simon? If you can hear me, squeeze my hand luv." He didn't squeeze. After a short while I let go of his hand, and slowly sat back down in the chair.

A few minutes later, a young nurse entered the room with a tray of tea and biscuits. I hadn't realised how hungry I had become, until I saw those biscuits. "We have a small room you can use if you get tired. There's a bed, if you want to have a bit of a sleep. Just let me know and I'll show you."

"What time is it please?" I asked.

"Five past ten," she said, as she left the room.

10.00 o'clock! What's happened to Laurence? Where had he got to? He should be here by now. Should I phone again? Maybe he isn't home. Of course! Saturday night! He could be at *The Feathers*. I could phone the pub. He would definitely come straight away, if he knew. I rose from the chair, looked at Simon, and left the room.

Over the telephone I could hear the noise of a busy

pub. The female voice that was speaking to me didn't sound like Melanie, the landlady. Whoever it was, had to shout so that I could hear her. "Laurence? Laurence Breakspeare? No, he's not been in all night."

"Have you any ideas about any other pubs, where I might be able to contact him?"

"No sorry," she replied, hanging up, obviously too busy to be bothered with some 'silly cow' chasing a bloke.

Well, I would just have to manage by myself. After all it is my husband. It's me who he needs. It's me who will have to take care of him now. Not Laurence bloody Breakspeare or anybody else, for that matter. As these thoughts came, so did the tears. I replaced the phone, turned to go back to the ward, and almost bumped into the young nurse who had brought the tea and biscuits.

"Eh, now then, what's all this? Come on, we can't be havin' you all upset. You look absolutely worn out. Come on, let me show you where you can have a bit of rest." She took my arm and guided me away.

"You're all so very kind. Could I just look in on Simon again first? Then yes …I think I will try to have a bit of a sleep." Suddenly I felt very tired. Simon was just as I had left him. The young woman led me a short distance to a quiet room. I took off my shoes, lay down, closed my eyes, and eventually drifted off to sleep.

12

I slept fitfully, through some very strange dreams. Then suddenly I awoke, chilled with sweat. At first I wasn't sure where I was. As my thoughts cleared, I slowly and stiffly climbed from the bed, and slipped my shoes on. Rubbing my eyes, I opened the door and peered out into the corridor. The hospital was a hive of activity. I quickly made my way to Simon's room. As I entered I heard voices. A man in a white coat and a senior nurse were standing beside Simon's bed. They both turned as I approached.

"Ah …Mrs Coleridge. Perfect timing …please come in," the man in the white coat said. "We were just telling Simon about the arrangements that have been made to transfer him to Southport."

I almost knocked the poor man over, as I reached for Simon. His eyes were open, and he smiled at me weakly. "Now then Jenny luv, come here and give your old man a big kiss." His arms were trying to reach for me. They couldn't quite make it. It didn't matter, as I bent over him and none too gently kissed him on the cheek. Once again I couldn't stop the tears from welling in my eyes.

"Oh Simon thank God!" I could barely get the words out.

"Shush luv shush, it's goin' to be alright… Come on, don't cry," Simon said, managing to give me one of his winning smiles.

The man in the white coat suddenly broke the spell. "Mrs Coleridge, I'm Dr Grainger. As I was saying, we shall be transferring Simon shortly after lunch. We have carried out all the necessary examinations, and feel confident that his condition is stable enough for him to travel the short distance to Southport and Formby hospital. Fortunately, Simon is basically a fit and healthy young fellow. In the spinal unit at Southport they have all the facilities required for Simon's rehabilitation. If you wish to stay here with him until then, that will be fine."

Then he and the nurse turned and left.

"Have you been here all by yourself?" Simon asked.

"Yes, but that's okay." I said. "I don't know what's happened to Laurence. I phoned him as soon as I could. I had to leave a message on his answer machine but I haven't heard a thing."

No sooner had I spoken, than the door suddenly opened and in walked Laurence. "Speak of the devil!" said Simon.

"I'm sorry I've been so long. I only got Jenny's message about 'alf 'n 'our ago. What on earth has happened?" he looked from me to Simon. "Good God

Simon, what have you done?"

Simon smiled weakly. "What 'ave *I* done? I 'onestly don't remember much about it old mate. I know I was out for a run. I've been told by the doctor that I was hit by a car or something, and that the bastard who was drivin' apparently didn't stop. An' now I'm up shit-creek."

Just then the door opened and a nurse came in and said, "Excuse me, but there's a policeman outside. He wants to know whether Mr. Coleridge is up to giving him a statement regarding the accident." I looked at Simon, and he nodded.

I turned to the nurse, "Yes alright, but please make it clear to him that he mustn't stay long, or say anything to upset my husband."

At this, I noticed Simon look pointedly at Laurence as he said, "Laurie old mate ...why don't you take Jenny and grab some coffee?"

I started to protest, but Simon was quite insistent. I knew that he didn't want me to get any more upset than I already was. So I relented, and gently kissed him on the cheek. "Right love, we'll leave you for a bit while we go and get a drink."

Laurence brought two cups of coffee to the table. We sat in silence for a moment or two. Then I told him the full implications of Simon's injuries.

He sat there in total shock. He just looked at the floor and sighed deeply. "Agh Jenny. Bloody 'ell! I'd no idea. Paralysed! I thought he'd just had a nasty bump. Y' know, just a clout. Oh Christ Jenny, I'm so sorry."

I'm sure there were tears in his eyes. I reached across and placed my hand on his arm. "There's something else I need to ask you about, Laurence. I know it won't be long before Simon starts worrying about the business."

Before I could go on, he interrupted me, "Jenny, please don't be worrying about that. I'll take care of things. I'll get on with sorting it out first thing in the morning. You and Simon have enough on your plates as it is. It's goin' to be okay, honestly." And he tried to smile reassuringly. At that moment I noticed the young policeman approaching us.

"I've taken your husband's statement, Mrs Coleridge. We'll be in touch as soon as we have any information. I just hope we can find whoever's responsible." With that, he nodded and left.

Laurence touched my hand, "Look Jenny, this is just a suggestion. What if we look in on Simon …then I'll drive you home, and then later this evening I'll drive us both over to the hospital in Southport."

"Oh thank you Laurence, that's very kind of you. But I don't want to be any trouble."

"Don't be daft Jenny; you could never be any trouble. Anyway, it's the least I can do."

Laurence took my arm as we left the coffee shop, and made our way back to Simon. He was sleeping when we entered the room. I kissed him softly. Then we left, and went out to Laurence's car.

13

The next few weeks were amongst the most difficult of my life: hectic, traumatic, worrying. During the daytime I was busy telephoning or e-mailing various organizations and companies, regarding Simon's accident. Most evenings were taken up visiting the hospital.

The worst time was in bed, at night.

That's when it would hit me.

I would just lie for hours, worrying.

I was so lonely. I hadn't slept on my own since we were married ...and of course, I missed making love. Sex was nearly always good for us. The only time it had been a problem was after the miscarriage. The doctor told me that I might not be able to have children. That hit me much harder than it did Simon. He wasn't as keen as I was to start a family. Adoption was briefly mentioned, but Simon made it fairly obvious that he didn't want to talk about it. Eventually we got our lives back on track, and gradually our sex-lives got back to normal but now, naturally, I was concerned about sex in the future.

Another important decision that I had to make was regarding my job. I knew that I couldn't go on working and manage everything else, so it was agreed that I should take long-term sick leave.

As for the business, Laurence was absolutely brilliant. He arranged for an agency electrician to join the firm. He sub-contracted work out when necessary, and just generally kept Simon's and my spirits up. He really is the kind of friend you need at times like these and he really has gone up in my estimation. He even helped me to make arrangements for having the bungalow adapted to Simon's needs. One of these needs, which for some reason Simon and I had shied away from, was the wheelchair that he would spend most of his time in.

Ramps would have to be installed inside and outside; doors had to be widened and a special shower fitted. The whole place was like a bomb-site.

Thankfully, we were already living in a bungalow – that at least was one blessing. We both would have hated it if we had needed to move.

I had a long chat with my mum and dad on the phone. It was such a fortunate coincidence that they just happened to live in Southport, only about a mile from the hospital.

I had managed to contact Simon's parents the day after he was taken to the spinal unit. It was without doubt, one of the most difficult telephone calls that I have ever had to make. Even though I tried to break the news gently, I felt that I had to give them the full facts. Naturally they were both distraught. They arranged for the earliest flight possible. They were at Simon's bedside by the next day.

Thankfully they are a pretty rational couple, and they have both been wonderfully supportive. Not just to Simon, but to me too. They are reasonably well off, and they quietly assured us, that we won't have any financial worries. "Just concentrate on getting well Simon. We'll do whatever we can to help."

At least we have that. A lot of poor souls would be in a far worse state. 'Count your blessings!' ...but, that won't help my husband to walk again.

If my life was thrown into turmoil, for Simon it was much worse. Because of his good general fitness, it wasn't long before the hospital staff was able to begin 'passive work' on the muscles of his legs. This would enable him to retain as much strength as possible. I was told that I would need to help with these exercises when Simon came home. Laurence said he would also give a hand. Simon jokingly said, "Laurence can keep his bloody hands to himself!"

At first, Simon seemed to be really upbeat about things. He was really keen when it came to doing the exercises. It wasn't long before they had him out of bed, and into the swimming pool. He was given electro-therapy, and was soon working with weights in the gym but, of course, for him it was a routine that never allowed him to escape from the fact that his life had changed forever. Then one evening about a month after the accident, there was drastic change.

I had been visiting Simon almost every day. I hardly ever missed. "Where were you last night?" he asked, in a very cold voice.

Taken aback, I replied, "Oh, I'm sorry luv, I was absolutely shattered. I thought you wouldn't mind just for once."

"You're bloody shattered! How the hell do you think I feel being soddin' well pulled from pillar to bloody post? Shattered? I'm fuckin' knackered."

I was totally shocked. It was such a change. I was so unprepared. I just didn't know what to say to him and I couldn't remember the last time he'd used the F-word to me. I tried to placate him, but it was to no avail. Then I started to cry. I just couldn't help myself. "If that's all you can do ...you might as well just bugger off," he said. Then he looked at me in a way that I'd never seen before.

"Simon please ...I'm sorry." I begged.

Then he turned his head away, and it felt as though he had punched me. I just turned and left the room in a state of utter anguish.

As I stood in the corridor sobbing, a young nurse came to my rescue.

She took me into a quiet office, sat me down, and telephoned the social worker that Simon and I had spoken to previously. She entered the room carrying two cups of tea. She was a stout, middle-aged woman with a kind face.

"A cup of the hospital's finest. Supposed to be a

'cure-all'. God's gift! We'll see." She reached down into a desk drawer, and pulled out a box of tissues. Passing the box to me she carried on, "Been giving you a hard time has he? Apparently he's been a bit of a 'bugger' all day. Wouldn't do his exercises – said it was a waste of effin' time. Pardon my French. It was bound to happen sooner or later. If you remember I did warn you both to expect it. It's a kind of delayed reaction. It's nothing personal. He has to lash out at someone …and it's nearly always someone they love. Unfortunately …that someone is you.

"It's suddenly hit him ...the full implications. He's now starting to ask questions. What's it all going to mean? And of course …the big one – is he really never going to be able to walk again? Is he forever going to be a burden to other people? And the other big one! Will he be able to have sex again? All these things are going to worry and concern him.

"These next few months are undoubtedly going to be, almost certainly, the hardest few months of your lives, but you will get through them. You are both young. You are a good, loving young couple. I really believe that and, of course, everybody here will give you as much help as we can. Once we can get Simon home things will gradually improve. I promise. Oh yes, there will be mood swings. He will have bouts of depression. We can prescribe medication for that. As I have said he will come to terms with things. He will adapt. You would be amazed by the resilience of people, Jenny. I know this may sound glib, but honestly, it isn't the end of the world. AMEN, end of lecture."

At last she stopped talking. I knew everything she said made sense. But it was though her words were coming to me through a fog. I just could not forget the way Simon had looked at me. That was even worse than the way he had spoken.

The next morning I climbed out of bed feeling pretty dreadful. I just didn't want to face the day. I had hardly slept at all for thinking about Simon, and the way had spoken to me but I knew that I had to pull myself together. I had to be strong for both of us. And anyway, the men who were doing the alterations would be here soon. A quick shower, then get the kettle on. Keep myself busy through the day, and fingers crossed; hopefully, he would be in a better mood this evening. I was just finishing my breakfast when the phone rang.

It was Laurence. "I was wondering whether you would like a lift to the hospital this evening? I haven't been t'see Simon for a couple of days and I know he'll be fretting about the job ...sixish be okay?"

I thanked him, and said that would be fine. Sure enough, there he was, on the dot at six o'clock.

On the way to the hospital I told Laurence about the previous evening. How Simon had spoken. How he had looked at me with such loathing. "It was awful Laurence. I know he can't really help it but it hurt so much. I just hope to goodness that it's better to-night."

Thankfully it was. As soon as we entered the room, I could sense it. Simon was sitting up reading. He smiled and said, "Hiya, you two." He paused for a moment, then said, "Laurie old mate, could you do us a favour? Could you give me and Jenny five minutes?"

Laurence simply nodded, turned, and walked out of the room. Then it was all smiles and tears.

"I'm so sorry sweetheart. I honestly don't know what the hell got into me. It's just that it's so bloody hard at times. Y' know."

I put my arms round him, and held him tight. I kissed his forehead, and then I kissed his eyes. I 'shushed' him and told him to stop worrying. "It's going to be alright. We're together. We'll always be together."

He nodded and said, "Yes luv, you're right. We will beat this bloody thing. Together! Now will you go and fetch Laurie? There's something I want to tell you both."

It was such a joy and relief to see him smiling. I opened the door and beckoned to Laurence. He could see by my face that things were much better. Laurence took the chair, and I sat on the edge of the bed. We both looked at Simon in anticipation. He was grinning. "They're going to try me out in a wheelchair tomorrow. Hopefully, in a couple of weeks I should be able to have a trial run at home. Do you think all the alterations will be done by then?"

"Oh Simon that's marvellous! Yes luv, they've nearly finished. All the major jobs are done. I'll make sure it's ready in time."

We were all smiling: such a difference from yesterday.

Laurence wanted to reassure Simon about the business. "Everything is fine. The lad from the agency is well on top of things. One or two bits, I've contracted out, so there's nothing for you to worry about." Then he gripped Simon's hand and said, "Look, I'll leave you two alone for a while. I'll be just outside in the corridor when you're ready Jenny."

Simon and I spent the next few minutes holding hands and kissing, and just generally expressing comforting thoughts.

"Jenny I really am sorry for being such an idiot yesterday. I'll make it up to you. I do understand you know. It really is okay if you can't make it sometimes."

He looked so vulnerable. So, almost childlike, I had to fight to hold the tears back. No! No more tears, only smiles from now on.

14

One afternoon about two weeks later, the sun was shining, and I was relaxing with a cup of coffee in the garden, when the telephone rang.

"Jenny luv …it's me, Simon. Guess what! They're letting me come home. Tomorrow morning. Isn't that bloody marvellous? Jenny are you still there? You've gone very quiet."

"Yes Simon, I'm here. That's wonderful news. Shall I need to come to pick you up, or will the hospital be bringing you?"

"I'll be coming by ambulance. I have to bring the wheelchair, and I think the ambulance crew will want to make sure I get settled in okay. And don't even bother thinking about coming to the hospital tonight. You just get some rest. I've got plans for you and me sweetheart, if you get my drift. I hope you do. So, right luv', see you tomorrow. I love you sweetheart."

"Simon; I can't wait. I love you too."

Thoughts raced through my mind, as I replaced the

telephone. I was really excited about the prospect of having Simon home, but I can't deny the odd moments of apprehension. It was going to be a big test for both of us. There were bound to be difficulties but as Simon had said, 'We'll beat this thing together'.

All the alterations and decorating were finished. I had worked really hard to make the house nice and tidy, just as Simon liked it. I must admit, the various adaptations did seem a little bit alien to me, but that would be a small price to pay once we got our lives back on track.

Laurence had been in touch. "When Simon comes home, do you want me to be there to give a hand? A bit of physical and moral support. Or would you rather be on your own? Whichever, I'll understand."

I appreciated the thought very much, and I thanked him, but I said, perhaps Simon and I should just do this together.

That night I hardly slept. So many thoughts and worries kept running through my mind. It had been just about six weeks since Simon's accident, but it seemed so much longer. How was he going to react to being back home? Home …yes, but under such different circumstances and being dependent on me for so many things – the sort of things that he had always taken care of himself. At least initially he would get support from the hospital, but sooner or later we would have to just rely on each other. And of course …sleeping together! That really was worrying me. I felt that as his wife I should be mentally prepared, but in truth I wasn't.

What was it going to be like? He couldn't move the

lower part of his body. What would he be able to feel? Of course he would be able to hold me. He would be able to touch me. He could use his hands. But what about when I touch him? What about when I touch his – when I touch his 'willy'? Will he be able to get an erection? We have had some advice from the hospital, but it was all a bit vague. I always refer to 'it' as his 'willy'. It's strange I know, but I've never been able to bring myself to say cock, or any of the other words. I don't even like penis. So, I always say 'willy'. Don't get me wrong; I'm not really a prude. It's just that certain things bother me.

Sex has always been fine between us, but I have to admit that I'm not the most adventurous of people. I'm not really into anything to kinky. Simon has never complained. Well not to me anyway. We usually 'do it' three or four times a week. It has been pretty frustrating since we've been apart. Over six weeks without sex! The longest we've ever gone. So now, it's just a little bit scary. Anyway, I'm sure that we will work everything out fine. We will just have to take things one day at a time.

The next morning I was in the shower before seven o'clock. By eight I'd had my breakfast. I sat trying to read the daily paper, but I couldn't concentrate. He'd just said that he would arrive in the morning.

What time?

Should I telephone the hospital?

No, just relax. Keep calm. That's what he will need – for me to be calm. Don't make too much fuss. Is everything ready? I had tried to think of everything. I picked up the paper again, and looked at the clock. 8.30 a.m. Every few minutes I stood and looked through the window, or went down the drive to the gate.

It was just after ten thirty, when I heard the ambulance pull up outside. I had to stop myself from running to the gate. Instead I walked calmly and welcomed him with a big smile, at the same time having to fight back the tears. "Hello luv …welcome home." I reached down, put my arms around him and kissed him hard.

The ambulance driver smiled and said, "Right Simon old lad …off you go. I've pushed you far enough this morning. It's all yours now." Simon looked at me and I could see that he was feeling slightly apprehensive.

Turning to the ambulance driver he said, "As it's such a lovely morning, I think I'll just go into the garden for a while. It seems to be ages since I had any fresh air. You know, being cooped up inside all the time."

"Okay Simon, but if you don't mind we'll just take a quick look inside to check out the facilities," the driver said, and gestured to his companion. At this Simon manoeuvred the wheelchair towards the rear garden, up the ramp and onto the patio.

"Crikey, you did that like an expert," I said, probably over-doing the enthusiasm. He just nodded and smiled.

The ambulance men came back out of the house. "That looks great. You've done a brilliant job Mrs

Coleridge. Right then, we'll be off. Take care Simon and behave y' self. If we don't see you again, all the best for the future."

I made coffee, and for the next hour we sat in the garden and talked. We talked mainly about the future. When would he be able to go back to work? What would he be able to do when he did start back? He wouldn't be able to go out rewiring, or doing any of the refits... "And in the warehouse I'll probably just be in the way. Christ Jenny, what the hell *am* I goin' to do?"

"Don't worry Simon, just give yourself time. We'll have Laurence over and we'll sort things out. Don't forget, there are always the orders to be arranged …and all the paperwork to be done. I'd like to bet he'll be very glad to have you back," I tried to sound as encouraging as possible.

"Yer right …bloody paperwork. Wonderful!"

And of course, we had to consider whether or not I should eventually go back to work. "Do you want to go back?" Simon asked.

I had always enjoyed my job. The people that worked there were great company. On the odd occasion, I would have a night out with a couple of the girls and working did make me feel independent.

"Well yes, I think I would like to go back if possible but only when the time is right," I said. Then I added, "Do y 'want to go into the house for lunch or shall we stay out here? I've done some pizza and salad."

"Let's stay here while the sun's out. We'll have to go inside soon enough," he said with a slight frown.

We ate in silence. I knew things were not going to be easy. I knew that we would have to take things a step at a time. I looked at Simon, smiled, then reached over and touched his hand. "I been wondering about the car," he said suddenly. "I think the 'Beema' is going to have to go. It's a shame, but I'm going to need something a bit more practical, something that will take the wheelchair. I'd need to get the 'Beema' adapted anyway. I'm not likely to be a 'boy-racer' anymore. I'll start looking into it in a day or two."

I was really quite shocked. Simon had always adored his B.M.W. Occasionally I had jokingly said that I wondered whether he loved it more than he loved me. Now he was talking about parting with it.

As the afternoon drew to a close it turned cooler, and it became evident that we should go inside. Simon smiled nervously and said, "I know you know that I've been putting it off. It just seems all a bit strange. It's only been a few weeks, but it seems so much longer. Anyway I'm being stupid. Yes, let's go inside." With that he wheeled his chair towards the ramp, and into the bungalow.

Later that evening we sat in the dining room, and had our first proper meal together for what seemed ages. I had prepared one of Simon's favourites – Fillet steak in a red wine sauce. This was accompanied by a bottle of Rioja. We finished off with tiramisu and Irish coffee. When I suggested that he should watch the television, while I did the pots he was quite indignant. "No, not likely! You wash, an' I'll dry. I can manage that, at least, and thanks for a lovely meal. Thanks for everything luv. Come here and give me a kiss."

Now it did feel good to have him home.

We sat and watched the TV and chatted. We were aware that occasionally we both took a surreptitious glance at the clock. "Are you tired? You look a bit tired. It is quite late." I knew that one of us would have to take the initiative sooner or later.

"Yes luv you're right. Bedtime, I think. I'll just pop into the bathroom." Simon steered his wheelchair out of the room. Right, this is it! The one thing that neither if us had spoken about all day. Good lord, how long had we been married?

We are husband and wife for heaven's sake. Pull yourself together woman. Go and make him feel as though he really has come home.

I went through into the bedroom. Simon was already in bed. I quickly undressed and climbed in beside him. He was looking up at the ceiling. I slowly put my arms around him and turned his face to mine. Then I kissed him gently but firmly. I began to kiss him with a little more passion, but as my hold on him became more intense, he very quietly said, "Do you think we could just cuddle up tonight Jen? I do feel pretty shattered."

He kissed me on the cheek, and then slowly turned his head away.

Laurie

15

After the accident, I was in a bit of an emotional turmoil. For some time afterwards I had strong feelings of guilt.

If, on that Saturday afternoon, I had gone jogging with Simon, instead of being with Harriet, there probably wouldn't have been an accident. Most likely, we would have been running somewhere else, as I didn't feel safe on that particular road. Therefore, Simon would, quite probably, not now be in a wheelchair. And where was I when Jenny needed me? Sorry Jenny, while you were worrying yourself sick at the hospital, I was too busy shaggin' or scoffin' bacon and eggs. So yes I did feel guilty.

On the other hand, I couldn't deny that there had been an 'up-side' to things.

Since more or less taking over the running of the business, I had sort of …come in to my own. I had never made so many decisions in my life. What's more, the business was doing fine.

No worries!

Well that wasn't quite true. I had got one worry. Now Simon's back home, how long before he wanted to get back to work, and I got my nose pushed out? After all, it was 'COLERIDGE ELECTRICS', Simon was the boss ...and to be fair, he had always been a good boss. The trouble was, he tended to be the boss outside work as well. Well, maybe that would change now but I wouldn't be holding my breath.

Oh yes, just in case you're wondering, I am still seeing Harriet. After our first night together and the accident, I wasn't sure what I wanted to do. She was very understanding. She said I wasn't to worry. I was to sort things out. Then, and only if I wanted to, perhaps I would give her a call. I phoned her two days after the accident, and we've been going out together ever since. And yes, the sex is still brilliant. I seem to be getting quite good at it. I am just a bit concerned though. Harriet seems to be getting rather serious. She's started using words like, 'commitment' and recently she said, "Wouldn't it be really lovely to have a bungalow like the one your friends live in?"

On the second evening of Simon's homecoming, I'd just sat down to my microwave dinner when the phone rang. It was his 'lordship'.

"Jenny and I were wondering whether you'd like to come over for your tea one evening?" Before I could reply, he carried on, "There's something I want to talk to you about. How about tomorrow? Sevenish?"

Same old Simon. Make it sound like an order.

"Hang on a mo'. Let me check my diary." I paused for effect. "No, that seems to be okay. I'm not seeing Harriet tomorrow," I said, trying to sound slightly offended at his not even mentioning her.

"Oh Christ! Sorry Laurie. I wasn't thinking. So it's still on then… you an' Harriet? Great stuff old mate. But like I was saying, there's something we need to talk to you about. You know, business stuff. She'd probably be bored to tears. She could come along another time… eh old mate."

"Yes, sure. Right, I'll see you at seven tomorrow evening." I replaced the receiver, picked up my dinner and stuck it back in the microwave. So, they wanted to talk to me. Business stuff? Were they going to offer me a partnership? Or perhaps, just a directorship. Or perhaps, the sack! Well I'd soon find out. One rather strange thing though. He didn't ask me if I was getting 'my end away'. Now that was not like the Simon I know.

The next evening as I drove over to Simon and Jenny's, I was still pondering over our impending 'talk'.

"Come on in old mate," said Simon as he opened the door. "Don't look so surprised. I can move about you know. These things are bloody marvellous," he added, patting the armrests of the wheelchair. I followed him into the lounge, and was disappointed to see that Jenny wasn't there. I wasn't sure what Simon had read in my expression, but as he pointed to an armchair he said, "She won't be long, she's just getting showered."

I had this immediate image of Jenny absolutely naked, sensuously applying soap to that gorgeous body. Christ! How I wished it were me doing the applying. I quickly forced myself to think of something else. "So come on, don't keep me in suspenders any longer. What's the big secret? I didn't sleep a wink last night," I lied.

"It's no big deal mate. We'll have dinner, and then we'll talk. Okay?"

"Okay." I replied resignedly. "Anyway, how are you feelin'? I bet it's good to be back home." Back home sleeping with Jenny! Having sex with her! But, now that's the thing, isn't it Simon old lad. Can you have sex? Can you give her what she wants? *What she needs?* I could old lad …given half a chance.

"Are you okay, Laurie? You're looking a bit odd." Simon was saying, as Jenny came into the room. Just in the nick of time.

"Hello Laurence. How are you? Dinner won't be long. I hope you're hungry. Hasn't he offered you a drink?" she said, going to the drinks cabinet.

"Just something soft please Jenny." *Like your lips, your breasts, your thighs, or...* For Christ's sake man …get a grip. They'll be wondering what the bloody 'ell's a matter with you.

We all enjoyed a sumptuous meal at the meticulously laid dining table. Although, Jenny you gorgeous creature, if I'm absolutely honest, salad isn't really what I would choose for dinner. But then again I would eat donkey's testicles if you served them. *Stop bloody looking at her. He's bound to notice, sooner or later.*

"Are you sure you won't have a glass of wine Laurence?" asked Jenny.

"No thanks, better not. Driving! Not worth the risk."

We sat quietly for a short time, while we ate our desserts.

Immediately these were finished, Simon announced, "Right, shall we take our coffee though to the lounge." Not so much a question, more like an instruction. Simon pushed his wheelchair past me, and made his way through.

Moments later we were all sitting comfortably in the lounge.

"Right, Laurence!" said Simon, with a somewhat serious expression on his face.

Oh, oh! I thought, this must be important. If he calls me Laurence, it's usually important. Simon put his cup to his mouth, and took a long drink.

He looked deeply thoughtful as he spoke. "I ...or should I say we, want your advice," he said in a serious tone. *Bloody 'ell, that's a first, I thought.* "As I'm sure you can appreciate Laurie, I'm wanting to get back to work. I can't see any point in chuffin' about. I don't want to be just hangin' about the house. We've decided that Jenny should go back to the pharmacy a.s.a.p. I'm not totally useless, and we feel that it's the best thing for her t' do."

I thought you wanted my advice. Looks to me like you've already decided I thought, maybe a little harshly, as he continued. "The only thing is old mate ...what am I going to do? Jenny thought I could be the pen pusher …but I'm not sure that I could cope with that. Probably send me up the soddin' wall. So, we wondered what you might think"

Partnership my arse! "Yes …great Simon! If you really feel ready, you should come back. Of course y' should." What else could I say? Bugger all! Then we chatted about our ideas for the 'best way forward', for the next half hour or so.

"I'm goin' to see about changing the car in the next day or two. I'm goin' to need something a bit more practical. Obviously I shall have to get something with hand controls," said Simon.

Bloody hell! Simon without his 'Beema'.

It was decided that Simon would come into work as soon as he got this new mode of transport sorted out. Then we'll just have to see how things go.

Jenny wasn't so sure about when she would return to the pharmacy.

"Once I know Simon is settled in, then I'll consider it," she said.

I looked towards the clock. Ten-twenty! Doesn't time fly when you're having fun?

I made my excuses, rose from my chair, and jangled my car keys. Simon was just about to speak, when Jenny cut in. "Simon was telling me, that you're going out with someone Laurence. Hillary, isn't it? You'll have to bring her next time Laurence."

"Harriet," I said, looking at Simon, and then smiling at Jenny. "She's called Harriet."

It was typical of him to tell Jenny the wrong name. "And yes thank you Jenny, that would be very nice.

Well, I'd better be off."

"Laurie old mate, talking about cars …are you still kick-starting that old 'Focus'? Simon asked. I just nodded. "Time you got something a bit better. We'll have a chat about it when I get back to work."

I walked out to the car. I didn't kick it. I just patted it and climbed in. It started on the first turn of the key.

16

One morning just over a week later, as I pulled into the parking space in front of the warehouse, I observed a new vehicle. It was one of those people-carrier things. I looked at my watch: eight-twenty-five. Thank God! I wouldn't want to be late on the first morning that his 'lordship' returns to his empire.

"Good morning Simon …welcome back," I said, as I entered the warehouse – and yes, I did mean it.

"That looks rather smart," I said, inclining my head in the direction of the new car.

"Yes, nice in't it?" Simon replied, rather absent-mindedly. I later found out that it was a V.W Sharan. Very posh! "The kettle's just boiled," he gestured towards the cups. He still seemed to be deep in thought.

"You didn't waste any time," I said gesturing outside towards his new car and pouring myself a cup of tea. "You managed to get into it okay then?" I added somewhat inanely.

"Yes Laurie …that's why I bought it," he said

patronisingly, before continuing, "Nice to see the old place still in one piece. What 'ave we got on today, anything special?"

The truth was, that business was a little quiet at the present. I hadn't had to use the agency 'sparkie' for several days. I was hoping that it was only a temporary blip.

As the day progressed, thankfully we became a little busier. Contractors and retail customers helped to make the hours pass. In between times Simon and I drank tea and coffee, and chatted about various things.

"So, how's it going with the lady friend then? Are you getting your leg over regularly? She looked as if she was a bit of a 'go-er'."

He really could be a crude sod at times.

"Yes, our relationship is going very nicely. Thank you for asking," I said, as sarcastically as I could.

"Oo' sorry I spoke," he said, feigning an apology. "No, seriously old mate, I didn't mean to offend. I hope it works out. It'll do you good." *Yes Simon, it is doing me good. But I would still love to shag your wife, you condescending chuff.* The harshness of my thought, quickly made me feel horribly guilty.

The next few days passed uneventfully. Simon quickly got into a routine. One lucky thing was that the warehouse, being a modern building, had a roller-shutter door, which gave easy access to Simon's wheelchair. Nor did he seem to have any difficulty manoeuvring it around the racking inside the warehouse. In fact, he made a point of letting me know that he could get about quicker than me.

At first, things were going pretty well. It really was good to have him back, but of course there's the rub. He is back; and he is the boss. Nor did it take long for me to get the message. Oh he's very smart with it. He doesn't use a hammer to crack a walnut but, as I say, he got the message across and of course I resented it. After all, who had kept things going this last two months? Who had made sure that you had a business to come back to? Me old lad, me!

When *The Feathers* regulars got to know of Simon's release from hospital, it was suggested that a 'welcome-home' party should be put on at the pub. I said that maybe I should 'run it' by his wife first, and then I would get back to them.

Jenny and I discussed it over the phone. I said that personally I thought it would be okay, but only if she was there as well.

"That sounds a nice idea Laurence. Can I leave it to you to organise it please?" Jenny said, in that sensuous voice... Would you like to come round right now and make long, slow, passionate love to me Laurence? Do you fancy a long, lingering shag? I sighed deeply, at my indecent thoughts. Dry mouthed, I said, yes, I would make the arrangements.

"Oh, and Laurence, I trust you'll be bringing your young lady. Harriet, isn't it?" Jenny's voice brought me back to reality. Serves me bloody right!

"Yes," I said, clearing my throat. "That's right Harriet. Yes, hopefully I'll get her to come."

It was set for the next Saturday evening. All the 'lads' would be there. Fantastic! "Will the 'twins' be in attendance?" I asked the landlady Melanie, looking meaningfully at her bosom, which was not on its usual magnificent display.

"Of course they will. I wouldn't want to disappoint my lovely lads, now would I?" she grinned cheekily. I shouldn't have really tried to surprise Simon. At first, when I suggested going to *The Feathers* one night, he seemed reasonably amenable to the idea.

"Just as long as there's no soddin' fuss," he stated but I guess he 'twigged', when I became more insistent that we went on the Saturday night. When Jenny said she would be coming, well that convinced him that something was going on.

"I've told you Laurie. No soddin' fuss old mate."

"Right, you're the boss. No soddin' fuss."

So on the night it was just a bar full of the 'lads', the usual hangers on. Oh …and a disco! ("Who's bloody idea was that?' Simon groaned) ...plus a few red balloons over the bar, and a red and white banner, a.k.a LIVERPOOL F.C. proclaiming "WELCOME HOME SIMON". Much back slapping, and wet snogs on Simon's cheek. The wet snogs would undoubtedly have gone down better if they had been from females, and not from 'the lads'! Melanie making a special trip from the other side of the bar, and a special showing of the 'twins', as she bent over the table to deliver Simon his pint of 'Stella'.

"Here you are darling, on the house."

It so happened, that Melanie had some competition in the 'bust department' on this particular evening. Harriet, who had said that she would love to come along, was giving her own ample bosom an airing. I have to say, she looked stunning. I was dead chuffed. Yes lads, she's with me! Melanie was just about the only person in the bar, who apparently didn't notice Harriet's cleavage. Simon certainly did. He would take a sly peek, and then leer lasciviously at me. I was hoping that Harriet hadn't noticed. "Great night eh. The lads 'ave done you proud, eh Simon?" I offered.

Every now and then, Simon looked in my direction. If looks could kill! "What? What?" I said in mock innocence. Jenny stood up and excused herself. "I'm just popping to the 'loo'," she smiled sympathetically. Was the sympathy for Simon? Or was it for me? Harriet stood up from her chair, bent rather exaggeratedly so that my face was very close to her breasts. This, I'm sure was for the benefit of Simon.

"Hang on Jenny, I'll come with you."

As soon as the girls were out of earshot, Simon gripped my arm. "Tell me something Laurie old mate. Why is it that women can never go t' the toilet on their own?"

I just shrugged my shoulders. By this time, Simon had drunk more than perhaps he should have done, and was looking rather 'worse for wear'. Well, who could really blame him? I sat there trying to think of a way to take his mind off all the 'fuss' that was going on all around him. I know that it must have been bloody awful for him, stuck in that bloody wheelchair hour after hour, especially as he had always been so active. No more running. No more squash. Christ Simon, I do hope they find the bastard who did this to you. Suddenly, I had what I considered a flash of inspiration.

"What about basketball? Plenty of people do basketball in wheelchairs. Table-tennis …or archery," I enthused.

"Archery! Bollocks to that. Who do you think I am, fuckin' Robin Hood? Trust you to come up with fuckin' archery. You know that darts is the one thing I'm no bloody good at."

No sooner had the girls returned from the 'Ladies' and sat down, when Simon announced, "Right Jenny luv, whenever you're ready. It's been great, but I think we should get off. I'm feelin' a bit knackered now." Without waiting for a response, taking his mobile-phone from his pocket, he telephoned for a taxi. "Cheers …see you in a few minutes."

Ten minutes later, he wheeled himself out of the pub as quietly as he could, leaving the 'good-nights' and 'thanks for comings' to Jenny. I looked at Harriet, and for a moment or two we said nothing. She eventually smiled.

"I'm sorry," I said.

"Why? He behaved more or less as I expected him to do. She's nice though. That's why I never mentioned Karen." I must have looked rather puzzled. "Karen!

The one Simon was trying to chat up, the first time we met," Harriet went on to explain. She glanced at her watch, "Are you ready to go?" she asked, picking up her handbag.

"Harriet." I put on my 'little boy lost' face. "Will I be staying over tonight?"

"Only if you're good. Very good!" she said, taking my hand.

17

After several pints of beer, my sexual performance on this particular Saturday night left something to be desired, and I wasn't the 'good boy' that Harriet had been hoping for. We both slept fitfully, but still managed to 'lie-in' until about 10 o'clock the next morning.

"Do y' fancy going out for a walk later Laurence? I don't know about you, but I could do with a bit of fresh air. We could drive out to a park, or somewhere," she suggested.

"Yes that sounds good to me," I said, at least trying to sound reasonably keen. We went, but to be honest it was one of those days when things just didn't feel right. We were both a bit quiet.

After a short walk and a cup of tea in the café, Harriet suggested that, perhaps we should go.

When we got back to her place I didn't even get out of the car, but made some rather lame excuse and left.

Well, it looks like being microwave and telly tonight, I thought to myself, somewhat morosely. Some ten or fifteen minutes later, I was just about to sit down and enjoy my culinary masterpiece, when I suddenly remembered something and cursed aloud, "Oh, soddin' 'ell, I've got to take the car in for it's M.O.T. in the morning." I ate my food with a minimum of enjoyment, then picked up the phone ...time to grovel to his 'lordship', so I dialled the number.

"Hello." It was Jenny's voice. Jenny's lovely, sexy voice. "Hello,' she said again.

"Oh hello Jenny, it's me. Laurence. Could I have a quick word with his 'lordsh'...? With Simon, please Jenny," I stammered, like a lovesick schoolboy. I thought I heard her chuckle before calling to Simon.

"Now then my old mate, what's up?" he said, in a manner not exactly full of patience or interest. I quickly explained my predicament, and it was agreed that he would pick me up at the garage at eight-forty sharp.

True to his word he was there bang on time. "When will y' car be ready?" he asked.

"I've to give them a ring about four," I replied. As Simon drove towards the warehouse he suddenly cursed. "Chuffin' 'ell, I've left some important papers on the table at home. That's with 'avin' my routine buggered up. I'll have to go and get them. I'll drop you off, an' you can open up." I just sat there and said nothing. We pulled up in front of the warehouse and as I climbed out he groaned, "I can't remember the last time I opened up late."

Before I was barely clear of the car door, he sped

away.

Sometime later there was a sudden loud banging on the main roller door. I put the pen down and slowly walked to the small door marked, CUSTOMER ENTRANCE. I peeked around the door and looked outside. "Open the bloody door f' Christ's sake," snarled his 'lordship', "It's going to piss it down." I quickly went back inside, and operated the switch on the roller door.

"Be careful," I said, as I put my hand out to protect him.

In his impatience and foul mood, he almost banged his head on the roller-door. "Doesn't look like rain to me," I remarked pointedly.

Trade was rather quiet that particular morning. Bloody typical …just what I needed, with him in a mood like he is.

"Tea or coffee?" I offered.

He waited a few seconds before snarling, "Anythin'! ...No, coffee. I'll 'ave coffee." Suddenly the phone rang. "Coleridge Electronics," Simon purred, putting on his customer-friendly voice. "I've got to go out," he announced, a few minutes later. With that he picked up his car keys, and wheeled himself towards the roller door. I could see that it wasn't easy for him to operate the switch, so I reached for it myself. The door opened, and he was gone.

I knew that I had to be prepared for his mood swings. Jenny had warned me. However, it was pretty obvious that something really had upset him this morning. Surely it wasn't just picking me up, or leaving papers at home. In all the time we had worked together, I couldn't remember a single instance when he had gone off, without letting me know where he was going. Obviously, if necessary I could contact him on his 'mobile', but I dreaded to think what sort of response I would get. *Hang on a chuffin' minute! Who been runnin' the whole soddin' shebang this last couple of months or so? I chuffin' have! So if his 'lordship' wants to sulk, chuffin' let him.*

He returned just after one o'clock carrying with him, that wonderful aroma of fish and chips. "I come bearing a gift, and seeking forgiveness," he simpered.

I said nothing. "Pop the kettle on, there's a dear," he said in a mockingly camp tone.

I still said nothing, but did his bidding. "Now then Laurence my old mate …tell me, 'ave I still got it, or 'ave I still got it?"

Even had I been going to tell him, I wasn't about to get the chance. "The phone call; earlier …was from the sports centre in Birkenhead? Well, I've been to see the manager. They need some major rewiring doin', and I've only got us the contract. About five thousand quids worth. Five thousand chuffin' quids worth! Apparently he remembered me from when I played squash there. Still got my card in his pocket. I'm so chuffed, I could jump out of this bloody chair."

I finally got the chance to break my silence. "Simon, that's fantastic! We'll need to contact the agency about a 'sparkie', and I must say it's nice to see that something's cheered you up. You were a right miserable sod this morning."

"Yes, sorry about that old mate. That's something I need to talk to you about later," he said mysteriously.

After our delicious repast of fish and chips, I busied myself with a sweeping brush, while Simon busied himself by perusing some very old copies of *Penthouse* and other 'gentlemen's' magazines. The sweeping brush came to a halt, as I had yet another flash of inspiration. Photography!

Of course!

Why hadn't I thought if it before? I walked around to where Simon sat in the area we loosely termed 'the office'.

"Photography!" I announced with a grin.

"What?" he said, looking puzzled.

"Why don't you take up photography? I'm not talking about the stuff you're gawpin' at in those mags. I mean proper stuff. Like weddings, and portraits. It would be perfect," I continued enthusiastically.

"Photography? Who d' think I am? David feckin' Bailey!" he said, raising his arms to the heavens. "No Laurence …but you have just given me a much better idea. You hold the camera …and then you can take pictures of me …racin'!"

"Racin'? What racin'?" I asked, intrigued.

"Wheelchair racin'. You know, like that Tanny Gray Whatsit. To be honest, I've been thinking about it for a while but I didn't want to say anything until I was sure.

Now I am! I'm going to do it Laurie. I am!' he said firmly. Then suddenly, looking at the clock, he said, "Aye now then, it's turned four. You'd better phone the garage, an' see if that bag o' bollocks you call a car is ready."

I dialled the number. The mechanic sounded cheerful. "It's failed mate. If you want to call in you can collect the 'fail-sheet'. It needs quite a bit doing. Front brake pads: hand brake, rear shockers ...on both sides, some electrics, an' a bit of welding. Other than that it's okay." he said happily.

"What's that going to cost me?" I enquired gloomily.

"About six hundred quid mate. That's when I've got the parts in." I was sure he was smiling. I put the receiver down quite calmly.

"Six hundred bloody quid!" I said between clenched teeth. "BOLLOCKS!" I yelled at the top of my voice.

After we closed up the warehouse, Simon drove me round to the garage. I asked the mechanic how long it would take to sort the car out. "Depends mate. On how long it takes to get the parts," was his cheerful estimate.

Suddenly but quietly, Simon took over. "Look mate," he said, speaking in a sarcastic manner to the mechanic. "Just do nothing until you hear differently. Okay?"

With that he gestured to me to follow him outside. "Look Laurie old mate, no disrespect, but that heap of shit's hardly worth six hundred quid. You'd just be wastin' y' money. Why don't you get something better?"

"That's all very well for you to say. You can go out and buy a car just like that. It's not that easy for me," I retorted glumly.

Simon looked at his watch. "Do you fancy a quick pint before I drop you off at home? We need to have a chat. I'll just give Jenny a call," he said, taking his mobile phone from his pocket. As usual, it wasn't a question. It was an instruction.

We entered *The Feathers* just as they were opening up.

"Good …nice and quiet. Get 'em in will you? I'll just 'ave half," said Simon, handing over a five-pound note. We sat in silence with our drinks. He seemed to be in deep thought. Then at last, he said, "This business about a car. I know that I don't pay you a fortune, but I know you understand the situation. Jenny and I very much appreciate that and we also appreciate the way you've kept things going this last few weeks." I was about to say that he didn't need to thank me, but he put up his hand to stop me, and carried on, "No Laurie, we would have been in deep shit without you. That's why I've decided to pay you a bit of a bonus."

Again I tried to interrupt him. No chance! He was determined to enjoy his moment of benevolence. He put his hand in side his jacket and pulled out an envelope, which he handed to me. Without saying a word I opened it and looked inside. The envelope contained a number of fifty-pound notes. I just sat and stared at the money. I was stunned.

Eventually I said, "Good lord Simon, how much is

there here? I can't accept all this."

"There's five grand. And I don't want another word about not taking it. I mean it, Laurie. It's up to you what you do with it of course, but you could buy a car. You should be able to get something reasonably decent for that."

I tried to protest, but it was to no avail. He had made up his mind …and that was that. I couldn't deny that the money would be very handy. Even though I was 'gob-smacked', in a strange way, I was rather disappointed. I had been thinking of asking for a possible pay rise. That was right out of the window now. "Right, thank you very much Simon. If you're sure. And yes, I'll start looking for a car straight away. I just hope you'll give me some advice. You know what I'm like with cars.'

"No problem old mate, but changing the subject, can I bend your ear for a few minutes?" he asked rather mysteriously.

"Of course …but I'll get us another drink first." I went to the bar feeling puzzled, and for some inexplicable reason, slightly worried.

I put the drinks on the table, sat down and said, "Right, I'm all ears." Simon took a long drink, and slowly put his glass down.

"Now, what I'm about to say is strictly between you and me. It's something that I don't find easy to talk about but you're my mate, and I simply have to talk to someone." He paused for a moment, as he took another drink. "Since coming out of hospital, there have been a certain number of problems that Jenny and I have 'ad to deal with. I'm sure you'll understand that." He paused again and then a sip from his glass. He was speaking very precisely, seeming to consider each word thoughtfully. Then suddenly he said, "Oh Christ, let me get to the point. It's about me and Jenny. We're having problems. Mainly at night: in bed."

He sighed, and looked down at the floor. I could tell that he was finding this very difficult. Slowly he raised his head, looked me in the eyes and said, "If you're finding this too embarrassing, just say so, and I'll shut up."

This wasn't the Simon that I knew. This wasn't a Simon in control. This was a Simon who was vulnerable. He looked lost. I wasn't used to a Simon asking for help.

"No it's okay …go on," I said. Even though I suspected that it would become rather embarrassing, I was genuinely concerned. I couldn't also help feeling curious.

"It's *sex,* of course. I can't …you know …get a hard on. Oh Christ, why am I telling you this?"

I then did something that I couldn't recollect ever having done before. I reached over and placed a hand on his arm. "Simon it's okay. Obviously it's up to you …but if you think it will help, then talk about it. Get it off your chest. We are friends f' Pete's sake, aren't we?"

I took my hand away, and sat back in my seat.

"Of course I knew …that it would almost certainly be the case. Y' know …'ave problems with the old todger," he continued, as he pointed towards his groin.

"The doctors, and the counsellor have warned me, but I still can't get my head round it." Suddenly, in spite of his mood, he laughed quietly. "Oh bloody 'ell! Can't get my head round it," he laughed again. Then he fell silent for a moment, before continuing. "That was one way that I thought it might work. She's never been keen you see…" I was looking at him rather bemused.

"Come on Laurie. Keep up. Jenny! She doesn't like going down on the old one-eyed trouser snake. Never has, bless her. She's tried her best …other ways. You know, with her hands. Or with her tits."

It was then that I realised that, no, I didn't really want to hear this.

I was actually starting to feel rather uncomfortable.

This was Jenny he was talking about: the same Jenny that I desired …the same Jenny that I fantasised about when I was in my bed. But it was too late now.

He had to talk. He had my ear. I was his friend. He had no one else to turn to.

Again he paused. "I'm sorry old mate. Not what you want to hear, but I just had to talk to someone. I don't know what to do. I shouldn't be dumping all this on you. Maybe things will improve in time. It's just that it's causing friction between us, me and Jenny."

I didn't know what to say. I hadn't a clue. I just sat there biting my lip and finding it very difficult to even look at him.

"Eh' look at the time," he said suddenly, looking at his watch. "Time we were off. Drink up old mate …an' stop looking so chuffin' miserable. It's me that's not gettin' his end away. You're the sex machine these days. How is Hilary these days?"

"Harriet! Her name's Harriet, Simon …and yes, she's fine thanks," I said tetchily, and then I wondered if that really was the case.

Simon drove the few miles to my house in silence. Then he just said, "Right old mate I'll pick y' up in the morning. Don't be late. An' Laurie, remember what I said, not a word. Not even to Hil'…Harriet, if you don't mind."

"No of course not. A' you gunna' be okay?" I asked.

He smiled wanly, and nodded. "Yer, I'll be fine. Don't worry. See you in the mornin'."

He started the engine as I shut the car door. I watched him drive down the road until he was out of sight, then I entered the kitchen and put the kettle on. I looked at the microwave, and then wondered what was on the telly. I felt for the envelope – full of money – inside my jacket pocket. I thought about Simon in his wheelchair. I took my cup of tea though into the lounge and sat down. No Simon my old friend, I wouldn't swap you places …for all your money. Just then I remembered something that I'd meant to ask Simon.

"Who is Tanny Gray Whatsit?"

18

The next day at work, both Simon and I felt a little awkward in each other's company. Neither of us spoke further about the problems that he and Jenny were having. We concentrated on business matters or, when time allowed, we discussed the subject of my getting another car. Should I buy privately, or should I go to a second-hand dealer? We trawled through local newspapers and motoring magazines.

"How much can you spend?" Simon enquired bluntly.

I was still feeling rather uncomfortable, about the money that Simon had handed me the evening before. "With what you gave me yesterday, and about another grand that I've saved, I suppose I'll have about six thousand. Although, I had thought about asking Harriet whether she fancied going on a holiday."

"A chuffin' holiday! When? Don't forget we've got that contract at the sports centre to sort out y' know. Don't go an' drop me in the shit with that. Can't you go a bit later?"

"Well yes …I suppose so," I replied: nothing more to be said then.

I really would have to get my own transport sorted out soon. I could tell that his 'lordship' was getting fed up of having to pick me up each morning. Also, I had to get a taxi whenever I went over to see Harriet. She very rarely came to my house. It wasn't the most salubrious place to entertain a lady. So I put my mind to it. *Come on Laurence stop chuffin' about, and get something bought.* And that's just what I did, a few evenings later.

Simon drove me over to a house in the village of Raby, to look at the car. When we got there, he just peered at it through his driver's door window. The newspaper advert had read; FORD FOCUS. 2009 59,000 MILES. ONE PREVIOUS OWNER. T&T. £4,950 o.n.o.

"Another soddin' Focus? Haven't you got any imagination, Laurie?"

"Not where cars are concerned," I said. "Anyway, I like the Focus. I know where everything is."

The chap, who was selling the car, said that it was a good car. Reliable: economical, comfortable, with plenty of T&T. To gullible me, all these things appeared to true. We took it for a short drive, and then I bought it.

"It got you here then," was all Simon said, as he entered the warehouse the next morning. He wheeled himself over to the sink and filled the kettle. "Tea or coffee?" he asked.

"Coffee," I said absent-mindedly. I sat down, picked up a newspaper, and without any real interest glanced at it. Simon placed my coffee in front of me; I slowly took a drink and then quietly said, "Simon, can I ask you something?"

He looked across at me and said, "That always sounds slightly ominous. Go on ask away. I'm not saying that I will answer though."

I took another drink, paused for a few seconds, and then said, "How are you ...really?" Before he could reply, I went on, "I mean stuck in that chair and everything." I still didn't give him the opportunity to speak. "I know you mentioned about things in the bedroom department, but what about everything else?" Finally, he managed to interrupt me.

"Why do you ask? Why now?"

I sighed deeply before continuing. "I can't help but worry about you – about both of you. You know – especially what you were sayin' the other night."

He poured some more coffee into both cups. "Yes, I'm sorry about that Laurie. I shouldn't have dumped that lot on you. Look, just forget I said anything. Jenny and me ...we'll sort it out and, of course, all the other changes are taking a lot of getting used to. One thing that did piss me off was havin' to get shut of the 'Beema'. I really loved that car." He paused for a second then went on, "As for this,' he gripped both sides of the wheelchair, 'I am getting used to it. Honestly! You 'ave to don't you? And I am serious about the wheelchair racin', and yes, maybe even basketball. I'm going to look into it. First thing I need to do, is to get some advice. There must be a club or association that I can contact. Anyway, look; I don't want you to worry. Jenny and me, we'll be fine. And as soon as that job's done at the sports centre, I want you to take that holiday."

"That's something else," I said with a frown. "That money you gave me the other evening. Can you really afford to be doing things like that? You get a five-grand contract, then give all the money to me."

"Look Laurie, stop worryin' about the bloody money. Strictly speaking I shouldn't say anything …and this is just between me and you. Dad's been very helpful, if you get my drift. So stop worrying. If I don't hear anything from the police in the next few weeks, I think I can take it that they're not goin' to catch the bastard who did it. If that's the case, then I shall see a solicitor about compensation. Apparently, that's a possibility. So like I say, don't worry. We'll get this job done, then you can take that holiday."

The next three weeks seemed to fly past. We had set on two 'sparkies' from the employment agency, to do the rewiring at the sports centre. They were good lads. Reliable, and expert in their work.

"Job done, and one satisfied customer, and the sports-centre manager said he'll put more work our way, as and when," announced a very pleased, rather smug Simon.

Having got the go-ahead from Simon, I broached the subject of holidays with Harriet. "I was wondering –

how would you fancy going away for a few days? You know, a proper holiday." After …what shall I call it…'our dip in enthusiasm', we seemed to be getting on much better. So I was hoping my suggestion would meet with her approval.

"Oh yes Laurence, that would be really nice," Harriet said, with a great big smile. All we had to do now was work out the where and when. It was decided that Harriet would make the arrangements. That night our sex was the best for some considerable time.

I was shocked. "Corfu?" Shocked doesn't start to describe it. "That means a plane! Flyin'," I said nervously.

"Well yes, that's the usual way to travel to Corfu," Harriet grinned at me. Then in mock shock-horror she said, "Don't tell me, that you've never flown before." We were sitting having Sunday lunch in a cosy pub. The restaurant was busy, and I was aware that people were looking in our direction.

"Harriet, I haven't even been out of the country, never mind havin' flown." I whispered.

"Well it's high time you did …and now is your chance," she said, still grinning. "It'll be great. You'll love it," she said quietly, taking my hand as though to reassure me.

Jenny

19

Simon and I had agreed that I should go back to work. Well, agreed as well as we seemed to agree about anything these days. His moods changed so quickly. One minute he was upbeat, then the next minute, he was really down. I did honestly try to help, and be understanding.

One major problem of course, was in bed. I'd never been very adventurous when it came to sex. I'm not prudish: just not very adventurous. To be fair, Simon was never one to try to persuade me to do anything that I felt uncomfortable with. Well not before the accident, that was. Right from getting married, I liked to believe we had a good and satisfying sex life. We had sex frequently and to the best of my knowledge Simon always climaxed. I quite often did. But that had all changed. Because of the way the accident had affected his lower body, he couldn't get an erection. At first we agreed that it would just need a little time, and a bit of patience. Unfortunately patience wasn't something that Simon was blessed with. What he didn't seem to realise, was that I needed sex too.

Maybe now that he seemed to be more relaxed about the business, and he was talking about taking up a sport, things would improve. Anyway, I'd made up my mind …I would go back to work.

The next morning, after Simon had left for work, I drove over to the pharmacy. Everyone seemed pleased to hear that I was starting back. The shop manager agreed that I should return on the following Monday. It was so nice to see them all again. Especially the girls.

As the journey home took me close to the company warehouse I decided to call in. Fingers crossed, it would be a nice surprise for Simon. So why was I feeling so apprehensive?

"Hello Jenny," Laurence said, with a warm smile. "This is a nice surprise. I'm afraid you've just missed Simon though. He's out visiting a client. Doing his Mr. Smooth Operator bit, to bring some more work in. Can I make you a drink? I was just about to put the kettle on."

I looked at my watch. "Yes please Laurence, that would be nice. Have you any coffee?"

"Anysing zat madam desires. Tea…cafe? Or perhaps madam would care for..." With this, his imitation French accent tailed off, as he pirouetted towards the kettle. Was it my imagination or was there something rather suggestive in his voice? No! Not Laurence – surely not.

Simon still hadn't returned some half an hour later. Glancing at my watch, I said, "Well thank you for the coffee Laurence. I'm going to get off now. Oh by the way …I hope you and Harriet have a lovely holiday. And don't worry about the flying; you'll love it. See you when you get back. Will you tell Simon that I'll have tea ready at the usual time?"

Shortly after seven o'clock that evening, I heard Simon's car pull up outside. I thought I heard the car door slam. If he was upset about something, he wasn't the only one. The meal that I had prepared earlier was spoiled. He could have at least, phoned.

"Laurie said you called in," was all he said, as he came into the kitchen. He looked at me, waiting for my response.

"Yes that's right. Where have you been? I said angrily. *The Feathers* I suppose." Before I could continue he pushed his wheelchair past me, and headed towards the bathroom. I think he may have banged his knuckles on the door-jamb in his haste, because I heard him curse the 'F' word.

The meal, of sorts, was eaten in silence. I washed the pots, and dried them. Usually Simon dried them, but this evening he didn't offer. We watched T.V, and had a solitary glass of wine. Shortly after half-past-ten, Simon went to bed. I followed a few minutes later. The bedroom light was already switched off. I quickly undressed, slipped on my 'nightie', and climbed into bed. Was this going to be the night when we didn't even kiss 'goodnight'? That had never happened before.

We lay there in silence for what seemed an age. I wasn't one to cry at the least little thing, but I felt very close to tears at that moment. Suddenly, we both sighed deeply at the same time. Then Simon took my hand and quietly said, "I'm sorry luv ...I'm such an idiot at times. I know I should 'ave been home for tea. The least I could 'ave done was phone, but I was in a foul mood because I didn't get that contract we were hoping for. Some bastard undercut me."

He squeezed my hand as he carried on. "I shouldn't take it out on you I know, or Laurence for that matter. The poor sod wondered what the hell he'd done. At least he won't 'ave to put up with me for the couple of weeks he's away on holiday. I am a prat sometimes I know ...and I know there'll be other contracts, but y' know me Jenny ...I just don't like losing."

"Shut up and give me a kiss." I whispered. I put my arms around him, and kissed him tenderly. As our kisses became more passionate, I felt his hand cover one of my breasts. I gently moved his hand and quickly took off my 'nightie'. Then carefully, but with some haste I took off his pyjamas. We were entering that place that we knew could lead us to awful frustration. Simon knew it, and I knew it but I couldn't stop. We were both totally naked ...and I loved it! I stroked his chest. The palm of my hand slowly touched one of his nipples. I felt it harden. As we kissed again my hand slowly moved down his belly. I stopped my hand as it touched the crinkly hair just above his cock. Oh yes, I can bring myself to say 'cock' now.

On one occasion when we arguing in bed, and I was being rather childish I suppose, Simon had grabbed my hand and thrust it roughly between his legs and said loudly, "It's called an effin' prick woman: a prick, or if you really are that sensitive, a cock."

Well weren't arguing now so I took hold of his soft cock, and I slowly began to work one hand up and down it. Then I moved my hand to his balls. I gently toyed with them. Then my hand moved back to his cock, but even though I knew in my heart that both of us were willing it with every fibre of our beings, the stiffness that we both craved, didn't come. Before Simon could become too distressed, I straggled him. I pushed my hips down to meet his. I lowered my chest until one of my small but perfectly formed breasts – Simon's words, not mine – was touching his lips. My nipple hardened as his mouth began to suck. Slowly he took most of my breast into his mouth. Oh god I love it when he does that. I pressed my pelvis very firmly into his pelvis, and I thrust myself into him. I kissed him and I pushed my tongue into his mouth. His hands held both my breasts, gently. He rubbed and tweaked my nipples. He really loves my nipples.

As our passion grew, it held certain desperation. I was silently praying that I could feel his cock harden. I reached down to take hold of him again. Was it? Was it getting harder? Yes surely! Oh please let it happen. I gently positioned myself and guided him so that he could enter me but, as had always happened since the accident, it was all to no avail. I knew when his body went still: when he just sighed. But this time there was a difference. Suddenly I realised that he was sobbing. Then very slowly and quietly he started to curse, "Oh Christ. Oh dear Christ."

He said it over and over again. Slowly I moved myself away from him and lay flat on my back. Then I felt the tears start to run down *my* face.

20

Neither of us slept well that night. In the morning as I felt Simon stir, I pretended to be asleep. Eventually he got out of bed, and into his wheelchair. I tried to sense his mood. He went quietly, and I hoped calmly, to the bathroom. A few seconds later I heard running water as he began to shower. I lay there feeling miserable. Try as I might, it was impossible not to think about last night. I could still hear his sobs: and the curses. A sense of absolute sorrow washed over me. "Simon, oh Simon, I'm so sorry," I whispered to myself.

I also felt a deep sense of outrage! I could kill the evil swine that has done this to us. We had been so happy. So, content. Now it felt as though we were being torn apart.

I still feigned sleep as I heard Simon coming out of the bathroom. I could smell him: the body spray, the aftershave. Strangely, I took some small comfort from that. Even as low as he must have been feeling, it was as though he was determined not to let himself go. As he dressed himself I lay still and quiet. He could manage by himself but, when things between us were good, I liked to help him. Sometimes he was happy to let me. Other times, he was liable to snap, "Leave me! I have to learn to do it for myself."

Then just as he was leaving the room he quietly said, "Right then, I'll be off then. I'll give you ring later." He sounded so sad.

After I had heard the car leave, I got up and showered. Back in the bedroom I stood in front of the full-length mirror, and looked at my naked body. Even though I had done this many times before, this time there was something different. Not in my reflection, but in the way I felt. I couldn't draw my eyes away. My hands suddenly gripped my buttocks. Tighter and tighter! Then they moved slowly onto my thighs. All the time I watched myself in the mirror. My fingers slowly drifted, feather light against my pubic hair. Then my hands moved upwards and I caressed my breasts. "Well Simon, even if you can't manage it, I'd like to bet that there are plenty of men who would love the chance." I whispered the words under my breath.

Even as the guilt came, I pushed it away. Then suddenly I was on the bed, and while one hand busied itself with bringing a nipple to full hardness, the other gently probed between my legs until it found its desired destination. Afterwards, I slipped on my dressing gown and went into the bathroom to wash. Still struggling with feelings of guilt, I went to the kitchen and made myself some tea and toast. I sat at the breakfast bar, and tried to concentrate on the newspaper. I couldn't stop thinking about what I'd done in the bedroom. I couldn't remember the last time I had done that. Until recently of course, I hadn't had the inclination. There had been no need. Well, now there is a need. It's my body, and if I want to …mastur' …do that, I will. This was stupid. Why should I torture myself? But no matter how much I tried to placate myself, the guilt would not go away.

Suddenly I realised that I needed to get out of the house. Fresh air! Yes that's what I needed. Right, where should I go? I looked out of the window. It was overcast: not the sort of day for going out for a walk. Where then? Shopping? Of course! That's what we girls do when we are depressed. Yes, I could 'bash the plastic'. A bit of 'splash the cash', would do me good before I go back to work on Monday, but where?

I could drive into Birkenhead. How exciting! Manchester is the place for shopping. I glanced at my watch. A bit late to go to Manchester …but I could go to Liverpool. Me …drive to Liverpool? In the past, on our rare visits to the city, Simon had driven. Could I drive through that tunnel? Even Simon hated driving through it. *"For goodness sake, stop being so stupid. Of course you can, you're a grown woman, not a child,"* I muttered to myself.

I put the kettle on again, and went out to the garage to get a map from my car. I sat with my drink and studied it.

I quickly dressed, and went out to the car. I wanted to leave before I had chance to change my mind. Half an hour later, I was approaching the tunnel entrance. I paid the toll, and drove into the gloom. I kept to the nearside lane, and held my speed to a steady thirty miles an hour. After what seemed an eternity I emerged into the daylight of Liverpool. Relieved yet childishly ecstatic, I grinned at myself in the interior mirror. A short time later I was parking the car, and heading for the shopping centre. What was I going to buy? What do I really need? It's not about what you need girl. It's about what you want! A coffee first, I think.

I found a pleasant little 'bistro' and ordered a cappuccino. This just wasn't working. After window-shopping for over an hour, and taking a leisurely lunch, I wasn't just tired, I was also bored. I decided to walk back to the car, and head for home. The weather had improved. The sun was trying to break through. If I got back in time, I could spend an hour relaxing in the garden.

Before leaving the car park I consulted my map. A lot of good that did! I still managed to get lost. All I had to do was head for the river, the docks, then towards the tunnel. So why couldn't I found my way? As I drove I became aware that I was passing a large park. At the entrance I spotted an ice cream van so I parked the car, got out and walked over. An ice cream would be nice, and hopefully some directions would be very useful.

"Sorry sweetheart, can y' come back when the queue's gone down a bit?" said the ice-cream man. I glanced behind me at the three people that formed the queue. I looked at my watch. It wasn't yet three o'clock. Plenty of time! I looked into the park, and decided to walk over to a bench, sit, enjoy my ice-cream, and watch the ducks on the lake. There were a number of men fishing. The sun shone through a few fluffy clouds. It was all very pleasant: all very tranquil. I sat considering whether or not to take a walk around the lake.

Finishing the ice-cream, I started to rise from the bench. Suddenly without warning, something 'whooshed' past me, almost knocking me over as it brushed my arm. As I sat back down, shocked and dazed, I was faintly aware of a voice shouting. I looked up just in time to see a cyclist skidding to a stop. The young man walked back to where I sat, extremely shaken. Before he could begin to speak I launched into a verbal tirade, "What the devil do think you're doing? You could have killed me you stupid beggar." The words flew from my mouth. The young man looked aghast.

"Me a stupid beggar? What about you? Did you look when you stood up? I don't think so!" We both glared at one another.

"Do you always ride that bloody thing like a maniac?" I asked him angrily.

"I wasn't riding like a maniac. As you would have been aware, had you been looking where you were going," he countered. But as he spoke his words started to tail off. He began to look slightly concerned. "Are you alright?"

"If I am, it's no thanks to you," I said, determined not to take any blame in my near escape from death! He laid the bicycle down on the grass, and asked if he might sit down.

Without waiting for a reply he did so. Then quietly he said, "Look, I really am sorry if I frightened you. I just didn't expect you to get up, and walk out in front of me like that."

"Like what? Like someone just getting up," I seethed.

He bit his lip and sighed, "You really are very cross with me, aren't you? Okay, it was my fault …entirely. Now please tell me, are you alright?" He looked genuinely concerned. It was then that I first really looked at him. Actually he had a nice face.

"Yes I suppose, I am okay." I said rather more calmly, and then went on, "It just shocked me but you're right, I suppose. It was partly my fault for not looking where I was going. I'm sorry for being so nasty to you," I said, smiling rather coyly.

"Well as long as you're sure." He smiled back as he rose from the bench and picked up his bicycle.

As he mounted his bike I said, "Excuse me …before you go, I wonder if you could help me. I have to find my way back to the Birkenhead tunnel. I got lost, you see. I haven't a clue which way to go. That's how I came to be in this park."

Once again he lowered the cycle to the ground. Sitting back down on the bench he held his chin, scratched his nose, and considered. "Right, the tunnel? You are quite a long way from it. Let me see. Do you know Liverpool at all?" I shook my head. "Okay …look, I've got an idea. I live in Bootle. That's in the direction that you need go. If you feel okay about it, we could stick my bike in the back of your car, and I could take you right to the tunnel entrance." He could obviously see the doubt in my eyes, because he quickly carried on, "Yes you're right of course, it's a stupid idea. I'm sorry. We've only just bumped into one another ...if you'll forgive the pun."

I looked at him again. I know it was foolish, but he did look perfectly innocent and he did have a nice face. I did need to find my way to the tunnel and he was going to show me – and it was broad daylight. What could possibly go wrong?

"No please, I would be very grateful. If you think we can get your bicycle in the car." The cycle safely stowed in rear of the car, he took off his helmet and got in beside me. That was when I saw the mop of stunning blond hair. He only spoke to give me directions.

As we approached the tunnel he said, "You'll have to drop me just here. I can't go any closer to the tunnel entrance with the bike." I stopped the car and we both climbed out. As he proceeded to lift his cycle from the car I thanked him for his help. "My pleasure," he smiled ...such a handsome smile. He really was very handsome ...and that wonderful blond hair. I had been secretively watching him in the interior-mirror as we had driven from the park.

"By the way," I said, "Do you happen to know the name of that park?"

"Yes, it's Sefton Park, any particular reason for asking?"

"Oh, I just thought I like to know exactly where we had bumped into each other." I grinned at him, more mischievously than a 'nice girl' should have done.

"Oh right, I see. Before you go, can I ask you something?" Without waiting for a reply he continued, "If I don't, I will probably regret it for the rest of my life. I was wondering ...do you think that there would be any chance of my seeing you again?" All the time he'd been speaking, he was looking anywhere but at me.

I was just about to explain that that would not be possible, when I stopped myself. Why not? No, no of course I couldn't see him again, even though I really wanted to. He was so handsome. This was madness! For goodness sake I'm a married woman. Even as I looked at him I heard myself saying weakly, "I don't come into Liverpool very often. It wouldn't be easy. I live on the Wirral you see."

He sighed, then said, "I would come over there, but I don't have a car, just the bike." He paused for a moment, then carried on, "There's a lovely building in the park, called the 'Palm House'. It's rather like a very large conservatory: all glass. They have concerts there: mainly classical." He was almost pleading, but also smiling – a smile I was finding very hard to resist.

"Do you like classical music?" he asked.

"Some," I smiled back at him, thinking, *come on, don't give up now*. He didn't!

"Next week they're doing Tchaikovsky, with the Liverpool Philharmonic."

"I love Tchaikovsky," I heard myself say. It was as if someone else were saying the words.

"Come with me then. Please!" He put his hands

together as if begging. Oh that smile! Suddenly I caught my breath. What the hell am I playing at? I must be going mad.

"Look I don't even know your name. You don't know mine …and here we are arranging to see one another." I was alright now. I had the situation under control. Just say, *thank you and goodbye*, get in the car and drive off. "Look, thank you for helping…", the words petered out.

Then he asked, "Could I phone you? Maybe, when you've had the chance to think about it..."

"No!" I said sharply. "Look I'll phone you …if that's alright. Do you want to give me your number?"

"If you have a pen and paper," he said, and again he smiled. This time, it was the smile of a man who knew he had got what he wanted. As I was getting into the car I suddenly asked him, "Well …are you going to tell me your name?"

"Colin," he said. "And yours?"

"Jenny ...and, just in case you're wondering, I will phone."

I drove home in an absolute daze. What on earth was I doing? I was a married woman. I was on my way home to Simon, my husband. I must be mad! I should forget that it had ever happened. Don't phone him. Just throw his number away. But I knew that I wouldn't throw it away. I would phone him. Then suddenly I panicked as I looked at my watch. Five fifteen! Simon would be home in less than an hour …and I had to face him.

21

At least I didn't have too long to dwell on what had happened earlier. I was busy preparing dinner when Simon arrived home. It was obvious that he was still feeling rather subdued. As he wheeled his chair through to the lounge he just about managed to say, "Hi."

Doing my best to act normally, but feeling full of guilt, I followed him. "Do you want a drink?" I gestured towards the drinks cabinet.

He sighed and said, "I'll have a whiskey please. Make it a double luv." I poured a 'large-one' from the decanter, and dutifully took it over to him. "Thanks," he said quietly, as he turned on the T.V.

"Dinner won't be long," I said, walking back into the kitchen.

As we ate our meal I tried to make small talk. "How was your day?"

"Not bad," he replied.

"You haven't forgotten that I'm starting back at the

pharmacy on Monday, have you?" I asked.

"No, I've not forgotten," he mumbled. God I thought, this is like trying to get blood out of a stone. Still feeling full of guilt, I suddenly blurted out. "I went to Liverpool today." Simon looked up from his food. From the look on his face, anyone might have thought that I had said I'd been to Mars!

"Liverpool! You went to Liverpool? What, you drove, through the tunnel?" His face was a picture. "What for? Why Liverpool?"

"Oh, just shopping: for clothes," I lied. I was rather shocked at the ease with which I told the lie.

"Good God," he said. That was as far has his interest went.

Later in the evening we sat watching television, saying very little to each other. I was dreading bedtime. My eyes occasionally glanced at the clock.

Quite suddenly Simon said – no, more like announced – "Oh, by the way, I've decided to sleep in the other bedroom from now on. I think it would be for the best: for both of us."

I looked at him in utter shock and dismay. "Simon, for goodness sake, surely that's not necessary."

Before I could continue, he said, "Jenny …last night was the final straw. I can't cope with it any longer. I'm sorry, but I think it's for the best, at least for the time being."

I jumped up from my chair and shouted, "Oh right, you can't cope. *You* think it's for the best. What about what I think Simon? This is not the answer. This is not just about you, y' know."

But even as I spoke, he wheeled his chair out of the room without another word.

That night, alone, I slept only fitfully. I had hated the lonely nights throughout the time that Simon had been in hospital, but this was much worse. My mind was in turmoil. It wouldn't give me a moment's peace. My thoughts jumped from Simon and his moods, to our problems in bed, then to the man that I had met in the park today. Try as I may, I just couldn't stop thinking about him. Colin! He was so nice. Nice? He is absolutely gorgeous! That lovely blond hair. That face! Stop it, you stupid woman. You must be mad! All night long, these thoughts tormented me. Or so it seemed. However, I must have drifted off to sleep eventually, because the next time that I looked at the bedside clock it had turned nine a.m. I'd overslept, and Simon had left the house.

I busied myself with housework throughout the morning. Dusting and polishing. Keep busy, I thought. But a little later, as I sat taking a coffee break, other thoughts took over. We couldn't go on like this; we had to sort things out. Maybe we should go and see a councillor. It's not as though we didn't still love each other. We did still love each other …didn't we? I placed my cup on the table, stood up and walked out into the garden. Did he still love me? Did I still love him? The answer had to be; yes of course we still loved each other.

Normally I would enjoy Saturday mornings: the

thought of the weekend and what it might bring: chores in the morning, followed by a lazy afternoon ...then, perhaps, an evening out at *The Feathers*, or some nice restaurant for a meal. Of course today was very different. Who knows what the rest of the day would bring? Simon should be home at about one o'clock. He usually closed the warehouse at twelve-thirty on Saturdays, but would he be on time today?

Subconsciously, I went into the bedroom, opened my wardrobe and took out my handbag. The same one I had used yesterday. I opened the small zipped pocket, and took out a small piece of paper. On it in faint pencil was a telephone number. I looked at the number for what seemed an eternity, sat down on the bed and looked at the telephone. I realised that my hands were shaking. My mouth was dry.

I went to the bathroom to get a glass of water, all the time looking at the piece of paper. Sooner or later I would phone him: Colin! *Don't be stupid! You can't! Get control of yourself.* I tried as hard as I could to talk myself out of it, but I knew that I would make that call. I put the glass of water down on the bedside cabinet, then <u>slowly picked</u> up the receiver and started to dial the number.

I slammed the receiver down. He probably isn't even in. He could be working. He could be out cycling. Through the park! I picked up the glass, took another drink and looked at the piece of paper again. I slowly picked up the receiver. This time calmly, resolutely, I dialled the number. After a few seconds I heard a man's voice. It was him!

"Hello," was all he said.

I just stood there with the phone in my hand, unable to speak.

"Hello," he said again.

Finally I said, "Oh hello, is that Colin?"

"Yes it is. Is that *Jenny*?

"Yes," I said, my voice barely audible, even to myself.

"I didn't honestly think that you'd ring. I'm so glad that you have," said Colin, his voice not much louder than mine. I was already beginning to panic. Dry mouthed, I felt the need to do this quickly.

"The concert, Colin," I interrupted. "When is it?" I had called him Colin! It was though I had broken down a barrier. Just saying his name excited me.

"Oh, the Tchaikovsky is Thursday to Saturday of next week. It starts at seven-thirty," he answered quietly.

"It will have to be Friday," I said, "Where shall we meet? I don't want to get lost again." We made arrangements to meet just outside the exit of the tunnel, at seven o'clock. "If for any reason I can't make it, I'll ring you," I said, quickly putting the phone down.

Simon did arrive home at lunchtime. He still seemed to be rather morose. He went to the drinks cabinet, and poured a large whiskey. "Do *you* want anything?" he asked quietly.

I shook my head. "No thanks. Lunch won't be long. I thought as it's so nice, we might eat outside," I suggested, feeling as though I was walking on eggshells.

"Yes …good idea. An' then, I think we need to talk Jen'. I'll take some plates out to the patio. Put some on my lap," he said, with just a hint of a smile.

As we sat eating our food, I looked at Simon, and considered just how his accident had affected our lives. At times he was barely recognisable as the man that I had married. I hope you can live with yourself, you lousy swine I thought, of whoever had brought this pain into our lives. I struggled not to say it out loud. Then Simon reached for my hand, and held it gently. I could sense that he was finding it difficult to speak. Then slowly he began, "Jenny, about last night. I just don't know what to do. It's killin' me Jen'. I know it must be the same f' you." He took a deep breath. "I feel as though I'm not a real man anymore. We used to be so good together. We were good together …weren't we Jenny?" I could see the tears beginning to well up in his eyes. I squeezed his hand, smiled and nodded.

"Yes Simon …and we still are."

Before I could continue, Simon cut in, "But things have changed Jenny." Then, echoing my thoughts, he said, "Christ I wish I could get my hands on the bastard who has done this to us. I'd bloody well kill 'im." Suddenly tears were running down his face.

I got up from my chair, put my arms around him and gently 'shushed' him. After a moment or two he composed himself, and as I sat back down in my chair he said, "Do y' think that perhaps we should talk to that counsellor again? It might help. I think that I probably overreacted last night. It was awful: being in bed alone

…without you. I'm so sorry Jenny luv. I know that I'm a bloody idiot at times. I promise I will try harder."

"Yes it was awful. But I do understand, y' know. We have to fight this together. Both, in bed …and out! And yes …perhaps we should get some advice. There's something else, Simon. You haven't said anything about taking up a sport lately. You really should try you know. I'm sure it would do you good." Then he smiled for what seemed the first time in ages.

"Yes y' right luv. I will look into it. Now come 'ere an' give your old man a big kiss." The big kiss given, I filled our glasses with wine and passed one to Simon.

"A toast," I said. "To us. To the future. Our future; together." We clinked our glasses together. "And stop worrying. You're still the man I married, all the man. "

As we sat there in a much happier frame of mind, I made a resolution. I would not go to Liverpool next Friday. I would telephone him – I could hardly bring myself to use his name: Colin – and explain. No! I wouldn't even phone. I just wouldn't go.

22

Over the next couple of days my spirits rose. Simon seemed more cheerful too. After our 'heart to heart' we went out for a meal that evening. We tried a new Italian restaurant in town. Well, new to us that is. Although it was a little tricky getting Simon's wheelchair through the door, the waiter was extremely helpful, and made us feel very welcome. We had decided to have a taxi so that we could enjoy a few glasses of wine, and we certainly did! That night, bedtime didn't seem too traumatic. We simply cuddled up together, and because of the wine, we were both soon asleep.

Monday saw me back at the pharmacy, which took a little bit of getting used to but after an hour or two, I was back into the old routine. Laurence and his girlfriend were back from their holiday in Corfu. This appeared to really please Simon, and I'm sure it wasn't just because of work, that he was happy to see Laurence. Although he would never admit it, Simon thinks the world of Laurence. I think that Laurence was the brother that Simon never had. So yes, hopefully things are finally beginning to get much better.

On the Wednesday evening as we sat eating dinner, Simon suddenly said, "Oh by the way, you know I was talking about taking up a sport. Well I've decided to have a crack at wheelchair-racing. I've been chatting to a couple of chaps on the Internet, and they were very helpful. They put me in touch with a company that builds the things. Only trouble is, they're in Loughborough. I hope you don't mind, but I've arranged to go down on Friday. Another problem is …I could be really late back. It crossed my mind that it might be better if I stopped overnight …depending on what time I get finished looking at the wheelchairs, that is. Apparently there's a lot to sort out. They 'ave to measure you up an' things."

He finally stopped talking. It had been ages since I had heard him so enthusiastic about anything. It was wonderful to hear. He was looking at me as if to say, go on, please say yes. I gave him a big smile and said, "I think it's a great idea. It's just what you need. I know you've been missing the competition. Friday you say? Just as long as you keep in touch. Phone me, and let me know how it's going. One condition though," I said, glancing at the dirty dinner plates. "I wash …you dry."

The following day at work my resolve weakened and I decided that I should phone Colin if only out of courtesy. After all, I did owe him an explanation as to why I wouldn't be coming to the concert. *Oh damn, I bet he's bought the tickets now*, I suddenly thought. It couldn't be helped. There was no way I could go now. Anyway, I didn't want to go did I? No, I'll phone him at lunchtime... But I didn't. I made some feeble excuse to myself.

By Friday I still hadn't made the call. As I struggled with my conscience throughout the morning at work, I finally had to admit to myself, that I had no intention of telephoning Colin to cancel our date. No, it wasn't a date! I was just going to meet him to explain why I couldn't go to the concert. I would be totally truthful. I owed him that at least. It wouldn't be a problem. I would be back before eight-thirty. Well before Simon got back from Loughborough.

"Are you alright Jenny?" asked Mr. Jones, my boss, "only you seem to be in a world of your own today." I made an excuse about having a slight headache. He smiled and made some remark about, taking more water with it.

I arrived home and started to prepare dinner. Suddenly I realised that I was making enough for two. Simon wasn't coming home to eat! I would have to hurry if I were to shower, dress, and get to Liverpool by seven o'clock. The sudden ringing of the telephone startled me. I slowly picked up the receiver. My mouth was dry as I quietly said, "Hello." I didn't want to speak to anyone at that moment, and especially I didn't want lie to Simon.

"Hi, it's me." It was Simon's voice. "Jenny it's going to be getting rather late to be drivin' back, by the time I've finished looking at these wheelchairs, so I think I will book into a B&B or hotel for the night. That's if it's okay with you?" Somehow I managed to say that it would be fine.

"Just make sure you phone me later. Make it just before I go to bed, say elevenish, if you can."

"Okay luv, will do. Love you."

"I love you too," I said. Then as I slowly put down the receiver, a sense of deep guilt began to trouble me.

After showering I stood looking into my wardrobe, wondering what to wear. It didn't really matter, did it? I wasn't going to go to the concert, so I didn't need to 'dress up'. I chose what I considered my least sexy bra and pants. Then a plain blouse and jeans. I put on a leather jacket, then picked up my keys, locked the house and climbed into my car.

Throughout the drive to Liverpool, I was every bit as nervous as the previous time. Of course, this time I was nervous for a very different reason.

As I approached the street corner where we had arranged to meet, I could see no sign of Colin. I stopped the car, turned off the engine and looked at my watch. Five past seven. I was a few minutes late. Maybe he wasn't going to come. Was I relieved, or was I disappointed? Before I could wonder any further, a taxi suddenly screeched to a halt directly behind me. I saw Colin jump out and hand the driver his fare. As the taxi sped away he smiled, opened the car door and got in.

"Sorry I'm late. Blessed taxi almost let me down. Hope you haven't been waiting long," he said rather breathlessly.

"No, I've only just arrived myself," I said.

I hadn't made any effort to start the engine.

"Right, I think we'd better be going. The concert starts at seven-thirty, and we have to find somewhere to park," he said. Again that smile! All my good intentions simply went out of the window. Before I could say anything I smiled back, and turned the ignition key.

"I must admit I've been wondering all week, whether or not you'd come. I'm so glad you have. You look lovely."

I started to protest. I certainly didn't feel lovely.

"Oh you do, really!" Colin gave directions towards the park, while I struggled with my feelings. Part of me felt riddled with guilt. Part of me was thrilled with excitement. What the hell was I playing at? We found a parking space, and set off to walk the short distance to the 'Palm House'.

We took our seats. The hall was almost full. The orchestra was already warming-up. Moments later, I sat there absorbed by the music. I do so enjoy Tchaikovsky, and I just love the 'Romeo and Juliet Suite'. I couldn't stop myself from taking the occasional sideways glance at Colin. I was very well aware that he was doing the same to me. When the interval arrived, Colin suggested that we went to the bar to get a drink. The bar was very busy, so I stood and waited while Colin went for the coffee. As we found a space to stand and drink, we both began to speak at the same time.

"After you," he offered. I paused to gather myself.

"Colin, there's something I need to tell you." I started slowly. He bit his lip and looked at me seriously. "I shouldn't be here tonight. Especially not like this, with you." Before I could carry on he interrupted,

"Why, because you're married?"

"How do y' know that?" I gasped.

"The ring is a bit of a giveaway."

How on earth could I have been so stupid? We just stood looking at each other in embarrassment. Before I could say anymore, Colin quickly continued. "Jenny, there's something I need to tell you. I have to tell you now but not here. Would you mind dreadfully if we missed the second half of the concert? I know it's a shame, but we do need to talk …and I imagine that you have to get home before it gets too late." I just nodded in agreement, my mind in a whirl.

We finished our coffee and as we walked to the car Colin asked, "What would you like to do? Find a pub or something. Or just sit in the car to talk?" I didn't want to be in the company of others. I felt the need for privacy. The car was parked in quiet side street, so we decided to talk there. We sat in silence for some minutes and then I said, "When did you realise? That I'm married, that is?"

He looked guiltily at me, paused for a moment, and then said, "More or less straightaway. As I said earlier,

I saw your wedding ring."

"So why did you ask to see me, knowing that I was married?" I snapped.

"I don't know. No, that's not true. It was as though I couldn't help myself. As we were driving towards the tunnel I couldn't stop looking at you. I just knew that I had to see you again." He took a deep breath, and was about to continue when I interrupted.

"You said earlier, that there was something you had to tell me. Are you going t' tell me that you're married as well?" I looked at him inquisitively. He hesitated, and even though an odd little smile, very briefly flitted across his mouth, I could see he was struggling to find the words, so I just waited patiently.

"No ...no I'm not married. There's no easy way of saying this, so I'll come straight to the point. I'm a priest. A Roman Catholic priest." Of all the things that he might have been going to say to me, never in my wildest dreams could I have expected this.

"A priest! Good God!" I said loudly, my hand flying to my mouth as I realised what I had said. "A priest. Why didn't you tell me when we first met? Oh my god!" Neither of us knowing what to say, we fell silent.

Eventually Colin coughed to clear his throat and said, "I'm sorry I didn't tell you straightaway but I was scared you wouldn't have seen me if I had."

Interrupting him, I said, "But I always thought that Catholic priests, were ...well..."

"Celibate. Is that the word you're looking for? Well yes I am. But it doesn't mean that I'm without normal feelings Jenny. You're not the first girl that I have noticed. You are however, the first girl I've ever asked out. I may be a priest, but I'm also a man Jenny. When I saw your wedding ring I just stupidly hoped, that maybe you were separated or something. As I said, stupid. Look I can see that you're upset. Perhaps we'd better go."

I looked at my watch. "Good heavens, it's almost ten o'clock. Yes I am going to have to go. Well Colin, it's been quite a night. I just don't know what to say. Will you be alright if I drop you of at the tunnel? Will you be able to get a taxi?"

"Yes I'll be fine. Before we go, can I ask you something? Would it be possible to see you again?"

"No Colin, I don't think that would be a very good idea. I shouldn't have even come tonight. I only came to explain that..." I shrugged my shoulders, and then continued. "I'm so sorry, but I think it's better if we don't meet again. In case you're wondering …it's not because of what you've told me – about your being a priest I mean, although I don't mind admitting it was a heck of a shock." Not waiting for him to reply, I added, "I do really have to go." I turned the ignition key, and started the engine.

Within a few minutes we were approaching the tunnel. I felt so very sad. Colin hadn't spoken other than to give me directions, to which I had simply nodded in reply. I stopped the car near to the tunnel entrance. I didn't switch off the engine. I sat looking straight forward though the windscreen. I couldn't bring myself to look at him.

"Well it looks as if that's that then. I'm sorry Jenny:

short and sweet, eh?" He paused, as though hoping I would say something.

After all my misgivings, all my feelings of guilt ...after what he'd told me, why did I still feel like this: still wanting to see him again? But no, it was impossible. Nor could I bring myself to tell him how I felt. I just looked at the windscreen.

"Right then ...I'll be off," he reached across and squeezed my hand gently. Then he got out of the car, and walked away. I was about halfway through the tunnel, when my mobile phone rang. It startled me so much, that I almost drove from my own lane into another car. I didn't dare to pick it up so I just let it ring.

After what seemed an age, it stopped. Suddenly I could feel the tears welling in my eyes. I wiped them with my sleeve. What was it I had said to myself only a few weeks ago? No more tears ...only smiles! That seemed so long ago now. I drove the rest of journey home as though in a daze. I had just locked the garage door, when my mobile rang again. "Hello, is that you Simon?" I said, trying to sound as normal as possible.

"Yes it's me Jenny. Where have you been?" Simon asked, "I tried to get you earlier."

"Oh right. Yes, I've been out. I just popped over to one of the girls for an hour," I lied. "I got a bit bored, so I called her to see if it was okay to go over. I've just this minute got in." My mouth was dry, and I felt terrible. Lying didn't usually come naturally to me. At least it hadn't done so before. I was on the verge of panicking. I could hear Simon's voice but I couldn't take in what he was telling me. Something about wheelchairs and how pleasant they had been, whoever they were!

"Simon luv it's a really bad line. I can't tell what you're saying," I lied again.

"Okay sweetheart, I'll get off then. See you tomorrow. I'll call in at the warehouse on my way home. If nothing's spoiling, I should be home before noon. Sleep tight. I'd send you a kiss down the line but the bar's full, and you know how shy I am. So I'll just say, good night luv."

Somehow I managed to say 'goodnight', although once again my eyes began to fill with tears.

I undressed for bed. Then I started to do what I usually did when I was naked in front of the mirror. I started to look at myself. I quickly looked away, riddled with guilt. For some inexplicable reason I found myself in the shower again. I suddenly realised, that I had already been in the shower just a few hours earlier. Not so inexplicable! I was trying to avoid going to bed. I had to force myself to climb beneath the sheets. As I lay there, the utter folly of what I had done came home to me. Madness! Crazy! You stupid, stupid bitch! And yet, for all that, thoughts of Colin pushed their way into my mind. Gorgeous blond Colin. Colin the Roman Catholic priest!

Laurie

23

The only trouble with taking a holiday is 'avin' to go back to work. Corfu was brilliant. It was my first time abroad, and the first time that I had ever flown. The flying? Great! The sunshine? Superb! The topless women? Fantastic! I've never seen so many bare boobs in my life, but now it's back to the grind and I wasn't exactly relishing it. You could never be sure what sort of reception you were going to get with Simon. I needn't have worried. He welcomed me like a long lost friend. "Morning Laurence." Bloody 'ell! *Laurence!* When did he last call me Laurence? "Good holiday? Christ, look at that chuffin' tan. Tea or coffee?" he said, holding up the kettle.

As we sat drinking, I enthused about every aspect of the holiday. "I was really apprehensive getting onto that plane, but it was magic! By the time we were coming into land I was really enjoying it. You could just about see all the island. The scenery on Corfu is marvellous. The beaches: and the women, nearly all bloody topless.

Tits of all shapes and sizes. And the bars at night. Fantastic! They 'ave this drink called Ouzo. It's bloody dynamite. I got well 'hammered' a couple of times."

"Did Harriet go topless?" Simon asked, with a leering expression.

"No, she didn't. She said she wasn't 'avin' any Greek blokes ogling her bosoms. And as you well know, she's got a right pair t' ogle at and some of them local lads are right randy buggers."

The following day Simon announced that he had to go to Loughborough on Friday. He was checking out a company that made racing wheelchairs. The next few days were pretty much routine. We spent the quiet periods doing a bit 'of stock taking. The holiday was soon forgotten. One part of it however, did still tend to occupy my mind. Every chance that she'd had, whether relaxing on the beach, or in a bar in the evening, Harriet made it clear, that she was becoming increasingly keen on our relationship developing into something more permanent. As for me, I wasn't quite so sure. Talk of commitment and involvement, frankly, scared me stiff. I really am very fond of her. In fact I think I'm falling in love with her, but when Harriet talks of, "It not making any sense, our running two houses." Well, that really does make me wonder if I'm ready to settle down again.

One thing I can't deny is that, since getting together with Harriet, my fantasising and foolishness regarding Jenny, has more or less gone. I've told myself to 'get a grip'. With Harriet I have something that I had never had with my wife, Molly: stability, plus, bloody wonderful sex. Sex with my ex-wife was a routine Saturday night 'quickie' if she'd had enough booze to loosen her up. The only thing that I could rely on Molly to do was nag. So all in all I've been pretty lucky... Lucky, when she 'buggered off' and very lucky when I met Harriet. I'm not going to meet a better one. So maybe it does make sense after all. My moving in with her, that is.

On Monday morning, after his jaunt on the Friday, Simon was in a very upbeat mood. That may have caused me to have what I can only think was a sudden rush of blood to the head. As we sat with our obligatory cup of coffee, I suddenly I found myself confiding, "I'm going to move in with Harriet."

Christ, where did that come from? I was supposed to be just thinking about it.

"Bloody 'ell old mate, that's a bit sudden in't it? Are you really sure? It's a big step y' know."

"Yes I know, but I am sure," I said, a bit too quickly. Of course I was anything but sure and I quickly changed the subject. "Anyway, how did it go down at Loughborough?"

Simon's eyes lit up. "Really well, they were very helpful. Mind it's not going to be cheap. Anything between three and four grand, depending on what spec' I decide on. The carbon wheels can bump the cost up. But if I'm going to do it, then I might as well do it right."

It was good to see him in such a positive frame of

mind.

"I'm going to phone them later this afternoon, to confirm my order. I shall need to go down again for a full fitting. I thought Friday, if that's okay?"

"Yes, sure," I said. "No problem."

In between customers, we sat drinking more tea and coffee. Simon enthused about his plans to get into wheelchair racing. "I chatted to quite a few people 'on line' about it. There's a disabled athlete's club in Liverpool that sounds good. If I was to go over one night, would you fancy coming with me? We could make a night of it."

I wasn't quite sure why he was *asking*. Usually it would come over as something of an instruction. Surely he wasn't worried about the prospects of coming into contact with other wheelchair users. No …as he said, we could have a good night out. It had been a while since we'd had one.

Thursday afternoon once again found us experiencing a quiet spell. "We're okay …there's that school contract coming up, and those two houses to rewire in Neston They'll keep us ticking over," Simon assured me. "Have you told 'er yet?" he asked.

"Told who, what?' I asked.

"Harriet. Have you told her that you're movin' in?" his eyes glinted mischievously.

"Oh right …no, not yet." I didn't particularly want to talk about it just then, but he sensed my discomfort and ploughed on.

"You want to get in there old mate, before someone

pips y' to it. Strike while the irons hot." Once again I found myself needing to change the subject.

"Are you still going to Loughborough tomorrow?" I asked a bit too sharply.

"Ooooh …a bit touchy old lad. Changin' the subject eh?" he smirked, and then quickly went on, "Loughborough? Yes I'll be goin' straight after breakfast. I'll probably stay overnight again."

The next day I made up my mind to talk to Harriet about moving in with her. If she was still up for it, then so was I. Later that evening I was taking a shower when I heard the phone ring. I struggled to hear the message on the answering machine, so I wrapped a towel around me, went downstairs and pressed the button.

"Hi Laurence, it's me," I heard Harriet's voice. She sounded rather odd. I cancelled the message, and dialled Harriet's number. After a few moments I heard her voice. "Laurence, I'm sorry but I'm goin' to have to put you off tonight. I've got go over to Karen's. She's had a big bust up with that chap she's been seeing. Apparently they had a big row, and he hit her. Sorry luv, but she sounds in a right state."

"Right, okay …of course, you have to go. Be careful mind. He's not still there, is he? Do you want me to go over with you?" I asked, suddenly rather worried.

"No, he's gone. Gone for good, all being well," Harriet reassured me.

"Right …but ring me straight away if there's any problem. Give Karen my best wishes. It's a pity though. I was going to tell you something tonight," I said.

"What's that then?" Harriet sounded intrigued.

"Oh nothing that won't keep," I said, trying to sound mysterious.

I sat watching the telly with a glass of beer in my hand. I wasn't really paying much attention to the programme. I was brought from my reverie by the phone ringing again. I looked at the clock. Nearly ten! Who the 'ell was ringin' at this time of night. I caught my unpleasant thought just in time. Of course it might be Harriet again. "Hello," I said rather worriedly. I was surprised to hear Jenny's voice.

"Is that you Laurence?" she asked. There was something strange in the way she spoke. "It's me, Jenny... Laurence, I'm sorry to bother you …but if you aren't busy could you possibly come over?"

It was then that I realised, that she sounded as though she'd been drinking. I started to feel worried. Christ …now I'm worrying about two women. I couldn't remember the last time that I had known Jenny to be drunk. "Yes of course. What's the matter?"

"No don't worry …nothing's wrong: just need to see you about something. I hope you don't mind." Her voice was definitely slurred.

"Okay Jenny, I'll be with you shortly."

As I drove the few miles to the bungalow, so many things went through my mind. Was she drunk? She certainly sounded as though she was. Was it something to do with Simon? And why did she want to see me? One thing I couldn't deny. Even though I had come to believe that my lust for her was a thing of the past, the prospect of being alone with her did fill me with a certain excitement. I'd never been alone with her before: so much for having got her out of my system. I parked the car in the drive, got out and rang the doorbell.

Jenny opened the door. It was immediately obvious that she was drunk. "Hi Laurence, come on through to the lounge." I followed her as she walked unsteadily ahead of me. It was then that I realised, that apparently, all she was wearing was a thin dressing gown. "Please sit down Laurence," she gestured towards the sofa. "Would you care to join me in a drink? I've already had a couple, as you may have gathered."

As she walked unsteadily over to the open drinks cabinet, I slowly sat down. "I'd better not. I've got to drive back." I looked at her, trying to fathom out what was happening. "Right Jenny, what this all about? Why are you drinking? I've never seen you like this in all the years I've known you."

"Can't a girl have a little drink if she wants to? I just felt like letting my hair down Laurence. An' you see …I don't get many chances to let my hair down Laurence. Simon doesn't like to see me drunk you know. But Simon isn't here, is he Laurence. He's in Loughbor …Lough…borough."

She was really slurring her words. "Laurence …dear Laurence, can I call you Laurie? Laurence sounds so formal, and I don't want to be formal tonight," she said, as she slumped into the armchair opposite me, splashing some of whatever it was, that she was drinking. Try as I might, and I wasn't really trying that hard, I must admit, I couldn't keep my eyes from roving from her legs right up to her face. The dressing gown was not doing a very good job of covering her. To make things worse – or better, if I'm truthful – Jenny was obviously aware of that fact. "Laurie, are you sure you won't have a drink? Just one little drink? You could always crash out on the sofa," she said, looking at me in a way that made my mouth go dry. I just shook my head and wondered, what the bloody 'ell is going on? Suddenly she dropped her glass on the floor.

As I stood to pick it up, she bent forwards and banged her head on my knee. "Oops," she slurred, giggling. As she straightened up, her dressing gown had fallen open. She made no effort to close it. She hadn't a stitch on underneath the gown. I just stared, as she slumped back in the chair. "Well Laurie what do you think? You've always wanted to see it, haven't you? No need to deny it, you naughty boy."

I just couldn't help but look. It was just as I had dreamed it would be. It was all there! The slim shapely legs, slightly apart: the fair pubic hair, the flat belly, the exquisite breasts. Oh Christ, those lovely breasts, with such perfect nipples. I could not believe what I was seeing.

After what seemed an age, I looked away and stammered, "Jenny, what the hell are you playing at? Cover y'self up." She just sat there. Not so much sat, but lounged. She even opened her legs slightly wider, and she was smiling: the smile that I had lusted after, oh so many times. Then she stood up from the chair, the dressing gown falling to the floor, as she came and sat on the sofa beside me. Totally naked! Before I could battle with my conscience, Jenny's arms were around me, and her lips were seeking mine.

I responded as most men would. I began to kiss her passionately. My hand found one of her wonderful, small breasts. I felt the nipple harden as she gently pulled my mouth to it. She took my hand and slowly pulled it down between her legs. She pressed it on to her soft pubic hair. My hand just seemed to freeze. Then I felt her hands tugging at my belt. Her fingers were reaching inside my pants. I nearly died! "Laurie, Christ it's so hard! That's how a man's cock should feel." And that is exactly when I came to my senses.

Suddenly I stood up, and pulled myself away. Jenny looked totally stunned. "Laurie, what's wrong? Come on, you know you want to. You know you want to fuck me. You always have. I've seen the way you look at me. It's okay; I want you to fuck me. That's why I asked you here tonight."

I just stood there shaking. She just lay back, naked and inviting. Eventually I said, "Jenny please …get dressed. This is wrong; we can't do this. I don't understand why you're doing it. Christ, you're married to my best friend." As I spoke I picked up her dressing gown. She had now drawn her knees up under her chin, and suddenly I could see her tears start to run down her face. I slowly sat down on the sofa beside her, wrapped the gown around her, and gently held her in my arms. "Shush, it's alright Jenny …please don't cry." But her tears flowed even more, and then she began to tremble.

Slowly the tears subsided, and the trembling stopped. Now she just lay quietly in my arms. I took a handkerchief from my pocket, wiped her eyes, took a deep breath and said, "Of course it's true what you say about my feelings for you. I have always wanted you, ever since the first time I saw you. Now I feel utterly ashamed of myself. But of course it's not me you want Jenny; it's Simon. Just Simon! I know you two are having problems. I'm sure you'll resolve them in time. I'm sorry Jenny." I felt so sad, so guilty.

After what seemed an eternity, she spoke. Very quietly she said, "Laurence would you mind waiting for a few minutes while I get dressed? Don't go, will you? There's something I need to say."

I just nodded and said, "I'll make a drink. Strong coffee, I think." She smiled weakly, pulled the dressing gown tightly around herself, and walked out of the room.

When Jenny came back she was wearing a pair of jeans and a blouse. She had obviously rinsed her face. She looked reasonably in control. After all, it had been quite a sobering experience, to say the least.

I handed her a cup of strong coffee. We both sat in silence for what seemed ages. Jenny sipped her coffee, and looked at the floor. I sipped mine and occasionally glanced at her. Putting her cup down very carefully, she began to speak, very hesitantly. "Laurence. The first thing I must do is say how sorry I am, for behaving as I have done tonight." I began to protest, but she held up her hand to stop me.

"No Laurence …I'm thoroughly ashamed. I took advantage of you. Knowing how you felt about me. I don't know what got into me, apart from too much brandy. They say that Brandy makes you randy."

She smiled, but her embarrassment was obvious. "I shouldn't joke about it. It's not funny. But you're right. It is because of the situation between Simon and me. But you see, it isn't just him that's getting no sex. I'm not getting any either and it's driving me crazy, Laurence. I'm still a young woman, and I have needs too, but I'm so sorry to have dragged you into all this." At that she fell silent, and she began to cry again.

I 'shushed' her again, and did my best to comfort her. "Come on Jenny luv …I didn't realise things were so bad. I don't know what to say but this isn't the answer. As I said before, it's certainly not me you want." Before I could continue, she cut in sharply.

"Laurence you're a lovely man, but you're right: I tried to use you and I'm deeply ashamed. Tonight, all I really wanted was a man's cock inside me. It's been so long since I felt that. There, now I've said it. That's the truth!" I sat there, shocked and dazed. Then quite suddenly she seemed to pull herself together. She sighed deeply and said, "Laurence, I know I've no right, but I do have to ask you a favour?" I just nodded. "Please don't tell Simon about tonight. I'm begging you. As I say, I know I have no right to ask, but it would break his heart. I've learnt something about myself tonight. I'm not the person I thought I was. It's not something that I'm proud of, but I promise you that

I won't put you in this position again. And once again, I am so very sorry."

I sat silently, thinking about the things that she had said.

Eventually I spoke, "Jenny, I'm not the person to judge you. What's happened here tonight isn't just your doing. I have dreamt about making love to you. No, that's not true: I've dreamed about having sex with you. I've lusted after you for as long as I can remember. So I'm every bit as guilty as you. So it would be a mutual favour. I need to know if you are likely to confess to Simon; or Harriet."

We agreed that it would be our secret: our shameful secret.

As I got into the car I was shaking. I glanced at the clock. Bloody 'ell, nearly one in the morning. Driving slowly home, my mind was in a whirl.

Suddenly it dawned on me. I would 'ave thought that Simon would 'ave phoned Jenny …what with him staying overnight in Loughborough. Christ, if he had phoned while we were 'at it'. Hell …and I've got to face him on Monday morning. I don't fancy that. Christ, I couldn't believe what had happened. What the hell had we done? I could never look at Jenny again without a sense of guilt and, if I were totally truthful, not without a sense of regret. I could have had sex with her tonight. She seemed desperate for it. She held my cock for Christ's sake. I sucked her breasts. I touched her pubic hair.

As I pulled up outside the house, I realised that I was still in a bit of a state. I made a distinct effort to calm myself then got out of the car and went into my rather unwelcoming house.

I thought about having a drink. Something strong! Brandy makes you randy, Jenny had said but instead I went upstairs, undressed, and having dropped my clothes onto a chair, I got into bed.

I lay there naked, and suddenly in my mind's eye saw Jenny's beautiful naked body. As my cock stiffened (she had used that word ... 'cock'!), I held it in my hand. Then I quickly climbed out of bed, and went to the bathroom.

A few minutes later as I climbed back into bed, suddenly the thought hit me. Oh Christ, what if Harriet's been trying to contact me, from her friend Karen's. Oh bloody hell Harriet! You don't deserve this. My guilt kept me awake for a long time.

Jenny

24

After Laurence had left, I just sat staring into space for what seemed an age. I simply could not come to terms with what I had done. It was like a dream, but if I'm honest …I can't say it was like a bad dream. Yes, I felt deeply shamed, but I also felt excited. How I had changed recently. Secret liaisons with men: almost seducing Laurence. Was I becoming an adulteress? Me, an adulteress! I was deeply shocked at the realisation that I was now a very different woman from the 'little Miss Innocent' of a few months ago.

I glanced at the clock. Almost two a.m. I'll never be up in the morning. That's when of course I'll have to face Simon, and no doubt tell more lies. Suddenly I remembered the phones. I hadn't wanted to be disturbed whilst I was seducing Laurie, so I had switched off my mobile, and switched off the house phones. After sorting this out, I went into the bedroom and quickly undressed. I stood in front of the mirror and took a long look at my naked body. As my hands began to touch, caress and probe, I thought, how could you turn this down Laurie? I had always known that he fancied me. How could I ever face him again? But face him I would. Sooner or later, I would have to. Just as I had to face the fact, that I was a different woman now. A very different woman!

Naked, I climbed into bed, and lay there deep in thought.

I knew now that I had to have sex.

I wasn't going to live without it.

Of course I knew what I really wanted.

He had blond hair: he was gorgeous looking, and he was a Roman Catholic priest.

I also knew that I would be contacting him soon: very soon! I couldn't sleep.

I lay thinking of Simon, Laurence and Colin, and sex! My hands started to move over my body. To those most intimate places, in a most intimate way. It was a long time before I drifted off to sleep.

I woke at about seven thirty. I felt terrible. Then the events of the previous night came flooding back to me.

Come on Jenny, you can handle it. You can handle Simon. Showered and dressed, with a cup of tea I began to feel a little better.

After breakfast I went through the lounge with a fine toothcomb.

I needed to be certain that no evidence of last night's indiscretion could be found. I read the newspaper and sat wishing that Simon would hurry up and get home.

I needed to get this over with as soon as possible.

At last I heard his car on the driveway. He wheeled himself into the kitchen as I was putting the kettle on. "Good morning Jenny luv. Put the kettle on please," Simon said brightly. I smiled and inclined my head towards the kettle. "Oh right y' already 'ave. A cuppa would go down a treat. Have y' missed me?"

His cheerfulness almost threw me. I had my back to him as I switched on the kettle. I had to force myself to turn, and smile naturally. "Hello gorgeous," I said kissing him warmly. "Of course I've missed you. How did it go in Loughborough?"

"Great: it's all measured up. Carbon wheels: the full works, it should be ready for delivery in a couple of weeks. I've just got to get fit now. Oh by the way: I tried to phone last night. I couldn't get through on either the house phone, or your mobile." My mouth dried, and I coughed to clear my throat.

"And I thought you'd forgotten. I was quite cross with you. Then this morning I noticed the receiver on the landline wasn't on properly, and the battery in my mobile was flat."

I couldn't believe how easily the lies came.

Even though I felt guilty, I knew I was going to phone him. Colin! What I didn't know was exactly why. Was it just the physical attraction? What else could it be? I kept putting it off, but on the Wednesday during my lunch break, I made the call. He sounded rather shocked when he heard my voice.

"Good heavens …is that you Jenny?"

I assured him that it was, and asked him if he would

like to see me again. He said that he would, but he was a little puzzled at my 'change of heart'. We made arrangements to meet on the Friday evening. I would have to tell Simon that I was having a 'night out with the girls'. More lies! It was becoming quite a habit.

Simon seemed a little put out when I told him that I was going out again, but he just said, "Okay luv, you go ahead. It'll do you good. I'll probably pop down to *The Feathers* with Laurie. That's if he's not tied up with Harriet." He made a crude joke about Laurence being tied up in bed. I pretended to chide his crudeness. Lies told, and an alibi contrived with work colleague Linda, I drove through the tunnel to my secret assignation. Secret assignation! I had to admit to myself that I really liked the sound of that. Colin was waiting at the same place as our previous meeting.

As he got into the car, he appeared slightly bemused.

"Hello," I said, as I smiled broadly.

"Hello Jenny …this is rather a surprise. I didn't think I'd ever hear from you again." I didn't say anything, but started the engine.

I drove away, then quietly said, "I haven't a clue where I'm going. Somewhere quiet, don't you think? Do you know a pub or somewhere that might be quiet on a Friday night? Or perhaps we could go to your place." That seemed to surprise him.

"My place? Well yes I suppose we could. We won't find anywhere else quiet tonight. I should warn you though, my place isn't exactly a palace."

I couldn't have cared less. I just wanted to be with him, and all the better if we were alone.

Colin had a second storey apartment in the centre of Bootle. And no, it wasn't the tidiest place that I'd ever seen. He fluffed up the cushions in an easy chair, and gestured to me to sit down. He moved some papers in an effort to improve things, and then sat down on the sofa opposite me.

"Can I get you a drink?" he offered nervously. "I haven't much in. I may have some red wine. Other than that it will have to be coffee I'm afraid."

I shook my head and said, "Nothing, thanks." I needed to talk, and I was aware that there wasn't a lot of time. "You must be wondering what I'm playing at …saying that I couldn't see you anymore, then ringing you out of the blue like that." Giving him no time to answer, I continued, "I just couldn't get you out of my mind. I did try, honestly." Then I went on to tell him about Simon, his accident, and about me: well, not everything about me! "Right, that's enough about me. Now tell me all about you. Everything!"

He paused for a moment or two, then said, "Not much to tell really. I was born in Sheffield. I was ordained there. Oh and I used to be a Sheffield Wednesday fan. Up the Owls!" He grinned at this and continued, "I came to Bootle four years ago. I'm the Catholic priest for the dioceses. What else?" He shrugged his shoulders and fell silent.

"You haven't told me how old you are," I prompted.

"How old do you think?" he teased.

"Oh, you shouldn't do that. Come on, don't tease. Tell me," I said.

"Thirty two," he replied.

"As old as that!" I teased in return, "and here's me thinking you were only about twenty-two. I was thinking you were going to be my toy boy," I said in a mischievous tone. We fell silent for a few moments. Then I said, "I'm afraid I have even more to confess." I just managed to stop myself from making some stupid joke, along the lines of, should I really be in the confessional box? I coughed and continued, "I'm not very religious. I don't go to church."

Colin looked at me for some time, and then said, "I come in to contact with a lot of the people who do go to church, but it doesn't always make them good Christians, or nice people. Anyway, I don't feel as though I'm in a position to judge you, or anyone else at the moment."

"*Why*?" I asked, my mouth dry with anticipation.

Again he paused. "There are no allowances within the Catholic Church for the thoughts and feelings I have about you. So what does that make me Jenny? Certainly not a shining example: not someone who can sit in judgement on others."

As he spoke, he looked straight into my eyes.

"So Colin, are you going to tell me what these thoughts and feelings are?" I asked the question very suggestively. I was totally under his spell. I knew then without doubt that I wanted to have sex with him.

"Jenny …I have never felt like this before. I can't stop thinking about you. To be honest, for quite some time now, I have had doubts about my commitment to the church. Since meeting you, those doubts have grown even stronger. When we met, I immediately felt different. I was different. Now I'm torn Jenny. Torn between my duty to the church, and my feelings for you. I thought when you said that you couldn't see me again, that I would get over you eventually. I will be honest and admit that I'm not sure whether or not I would have done. What I can say is that when you phoned to ask if I wanted to see you again, I was so happy. I can't put it into words. Now you're here …and I just don't want you to go, even though I know you must. So now you know everything. There is however one thing that I do need to ask. Why did you change your mind about seeing me again?"

I knew that I had to answer his question carefully, and truthfully. "As I said before Colin, I just couldn't get you out of my mind. I just knew that I had to see you." As I spoke, I quickly got up from the chair and sat on the sofa beside him. We sat looking at each other, and then I placed my hand behind his neck and pulled him to me, until our lips met. We kissed gently. I could sense his awkwardness. I tried to stimulate him by kissing him more passionately, but he pulled away. He looked uncomfortable: awkward. But I was in no mood for another rejection. I needed to gain his confidence. For the first time in my life, I felt in control. Sexually!

In the past it had always been my husband who had instigated sex. Now it was my turn. "Colin, must ask you something. Have you ever been with a woman? I mean …you know …had any physical experience before you became a priest?"

I sensed his embarrassment as he shook his head, took a deep breath, and said, "No, not really."

"Well, I think perhaps it's time you did," I said, standing up. I was wearing a simple dress that buttoned all the way down the front. Easy access! Slowly I began to undo the buttons. I watched Colin's face as I did so. He was transfixed. I let the dress fall to the floor. I stood there wearing just a tiny black bra and panties, with stocking and a suspender belt. I held my hands out to him and he came to me like a little boy lost. We kissed again. This time the passion poured from both of us. I pushed him roughly back onto the sofa, pulling his t-shirt from his body.

I saw that his chest was smooth and hairless, unlike Simon, who was covered in thick black curly hair all over his chest and shoulders, Colin looked so beautiful. I had to have him. I felt his clumsy attempt to undo my bra. I quickly unhooked it and dropped it on the floor. As his hand covered one of my breasts I brought his mouth to the other. He took my nipple and began to gently suck it. I found myself making encouraging noises.

He obviously needed a woman's guidance, and I wasn't about to let him off the hook. I unbuckled his belt, and said, "I think we should have these off." I pulled his jeans and pants down, and threw them to the far side of the room. He was now totally naked. I looked at his cock. It was throbbing! My mouth was dry, and I struggled to find saliva as I took his cock in my hand, and stroked it up and down. Up and down. It was so hot! So hard! As my mouth moistened, I put his cock to my lips, and kissed it. Then without thinking, it was in my mouth. Slowly and gently I sucked him.

He moaned in ecstasy. I had to have him inside me. I eased my head away before he 'came' and quickly pulled off my panties. Then before he could do anything, I straddled him. I guided him into me. He was putty in my hands. I had never felt so in control before. I began to slide myself up and down his gorgeous hard cock. Within a few seconds I sensed he was about climax. I wanted to prolong this fantastic feeling, but thankfully I retained enough sense, to ease my body away just as he did 'come'. The noises he made were music to my ears. He was in ecstasy and I had sent him there! After a few moments he became quiet.

I was aware of his growing embarrassment. He suddenly seemed more conscious of his own nakedness, than mine. Without speaking he rose from the sofa, picked up his clothes, and quickly dressed. He then handed me my bra and pants. As he did this he smiled shyly. I took my time as I dressed in silence. It was obvious that he didn't know what to say so I tried to ease his embarrassment by asking, "Are you okay?

Colin smiled and, rather breathlessly, said, "Good heavens yes, I feel fine – fantastic – amazing! How are you? Was it alright for you?"

Short but sweet my darling ...short but sweet, I thought. But instead I said, "Of course ...it was wonderful." I then surreptitiously glanced at the clock. Time I was going. "Can I use the loo Colin? Then I really must go."

As he pointed the way, he grinned and said, "That's

right, use me, then cast me aside."

Afterwards, he walked me out to the car and we kissed 'good night'. "I'll give you ring soon," I said as I got into the car. I could see the doubt in his expression. "I will. I promise. Oh, and by the way …don't worry, I am on the pill." I lied. I don't think this had even crossed his mind, because suddenly, a rather surprised look of relief crossed his face. He gave me a brief kiss, and then I closed the car door and drove away.

I drove home at speed. I was hoping I would get back before Simon. Good Lord …Simon! What would he do if he ever found out? He'd go crazy. It would hurt him so much. He might even kill me! I must be going crazy myself, but I had just had sex for the first time in …what: weeks, months? Short and sweet, it may have been, but it had still been sex! Poor Colin: had he really been a virgin? Well he certainly wasn't now. And who had, 'taken his cherry'? Me! I had! Jenny you really are a naughty girl. I smiled at myself in the interior mirror.

I drove onto the drive, flicked the remote at the garage door, but when it opened I saw that Simon's car was already inside.

"Hi luv. 'Ave you 'ad a good night?" he said, smiling at me as I entered the kitchen. He went on, "Been anywhere nice?"

I felt dry-mouthed and awkward. "Oh just to a couple of pubs in Liverpool. You know me and pubs. I just went along with the girls. It was okay, but it's not really my scene. Anyway, what have you been up to?" I asked trying to change the subject.

"Me and Laurie just went to *The Feathers*. We 'ad a game of darts, and a quiet drink. Oh yer', Laurie 'as put his house on the market. He's definitely moving in with Harriet. Are you listenin' to me? Are you okay? You seem a bit quiet. Is there something wrong?" Simon looked at me quizzically.

"No, I'm just a bit tired," I replied, feigning a yawn. "I'm going to make a cocoa, and go to bed. Are you coming?"

I needed to ease any possibility of tension building between us, so I was relieved when he said, "No, I think I'll watch the telly for a while. You get off luv, you do look tired." I made my drink, and headed for the bedroom.

"Goodnight Simon."

Hopefully I would get to sleep before Simon came to bed.

"Goodnight Jen'," he said, almost absent-mindedly.

Laurie

25

A couple of days later, I was still struggling to come to terms, with what had happened between Jenny and myself. As much as I told myself to put it behind me, I was finding it very difficult. Of course, it was still worrying me as I drove over to Harriet's that evening.

We were just finishing our tea when Harriet said, "Laurence, there's something I have to tell you." She looked rather serious, and slightly worried. I just sat silently anticipating something that I didn't want to hear. Like, I don't want you to move in with me after all. That would be bloody typical of a woman. Especially, I was just about to announce that, that was exactly what I would like to do.

She paused and then said, "There is only one way of saying this, so I might as well come straight out with it. I'm pregnant!"

"What?" I gasped. Harriet calmly said it again.

"I'm pregnant."

I barely let this tremendous news sink in, before I

leapt from my chair, dashed around the table, and grinning from ear to ear grabbed her in my arms. "You mean we're going to 'ave a baby? That's chuffin' fantastic! Oh my god …Harriet, that's brilliant."

Suddenly she was smiling. However, it was a rather uncertain smile. "Are you really pleased? Really? Honestly?"

I just kept on grinning. I nodded, and grinned. I was going to be a dad! How could I not be pleased? Pleased? I was chuffin' ecstatic!

"You are really sure?" I said hesitantly.

Harriet smiled and replied, "Yes I'm sure. I've done the test twice."

"So …how do *you* feel about it?" I asked, pensively.

"Now that I know you're happy …then so am I. Actually …delighted, and very relieved," replied Harriet. She had a huge smile on her face.

"So come on then, when is it due? Did it happen that last night on holiday …when we were both rather Brahms and Liszt?" I went on excitedly.

"It's due in April. And yes, I think it must have been that night," she replied. Conceived in Corfu! So then I asked her whether she still wanted me to move in. "Yes, of course I do," was all she said.

"Just as well," I said, "I've just put my house up for sale." That night in bed, I hardly dared to touch Harriet.

"Don't be silly, I'm not made of china. I won't break," she said.

Even so, all we did was hold each other close, until we drifted off to sleep.

The following day, Simon asked me whether I fancied a drink in *The Feathers* that night. When I hesitated, he said, "Don't let 'er start making the ground rules old mate. That's the beginning of the end." Who was I to argue with my lord and master?

"About eight," I suggested. I had been looking for the right moment to tell him the news. Over A pint would be perfect.

Jenny offered to chauffeur us to and from the pub, so that we could have a few pints. It was the first time I had seen her since the other night. I felt very awkward, and I struggled to hide it but she never batted an eyelid. She did however decline Simon's suggestion that she might stay for a quick one.

"I'm glad she didn't come in to be 'onest. There's something thing I want to ask you," said Simon seriously. I nearly spilled my beer. What the hell was he going to say? He took a drink from his glass, then said, "It's Jenny. She seems to be acting a bit strange lately. I just wondered whether you'd noticed anythin', or whether she'd said anythin' to you. Y'know …about somethin' that might be botherin' 'er."

I struggled to stay calm. Eventually, trying to keep a non-committal expression on my face I replied, "No, I haven't noticed anything and she certainly hasn't said anything to me. Anyway, what do you mean …actin' strange?"

Simon took a deep drink before continuing. "Well she's started going out with the girls from the pharmacy. An' she's being really vague when I ask 'er about it. Well you know Jenny …she's never been one for goin' out. Now she's talkin' about doin' a computer course in Liverpool." I had to seem ignorant regarding Jenny's behaviour, but even as I spoke I couldn't help thinking, Christ Simon old lad, if only you knew. Suddenly I wondered, does he know something? Is he trying to 'set me up'?

I took a sip from my glass, and spoke as calmly as I could. "I'm sure it's nothing. She perhaps just needs a change. You know ...a bit of space." I had to change the subject. I looked over to the dartboard. "Fancy a game?" I asked.

"Go on then. Get another drink in first though, eh." As I took the drinks back to the table, an odd thought crossed my mind. I hadn't given Melanie's voluptuous bosom or cleavage, even the slightest glance.

I took my Schofields from my jacket pocket, and put on my serious darts face. Simon obviously found the game much more difficult now, since he had to throw from sitting in his wheelchair but, to his credit, he never mentioned it.

"301?" I asked.

As he was poised, about to throw his second dart, I calmly said, "Oh, by the way ...I've got some news. I'm goin' to be a dad."

His dart didn't even hit the board. His face was a picture. Eventually he looked at me and soberly said, "Bloody 'ell old mate, just f'r a minute I thought you said that you were goin' to be a dad." I said nothing. I just took a drink from my pint. "You not chuffin' kiddin' are you?" he asked grinning at me.

I grinned back and just said, "No ...I'm serious."

"Well that's buggered me up for darts," said Simon. "I think this calls for champagne. I take it you are happy about it?" He could see from my broad smile that I obviously was. This was the signal for him to take charge. "Melanie my darlin', could we 'ave a bottle of your finest champagne? It's celebration time. Bring a glass f' yourself as well," he shouted cheerfully. The few customers in the bar looked up curiously from their drinks. Melanie was over in a shot.

"So what's this all in aid of lads?" she asked, as she sat down, her arms folded beneath that splendid fulsome bosom. That, of course, gave it even more exposure.

"Laurie's 'ere 'as just told me, 'e's gunna' be a dad," Simon said to her cleavage. Melanie pulled my head to that wonderful chest, and hugged me to the point of almost suffocation.

"Congratulations Laurie luv ...that's wonderful news," she said, releasing my embarrassed face. She poured the champagne, and proposed a toast. "To Laurence, the soon to be dad." Personally I wouldn't normally thank you for a bucketful of champagne.

I'd rather stick to my pint of bitter, but I had to admit ...this was a rather special occasion.

Suddenly Simon said, "Eh' shouldn't the girls be 'ere? I'll give 'em a ring shall I?" The last thing I wanted just now was to be face to face with Jenny, and Harriet. I made what I hoped was a plausible excuse for not phoning Harriet, but of course I had no say in whether Simon should call Jenny or not.

When Jenny sat down at the table she just glanced

questioningly at the almost empty bottle of champers. She was coolness personified.

"Come on then …what's so important that you've dragged me away from my Pavarotti?" She addressed the question to Simon. It was as if she fully expected that 'the surprise' would centre around him. I wasn't the type of person who had, or sprang surprises but, for once, Simon didn't take centre stage.

He just pointed at me and said, "Go on then, tell her."

As I told Jenny my news, I poured her the last drop of champagne. I looked her directly in the eyes as I did it. Just for the briefest of moments, I thought I saw her losing her composure, but she recovered it in a flash. *Very commendable Jenny,* I thought. Then she kissed me softly on the cheek. "Congratulations …that's wonderful, Laurence. Please give Harriet my congratulations too."

I was rather quiet as Jenny drove us home. Simon more than made up for it. He was pleasantly merry and he continued to extol my virtues between the bed-sheets. Jenny was also rather quiet. I was really relieved, when we got to my house. Climbing from the car I quickly bade them both 'goodnight'.

The following morning at work, Simon was feeling slightly the worse for wear. "Remind me not to drink 'plonk' ever again," he groaned. We busied ourselves with tidying shelves and making tea or coffee. Suddenly Simon said, "D' y' know, I couldn't get to sleep last night. I kept thinking about you becoming a dad, and it set me thinking. Perhaps it's time me 'n' Jenny tried again. What d' y' think old mate? D' y' think I'd make a good dad?"

I thought about this for a few seconds. What was this all about really?

Had my announcement truly set Simon seriously thinking about starting a family? Or was it that he was jealous, of the fact that I was going to have something that he didn't have? Of course, I didn't have the 'bottle' to put this to him. "I think you'd make a great dad …and I think Jenny would make a great mother but 'ave you discussed with her? I don't mean to pry but …I mean, perhaps there's more to consider …you know …with your special needs." I was floundering. "Oh Christ Simon, I wish I hadn't started this."

"Laurie old mate, it's okay. I suppose you're wondering how I would manage to do it anyway: become a father, that is." I started to protest but Simon continued, "We've been told by the counsellor that it's possible. Something called Inverted Fornication."

"Invitro Fertilization," I said without a hint of a smile.

He ignored me, and carried on, "I won't embarrass you with all the sordid details, but the more I think about it the more I like the idea. Yes, I'm goin' to talk to Jenny about it this evening."

26

A few days later, Simon took delivery of his new racing-wheelchair. He was of course, extremely excited. "Bloody 'ell old mate, it's chuffin' brilliant. I bet it'll go like shit off a shovel. You'll 'ave t' come over an' 'ave a look. It's bloody great."

After we had finished work that evening, he insisted that I follow him home, to view this masterpiece of magnificent workmanship. Indeed, it could not be denied that it was very impressive. "An' so it should be old mate ...f' what it cost. It set me back over four grand. Anyway, all I've got t' do now is get fit ...an' then I'll be lookin' t' 'ave a go at racin'."

He was so excited; it was hard not to get caught up in his enthusiasm. Such was his excitement; it was difficult to get him to concentrate on work for the next few days.

One morning over coffee Simon said, "I've been in touch with that club in Liverpool ...the one that specialises in disabled athletes. I'm thinkin' of goin' over tomorrow evenin'. D' y' fancy goin' with me," he enquired. "We could make a night of it."

I wasn't really up for one of Simon's 'nights out'. Now that I'm going to be a father, I would be expected to behave in a responsible manner, but it would have been rather churlish to desert an old friend in his hour of need. Anyway, I wasn't a father, yet.

The following evening Simon picked me up from home, and we set of for Liverpool. As we exited the tunnel, he sighed with relief. "Thank god f' that. I hate bloody tunnels." Surprise, surprise! I looked away, and smiled smugly to myself. After numerous conflicting directions given by helpful Scousers, we eventually located the sports-club in Walton.

For what seemed to me to be an age, Simon and his new friend discussed training regimes and schedules, interval training, heart monitors, and special diets that apparently contained loads of carbohydrates, such as pasta, and isotonic drinks. Even I know about the benefits of pasta, and isotonic drinks.

After what seemed an eternity, Simon finally shook hands with the chap, and announced that we could leave. Ignoring my obvious sigh of relief, as we climbed into the car, he said enthusiastically, "Well that was all very interesting. At least now I know what I have t' do t' get racin' fit." *Oh bloody goody*, I thought but I kept it to myself.

"Right Laurie old mate, I think it's time for a drink. What's it t' be, a pub or a 'gentleman's club'? Of course we could do both." I brought him quickly back down to earth.

"Hang on Simon, we've got work in the mornin', and I don't want be too late gettin' back."

Simon drove into the city centre, and we headed for the 'action' as he liked to call it. Once we were parked, and Simon was comfortably in his wheelchair, I offered to push him. He declined with good grace. "No thanks old mate, I need to do it myself. Call it trainin'. Mind you, I may need a push back t' the car, when I've 'ad a pint." We found ourselves in Queen's Square, outside a club called *The Arena*. "Spot on!" Simon declared. *The Arena!* How apt. Must be an omen."

While Simon, who found his wheelchair no disadvantage at all, flirted outrageously with several young women (he used it to great effect as a chat-up line), I found myself just wanting to get back home to Harriet.

It was decided that we would go back to Simon's, and then I'd get a taxi to my place. "Don't want to risk it with the 'busies' any more than necessary, old mate," Simon said, gravely. Even I was conscious of the *fact that* I was rather subdued, as Simon drove us home. "What's up with you y' miserable sod? Y've been a right pain in the arse all night. Is it becos' y'd rather be watchin' the telly with y' girl-friend?" he said, with a strong hint of sarcasm.

"No …it's just one of those nights," I lied. The truth was, that I knew that I would come face to face with Jenny when we got back Simon's and that was something that I wasn't relishing.

"Come on in an' I'll phone you a cab," said Simon,

as we got out of the car, and entered the bungalow. "Go through to the lounge, an' Jenny'll get y' a drink," he added, as he reached for the telephone. I could hear the sound of the television, which meant that Jenny was still up. I had been fervently hoping that she might be in bed. I entered the lounge feeling extremely ill at ease.

"Oh, good evening Laurence …how are you?" Jenny asked, as calmly as you like.

"I'm okay," I said quietly, looking at her quizzically, trying to stir some sign of guilt, but no, nothing: I couldn't believe how utterly calm and in control she was. This woman, who had attempted to seduce me only a few nights ago, sat on the sofa, her legs curled under her, a glass of 'something' in her hand. She was wearing a short dressing-gown. Her hair was wet. She had obviously just showered.

When Simon entered the room, he went straight to his wife and reached for a kiss. "Hiya' luv." He then turned his attention to me. "Y' taxi'll be about twenty-minutes old mate. Hasn't she got you a drink?" he smiled good-naturedly at his wife. "Come on Jen', what sort of hostess will our Laurence think you are?" I nearly choked. I dare not even look at Jenny.

Suddenly she chuckled loudly, and said suggestively, "What would you like Laurence?"

I coughed to clear my throat, and shaking my head simply said, "Nothing thanks." Simon bless him, in all innocence made matters worse.

"Come on Laurie, 'ave a 'short'. The mood you've been in tonight, y' could do with a good stiff one." Jenny's chuckle turned into full-blown laughter. Simon looked at her with a rather puzzled expression. "What's so funny?" Jenny just put a hand to her mouth, and shook her head. A blessed silence fell over us for a few moments. Then out of the blue Simon dropped his bombshell! "Y' know Jenny luv …I've been thinkin' …perhaps we should take a leaf out of Laurie 'n' 'arriet's book, an' try for a baby!"

If there had been any awkward silence before, it was now deafening. Fortunately for me, I was literally saved by the bell. The front-door bell. My taxi had arrived. Thank god!

On the journey home, I tried to take in the full implications of what Simon had said. Was it just the beer talking? Not if, as he said, he had been thinking about it for a day or two. Had he thought it through? Could he father a child? Perhaps artificial insemination was possible ...but what about Jenny? How would she feel about motherhood? Suddenly I stopped this train of thought. What am I gettin' all worked up about? It's none of my business what they do f' Christ's sake. The taxi stopped outside my house. I paid the driver, then entered my rather shabby two-up, two-down. I tried to recall how long I had lived there. One thing I was sure of, I was more than ready to leave, and move in with Harriet. Within a few minutes I undressed in slipped into bed.

I didn't want to lie there thinking of Simon and Jenny, but that's exactly what I did. 'Jenny, how could you? Bloody hell! And you Simon; what a twat! It's just like you.' He couldn't soddin' well stand t' see me have anything, unless he could have it too.

Jenny

27

After Laurence had left, I went into the kitchen to make some cocoa. Any excuse to have time to myself, to think about Simon's bombshell. A baby! We hadn't discussed the subject since I had miscarried, even though it was almost four years ago.

I was so deep in thought that I hardly heard Simon enter the kitchen. "Jenny luv, I'm sorry. I didn't think. I'm such a prat. It must be the beer."

I turned my back to him as I said, "Simon I'm really tired; could we talk about this tomorrow?' We'll talk it all through after dinner."

I passed him a mug of cocoa, and took mine through to the bedroom.

Simon followed me through, undressed, eased himself into bed and was soon asleep. I slept very little that night.

A baby, for god's sake. Me: have a baby!

Me: a woman who was having an affair ...but was I really having an affair? Not if I was to put a stop to it.

End it!

Now!

After all, Colin and I had only had sex once, and that's all it was. Sex! And Simon and I could have sex in a way. After all, you didn't have to have full intercourse to have sex did you? And I didn't love Colin, I loved Simon. I had arranged to go round to Colin's apartment on Thursday. I would tell him there and then, that I couldn't see him anymore. It definitely had to stop.

The next morning I found myself blessed with a very unpleasant cough. I would have to get hold of some antibiotics when I got to work. By that evening my cough had become a full-blown cold. After a rather subdued dinner, I suddenly asked Simon, "Did you really mean what you said last night, about us trying for a baby?"

He looked rather pensive, but eventually said, "Yes actually, I did. I know with everything that's happened it won't be easy, but don't you think it would be worth trying? Just think Jen' …a child of our own." Before I could interrupt, he continued, "And before you ask, this is not just because Laurence and Harriet are havin' one. Regardless of what he may say or think. I know it must seem rather odd to you at the moment. What with me not being able to get an erection, but if you remember what the doctor said …if the sperm can be taken out of me, then it can be put into you."

We continued to discuss the subject at great length, and agreed to see our G.P in the very near future.

The following morning, I reminded Simon about my impending Thursday evening computer course. This was a lie that I had thought up in a moment of inspiration. Another lie! How easily they came these days. I was starting to thoroughly dislike myself. Well, it would soon be over. I must finish with Colin. Simon looked up from his newspaper.

"Thursday evening? That's a coincidence. I'm goin' over to see that chap at the sports centre in Walton, on Thursday evening. I could drop you off. Then pick you up after, and we could go for a drink or something." I was completely taken aback. I had to think of something quickly.

"Oh no …that's alright, I'm going to go straight from work. I want to do some shopping in Liverpool first and I'm not sure what time the class finishes," I stammered. Lies, lies, and more lies!

My cough had subsided considerably. Hopefully just a twenty-four hour thing, but I knew that I should finish the course of antibiotics. Before driving away from the pharmacy on Thursday evening I telephoned Colin. "Can I come over right away? I'll explain when I get there."

Colin had obviously made a big effort to smarten his apartment up. Before I could compliment him however, he took me in his arms and kissed me passionately. All the resolve that I had been building up just faded away. I had intended to tell him straight away... *As soon as you walk in the door* I had told myself. One kiss changed all that!

Before I could even begin to control the situation, as I had done on our last encounter, Colin swept me off my feet. He carried me into his bedroom, and quickly placed me on the bed. I had no say in what happened next. He literally pulled my clothes from my body. In seconds I was naked. He stood up and quickly removed his own clothing. As he slipped off his underpants, his cock was suddenly there. What a cock! I could not take my eyes off it. He lowered himself onto me, and began to gently kiss me all over. My lips, my neck, my breasts, my nipples, my belly ...then ...oh so slowly, his tongue was inside me. I felt as though I would explode. This was heaven: sexual heaven. How long this exquisite sensation lasted, I'm not sure. I became aware that he was clumsily trying to put his cock into me. I held that big, hard thing, in my hand for a few moments, making him writhe with anticipation and lust ...and then slowly I guided it into me.

It is said that sex, like most exercise, whets the appetite. Well, I could hardly eat a thing that evening. Colin had obviously put quite a lot of thought into preparing our meal. I was also acutely aware that I had become very quiet. At first Colin seemed not to notice, but eventually he said, "It's pretty obvious that something's wrong. What is it?"

Gradually, I told him everything: that the sex with him had been fantastic ...but that was all it was. Sex! ...How dreadfully guilty I felt, deceiving Simon like this: how it was Simon that I loved and not him: how Simon and I were considering starting a family: how I couldn't go on like this, and that we had to stop seeing each other. There, I had finally managed to say it.

Colin looked totally crestfallen... "But Jenny I'm crazy about you. I've decided to leave the church." He put his hand up as I began to protest. "No Jenny, I have made up my mind. Even before I met you I was seriously considering it. I've had doubts about my commitment to God for a long time – perhaps even right from the beginning. Finally, meeting you has made it all clear to me. I need you Jenny. I want to be with you." He looked at me pleadingly, but I had to be firm.

Suddenly I had to get out of there. I wanted to be with Simon not here with this other man; this other man who had, apparently, changed from the shy innocent into someone totally different. Quietly I began to cry. Colin took me in his arms, and gently comforted me. It was as though he fully understood.

He left the room, and returned with a box of tissues. He passed me one and then, holding my coat, he said quietly, "You know how I feel about you, but I can't try make you do something that you'll regret. However, if you ever change your mind...well...you know where I am." Colin walked me outside to my car. He was very upset.

I felt so terrible for treating him this way, that I didn't even notice the rain. "I'm so sorry Colin. I do wish you all the best for the future. I'm sure you'll meet someone soon." If only it were possible to see into the future! Now, all I wanted to do was get away. I felt so ashamed.

"One last kiss?" he asked wistfully.

I placed both hands on that beautiful blond hair, and kissed him tenderly. Then, as I ran to the car, I did realise it was raining, so I quickly got in, started the engine, switched on the windscreen-wipers and quickly drove away. I was almost home when, suddenly, a shocking thought occurred to me. *Had Colin 'come' inside me?* Thank God I'd had the sense to take 'the pill'.

Laurie

28

"Good morning Laurie," said Simon as he entered the warehouse the following day. He sounds bloody cheerful, I thought moodily.

A rather glum, "Morning", was all I could manage. He didn't seem to notice. I put the kettle on as a matter of course. As I turned, I noticed that he was looking at me in a rather odd way.

"Well?" he said.

"Well what?" I asked, genuinely puzzled.

"Chuffin' 'ell Laurie, are you blind? Can't y' see?" he said, pointing to his chin. He'd shaved his beard off! His glorious black beard.

" Good god …you've shaved y' beard off!" I exclaimed.

"My, you're bloody sharp this morning old mate. Mind you, not as sharp as my razor. So …what d' y' think? Smart or what?" Simon grinned.

"But why Simon? I always thought your beard was

y' pride an' joy. What's Jenny had to say about it?" I asked.

"She doesn't know yet. I did it after she'd left for work. She'll probably go ape-shit …but what the hell, it's my beard, and if I want to shave it off I soddin' well will."

"But why?" I asked again.

"I just thought if I'm goin' in for this wheelchair racin' caper, I'd be better off clean-shaven. Y' know, more aerodynamic and if we are goin' to try f' a kid …well I don't want to go scarin' the shit out of the poor little sod, do I? No doubt, there'll be enough of the 'sloppy green stuff' anyway."

I was silent for a few seconds. Finally I said, "So you're serious then, about having a child?" For some reason I couldn't bring myself to use the word, baby, and right at that moment, he sensed my mood.

"What's wrong Laurence? You seem to be a bit grumpy this morning. Surely it's not because me 'n' Jenny are talkin' about tryin' for a kid, is it?" Simon looked at me quizzically. I said nothing. Feeling rather foolish, I just shrugged my shoulders. "I thought you'd be pleased. You 'n' 'arriet; me 'n' Jenny: a kid each: growin' up together, playin' together," Simon said very quietly.

I sighed deeply. "Yes, you're right of course. It would be great. It's just me bein' a prat, but Simon, how are you going to …well you know, how are you goin' to do it, if you can't …you know …get an erection?"

Simon took a long swig from his now nearly cold

coffee. Wiping the back of his hand across his mouth he said, "That's just the point. You don't 'ave to get an 'ard-on to 'ave a baby." He paused for effect. He was now in his element. *All he needs now is a white coat and a stethoscope,* I thought. "No, you see Laurie old mate, if the woman can arouse the man sufficiently …y' know, by playin' with his todger, she can make him shoot his load. He doesn't necessarily 'ave to 'ave an 'ard on. Of course, y' have to have somethin' handy to catch the old spermatozoa in. Then just pop it in the fridge an' take it to the clinic the next mornin' an' Bob's y' uncle. Or, y' baby.'

Simon really did have a way with words. Play with y' todger! Shoot your load! How eloquent! Byron, eat your heart out! But that's Simon; you have to take the rough with the smooth.

Later that afternoon Simon asked me to accompany him to Walton again, to see his coach. I agreed with proviso that we, "Come straight home afterwards: no boozin' in Liverpool."

"Fair enough. We'll 'ave one in *The Feathers* afterwards, instead," he said with a grin.

It was later than Simon had planned when we arrived at the sports club. Having chatted with the coach, Simon thanked him for the training schedule, and we walked back out to the car. It began to rain as we headed towards Bootle, and the tunnel. It was also just starting to get dark. As the car slowly approached a busy road junction, my attention was drawn to a man and woman standing across the road. I could see them both clearly in the light of a street lamp. He was quite tall, with a shock of vivid blond hair. She was petite, and very pretty. *She was Jenny*! Christ! Was it? Yes, it was *definitely* Jenny. I looked quickly over to Simon. He was concentrating intently on the busy road junction. Thank God!

As the car moved forward I glanced again in the direction of the couple. They were kissing. Jesus Christ! I looked again at Simon. He was totally unaware of the shocking scene that I had just witnessed. My mind was in a whirl. Do I say anything? Dear God, what the bloody hell was she playing at? First me, now this! No don't say anything. Face her with it first. The bitch! The poor bastard is gettin' all excited about 'avin' a baby an' she's out …what? Shaggin'?

"You're quiet old mate …not still sulkin' are y'?" Simon asked as we made our way back through the Wirral.

"No of course not, I'm just feelin' knackered," I lied. "If it's all the same to you, I could do with skippin' *The Feathers*. Can y' just drop me off at home?"

The following afternoon, while I was at work, I got the news I had been hoping for. The estate agent phoned to say, that someone had offered the asking price for my house.

Fantastic! Now I could make the move to Harriet's. Our relationship had been getting better all the time. We really were in love. I had instigated a sort of partial curtailment to our sexual activities. "We have to think of the baby," I'd insisted, "and you too of course." I'd added quickly. Even so, we still managed to keep each other sexually satisfied. No, any problems I had lay in a totally different direction.

I had to do something. I couldn't just stand by and watch my best friend destroyed, but what could I do? I could go and have it out with Jenny. Or may be better still, have it out with that blond-haired bastard that I'd seen kissing her. Yes, that's it. I'll drive over to Bootle, and confront the bastard. Easier said than done. I thought. I could finish up gettin' my head kicked in. He did look a rather big sod, and I'm not exactly the bravest of men. Re-enforcements! I could take one of the lads with me, but who?

Who could I trust to keep his mouth shut? Tony? No, not Tony, and certainly not Ronnie. Who then? No, I'd better go on my own.

I had just replaced the telephone receiver, when the sudden sound of Simon's voice made me 'jump'. His wheelchair was so quiet that I hadn't heard him enter the office. "Who was that on the phone?" he asked. After what I'd seen last night, and my thoughts about going to Bootle to try to sort it, my nerves were on edge.

Gathering my wits as quickly as I could, I explained that it was the estate agent ringing to give me good news regarding my house sale. I went on at some length regaling Simon with all the benefits, and pleasures that were waiting for me: anything to take my mind off Jenny, and her bloody disloyalty.

That evening as Harriet and I were having dinner, I announced that I had to pop out for a couple of hours. The sooner I got this over with, the better. As I drove to Bootle my resolve was tested to the full. Just what was I going to say to this big blond bastard? *"Ay' you! Are you shaggin' my best mate's wife?' Cos' if you are..."* I would just have to wait 'n' see when I got there.

I was surprised how easily I found the road where I had seen Jenny and 'him' kissing. As I parked the car it suddenly occurred to me that he may not even be in.

Whether this was wishful thinking or not, I'm not sure.

Eventually I got out of the car, and approached the door of the apartment building.

There was a plate with several names on it. A push button was beside each name. I hate those bloody things. I hate them at the best of times, but now …what the hell do I say into it? *"I want to speak to a big blond-haired man?"* I looked at the nameplate, and tried to work out a rational way of going about it. All but four of the names were female. I suddenly stabbed my finger at a name. A rather muffled, elderly male voice said, "Hello." Well, that's not him, I thought.

I hadn't a clue what to say, but finally mumbled, "I'm looking for a blond-haired fella'. I think he dropped 'is wallet in the road. I'm tryin' to find 'im." "Oh that'll be Father Johnson, at number six," said the elderly voice. My mind went blank for a second or two. Father Johnson? Who the hell's Father Johnson? A priest? No, it can't be him. Never the less, I pressed the button marked '6'.

"Hello," said a strong young male voice. Instinctively, I knew it was him.

"Sorry to trouble you …Father, but I have to see you urgently." I said cautiously. I heard the security lock release, and entered the house. First floor he had said. "Bollocks!" I cursed, as I banged my shin on the pedal of a bicycle that was standing in the gloomy passageway. I was about to knock on the door, when it opened, and there he was. There was no mistaking him. Tall, blonde, and it could not be denied, very handsome. He smiled warmly as he said, "Come in …now what all this about urgency?" *You smarmy bastard. I'm goin' to beat the shit out of you,* was the first thought that leapt to mind, but instead I just stood there in silence.

He looked at me, obviously somewhat puzzled but there was also the look of a man in control. He knew a troubled face when he saw one. "Come and sit down," he said, directing me to a chair.

I declined the offer. I needed to stand to tell the bastard what I'd seen, and what I was going to do about it. He was wearing jeans and a T-shirt, but as I glanced across the room, I saw a black suit and shirt with a 'dog-collar', placed on a clothes hanger. He is a priest! Bloody ell! But it's definitely him, I thought.

"I'm here about Jenny," I blurted out.

He looked extremely shocked. Then very quietly he said, "Oh …right …I see." He paused for a moment then continued. "As Jenny told me that her husband is confined to a wheel-chair, do I take it that you're a friend of his?"

"I'm Simon's best friend. He means a great deal to me. And you'd better believe it" After all my intentions of violence, bizarrely it all turned out to be rather civilized. He asked my name. Then he made some tea. As he poured the tea, he gestured towards a chair. This time I took the seat, and then taking a sip of tea, I began to speak. He listened like 'a man of the cloth', while I told him everything. Well almost everything. It became obvious that he already knew most of what I related. I didn't mention Jenny's attempted seduction of me.

When I finished speaking there was a slightly uncomfortable silence. Then quite suddenly he said, "Jenny has already told me, that it's all over between us so I've decided to move back to Sheffield."

I looked at him askance. Seeing my puzzled expression he said, "Of course …sorry, how would you know? That's where I originate from. Sheffield. As I say, I've decided to go back. So I'll be …what do you say, 'off the scene', quite soon."

The really strange thing is that I actually started to feel some sympathy for him. After all, he wasn't the only one to fall for Jenny, and her charms. He was silent for a moment or two then he asked, "You said that to the best of your knowledge, Jenny's husband knows nothing about our affair. Am I right in thinking that that's how you wish it to stay?" I just nodded.

I began to wonder, what good I had done coming here after all? It would seem that it was all over anyway. Suddenly I felt rather foolish and just wanted to get home to Harriet. I got up from the chair and walked towards the door. Then very quietly and as menacingly as I could, I said, "As I've already said, Simon means a great deal to me. If you ever go back on your word, I'll make sure you'll regret it."

"I won't," was all he said.

I stood outside the apartment holding onto the car door for a few seconds, before climbing in and driving off into the night ...thinking *still – I ought to 'ave thumped the twat if only once, for Simon!*

29

The following week was, at least for me, something of an anti-climax thank goodness. After the events of the last few weeks I was ready for the 'quiet life'. At work Simon was his usual rather bullish self: nothing out of the ordinary there then. Business was just about ticking over. "I have to go out and check up on a couple of rewiring jobs. One 'private', and one at that girl's school in Heswall. I'm rather looking forward to that one. Some o' them young lasses are right little crackers," he said with a leer: nothing out of the ordinary there then.

The chap who was buying my house was keen to get on with it, and I was keen to oblige. Harriet was coping in grand style with our pregnancy. No morning sickness. Well, not yet. No peculiar culinary requests, so far. So as they say, 'All quiet on the Western Front'.

This respite came to a sudden end, one morning about a week later. I had opened up the warehouse as usual and I had put the kettle on as usual, when his 'lordship' arrived moments later. It was obvious that he was in a highly excitable state. As is my way at times, I pretended not to notice.

"We should be suppin' champagne again this mornin' Laurence my old mate, not chuffin' tea. I come bearing tidings of great joy," he announced dramatically. I just stared at him.

"Come on, don't be a twat …ask me," Simon insisted.

Finally I let my face slip. I grinned and said, "Go on then…spill the beans." He paused for effect.

"Not far off old mate. Whilst it wasn't beans that I spilled, stage one has been successfully carried out." I had a good idea what he meant. I was hoping to be spared the gruesome details. Not a chance!"Last night Jenny took me in hand, if you get my drift. Having done the necessary, the seed of my loins was transferred to a suitable container: i.e. a plastic bottle. Jenny's goin' to drop it off at the clinic, on her way to work."

His face was a picture of happiness. Even though I cringed mentally at all the gruesome details, how could I not be delighted for him? I hugged him as I said, "Simon, that's fantastic."

"Thank you Laurence, but of course as Jenny's says, it's only the first step; the tricky bit's yet to come."

Just a few days after his inspection of the rewiring job at the girl's school, Simon brought more shock news. This time his mood was slightly more subdued. "We had a visit from the 'busies' last night. Guess what? They've traced the driver of the car." I didn't catch on immediately, so he continued, "The driver who hit me, it turns out that 'is girl friend goes to that school I visited the other day. She saw me in the wheelchair and apparently 'er conscience got the better of 'er. She admitted it to 'er parents, and they took 'er to the police-station. Seems she comes from a decent family, but she's been knockin' about with this lad who they consider a bit rough. It was him who was drivin'. Seems he had taken his brother's car without him knowin'. No licence ...and no insurance.'

Simon fell silent and I couldn't help but noticed that he didn't seem exactly ecstatic. I was about to say that it was good news, but thought better of it. Simon suddenly went on, "It'll go to court of course, as it should do. It's just that I'm not sure: you know, having to face him – he's only fifteen for Christ's sake."

It was then I realised that Simon was on the verge of tears. I'm ashamed to say it, but I felt embarrassed. In my eyes, he had always been, 'Big Strong Dependable Simon'.

"I'll stick the kettle on." Was the best I could offer.

We were both very quiet as we drank our tea, both of us very thoughtful. Eventually I broke the silence. "As you say, it's only right that it goes to court. These young kids have to realise the consequences of their actions. He could 'ave bloody well killed you."

"Instead of which ...I'm just committed to a life in this fuckin' thing," said Simon with a sigh. I wished the ground would open up and swallow me. But I had no cause to feel sorry for myself, so I said, "We'll all be there with you y' know. All the way, supporting you."

Simon looked up from his cup, sniffed, and said, "Yes, I know. Thanks old mate."

Jenny

30

When I arrived home from Bootle, Simon was already there. I could hear his wheelchair moving about. "That you Jen'? Late, aren't you?" he called. "Yes, sorry luv." Was all I said, as I entered the kitchen. Simon had his back to me.

Suddenly he spun the chair around, knocking a cup from the table. "Oh bollocks!" he cursed, as it smashed into several pieces. I didn't say a word as I reached into a cupboard for a small hand-brush. Just then, as I bent to sweep up the bits of pottery, my attention was drawn to Simon's face.

"Good heavens, what happened to your beard?" I asked incredulously. He just grinned inanely.

"I shaved it off. What d' ya' think?"

I just didn't know what to say or how to react. Unexpectedly, I felt I was about to burst into tears. I turned, and quickly walked into the bedroom.

As I had been driving home from Colin's earlier in the

evening, I had found it very difficult to reconcile myself to the fact, that I would probably never see him again. However what happened later that night only made my resolve all the stronger. When Simon came to bed I was just drifting off to sleep. He kissed me 'good-night', and said, "Sorry luv, I should 'ave asked you first", as he turned his head away. I don't know whether it was guilt or what but suddenly I felt very drawn to him. I put my arms around him, and started to gently kiss the back of his neck. I touched his clean-shaven face.

It wasn't a sexual touch. Well not at first, but Simon quickly made it so. Firmly he took my hand and put it between his legs. When I didn't respond, he placed it onto his soft cock. I knew instinctively what he had in mind. The *suitable receptacle* had been on his bedside cabinet since we had talked about trying for a baby. His hands began to tug at my nightie. "Take it off," he whispered.

Even as I did, my conscience was troubling me. Sex with two men in one night. What does that make me? A tart? A slag? *Stop it you stupid woman, before he suspects something.* I began to act like the 'good little wife' that Simon knew me to be.

I did what he wanted. I began to play with his soft little cock. I gently stroked it. My hand encircled it and plied it, and I put all my thoughts into making that 'thing' become hard. I was concentrating so much that I was hardly aware of his fingers probing inside me. Then suddenly I was. I don't know how I stopped myself from pulling away. This didn't feel right. After the passion of Colin this wasn't sex.

Then Simon was roughly pushing my head down towards that 'thing'. I had always made perfectly clear to him that doing that was something I would rather not do. But I had done it to Colin, hadn't I. Did I enjoy doing it to Colin? The answer had to be, yes. So, right then …I would do it for my husband. Like the 'good little wife' that I am, I allowed my head to be forced over 'it'. I took it into my mouth. It felt so strange. Colin's had been big and hard! This was small and soft. Like a marshmallow, I thought, rather bizarrely.

I felt the need to giggle, but thankfully I couldn't. However, I knew my duty. My head began to move up and down, as my lips and tongue sucked and licked. Then I thought I sensed a slight change. Simon was definitely becoming …what? Agitated? Worked-up? Again I became aware of his fingers. Whether by design or accident they found the 'magic-spot'.

Of course this helped, as I began to enjoy it. And yes, something was definitely happening to Simon. He was becoming extremely agitated. He was moaning with pleasure. I knew then that he was about to 'come'. I felt him reach for the container. Suddenly he pulled himself away from me, as he fumbled between his legs.

"Yes! Yes!" he shouted. "Got y', y' little bugger." I was stunned by his noisy reaction. Simon however, was absolutely jubilant. "We've done it luv …only bloody done it!" he whispered excitedly.

I didn't know how to respond, but Simon didn't seem to notice.

"Oh Jenny luv you've made it happen. We've got it

in the bottle. You'd better pop it in the fridge quick, before anything happens to it." I could hardly take in what had occurred. I managed to ask him whether he had put a lid on the container. "Of course I 'ave. We don't want the 'genie' getting out of the bottle, do we?"

I still felt stunned as I walked into the kitchen. I looked at the small brown plastic bottle. Is it possible, that a baby could come from what is in there? I thought, as I carefully placed it in the refrigerator. Of course, I would have to drop it off at the clinic in the morning. I sat down on a kitchen chair for a few moments deep in thought. When I got back into bed Simon was sound asleep. I couldn't help but sense his contentment, and regardless of any sense of loss that I had felt earlier in the evening regarding Colin, now that same contentment began to wash over me.

A few evenings later, Simon and I were presented with a tremendous shock. We had just finished our dinner when the front door bell rang. It was the two young police officers who had attended Simon's accident. "Good news, I hope," the young man announced, as they entered the hallway. I gestured that we go through to the lounge. They followed me and both took a seat.

"We've traced the driver of the car that knocked you down Mr Coleridge. Some young lad who took his brother's car without his permission," the young man continued. Both Simon and I were so shocked that neither of us reacted at first. The policewoman took her cue. "Naturally we shall be applying to the C.P.S." I looked at her in puzzlement. "The Crown Prosecution

Service," she explained.

She went on to say how they had received information from a fourteen-year old girl, who had been travelling in the car at the time of the accident. Apparently the boy, who was only fifteen, had been in trouble before, for so-called joy-riding. "Well this time, he's going to find himself in more trouble than he can handle. If I get my hands on him, he'll wish he were dead," I said emotionally.

I glanced at Simon, and was surprised to see that there was no similar reaction from him, but I didn't comment. I would ask him after the police officers had gone. If they sensed anything, they didn't mention it. No doubt they've seen all the different reactions before, I thought.

"Right, we'll say 'goodnight' then. We'll keep you posted about any further developments," said the policewoman, gesturing to her colleague that it was time to leave. I was still trying to take in the implications of the news as I said 'goodnight' and closed the door.

To say that the last few days have been eventful would be putting it mildly. What with finishing with Colin, Simon shaving off his beard – I still can't get used to it – and the impending court case. And now I've received another shock. Shirley, one of the girls that I work with at the pharmacy, told me about an argument that she'd had with a woman customer. Apparently the woman had taken antibiotic tablets that she'd purchased from the pharmacy. She said that she should have been advised that taking antibiotics could have serious consequences, regarding their effect on the birth-control pill. She wasn't advised, and now she was pregnant!

"Jenny, are you okay? You've gone as white as a ghost," Shirley exclaimed. All I could think of was the fact that I had done exactly the same thing, only a few days earlier. I too had taken antibiotics, and then I'd had sex with Colin. Oh my god, could he have made me pregnant already?

At lunchtime I changed my routine. Instead of my usual sandwich, I walked into town and ate in a small, quiet café. I needed to think. I had to work this out. Timing could be crucial. 'I must get things moving regarding the Invitro Fertilization. I simply had to get Simon's sperm implanted inside me …quickly!'

Laurie

31

Oh goody, it's that time of year again. The start of the football season; therefore my cup runneth over. "We're playing Celtic in a pre-season friendly on Saturday," announced Simon over coffee. "We'll 'ave to find out what the procedure is regarding this thing," he added, patting his wheelchair.

I would like to say that it was a pleasure, to be out with 'the lads' again. Try as hard as I might …and to be honest, I've never tried all that hard, I've never really felt like 'one of the lads'. We had arranged to meet up in the pub, aptly named, *The Ball*, close to Anfield: Liverpool's ground.

"Right lads, just a 'swift one', then we'll get off," instructed Simon, handing me a twenty-pound note. We weren't exactly mob-handed today. The 'terrible duo', Ronnie and Tony had made it, along with two more. Christ, what were they called? Jez' and Mick. Yes, that's it. Simon checked his watch, quickly drank his beer, and announced that it was time to head for the match. "Right lads, me 'n' Laurie will find a steward, to show us where the wheelchair entrance is. We'll meet up in 'ere after the match. Okay?" said Simon, showing his qualities of leadership again.

The others were already back in *The Ball* when Simon and I entered.

"Chuffin' nil-nil! Wor' a soddin' waste o' money that was," proclaimed Ronnie, beer running down his chin.

"It was a right load a shite," contributed Jez'.

"Shush," whispered Simon, putting a finger to his lips, as he struggled to control a giggle. He gestured surreptitiously, in the direction of a group of noisy Celtic supporters. These Scottish 'gentlemen' already looked somewhat the worse for drink. Simon looked at me knowingly. He drank the last of his coke and said, "Well Laurie old mate I don't know about you, but I'm ready to make tracks. Time to get home to the wife."

The 'lads' took the hint, and picked up their glasses in order to finish off their drinks. "We'll see y' in *The Feathers* tonight then," said Tony. *That's something to look forward to*, I thought blissfully.

By now Simon was heading in the direction of the pub door, when his wheelchair accidentally bumped into a rather large Celtic supporter. The first thing I heard was the smashing of a glass, as it hit the floor. The second thing I heard was, "You clumsy crippled bastard!" This was growled in a drunken, and very vociferous Scottish accent. Without really looking, the

Scotsman just lashed out, catching Simon a vicious blow to the side of his head. Simon was almost knocked from his wheelchair, and that's when all hell broke loose.

Now I'm not the bravest of men, but to say that this four-eyed twat saw red, is putting it mildly. Goggles or no goggles! It wasn't exactly a punch that I threw – more a flailing arm. I doubt very much that the Scotsman was even aware of it, but he was certainly aware of the chair that was brought down on the back of his head so skilfully by Ronnie. Then it was absolute mayhem. Tables, chairs, pint-pots, and bodies flew in all directions.

It was nearly seven o'clock, when we finally left the police station that evening. Fortunately for all of us the police eventually accepted our version of the events, and not without a certain amount of good humour. Simon and I then phoned home to explain to Jenny and Harriet that we'd be slightly late getting back. It also occurred to me that it might be prudent to give *The Feathers* a miss tonight!

I got a right 'ear 'ole bashing', as soon as I walked through the door.

"Just look at the state of you, y' silly beggar. What the hell do y' think you're doing, fighting at your age? And you could have broken your glasses." shouted Harriet angrily. I just stood there, feeling somewhat abashed. Eventually she calmed down long enough for me to explain. Suddenly I felt quiet exhausted.

Later, in bed, Harriet gently drew my rather sore head to her warm and fulsome bosom, and said, "Actually, to be truthful, I'm rather proud of you, 'Big man'. I know you were standing up for Simon. However, it's not exactly the right example to be setting to our child." I sensed her gently patting her belly, as she chided me. I just smiled to myself in the darkness.

I lay there for a while, running a mental replay of the fracas in the pub. My superbly executed Muhammad Ali-like right cross, which sent the burly Scot crashing to the floor, with his kilt up around his neck. Thank God he was wearing underpants. In truth this would be my flailing arm, which probably caught him on the shoulder. My memory of events may have been slightly blurred. However I did recall with clarity, his huge fist heading towards my face, and the timely intervention of Ronnie's use of the pub chair on the back of the giant's head. I also recollected the several tartan-clad gentlemen and jolly Scousers, who then joined in the rearrangement of the pub's furniture and glassware.

The irony is – I've always looked on the Scots as lovely people ... which of course they are.

Jenny

32

Was I being silly? Maybe, but I couldn't help but worry. The fact was that if the antibiotic tablets had affected the morning after pill, I could already be pregnant by Colin. Heaven knows what that would do to Simon. God knows what it would do to us. These thoughts, and many more, worried me sick as Simon and I waited in the I.V.F. clinic to talk to the consultant. I was extremely relieved when he said, "I see no reason to delay matters. Indeed the sooner we get on with things, the better. I will arrange for you to have a scan immediately."

The very mention of a scan set the alarm bells ringing. Oh my god, if I had conceived through Colin just a couple of nights ago, would anything show up in a scan? I was so naïve in these matters, that the very thought sent me into a blind panic. I looked at the consultant and said as convincingly as I could, "A scan? Do I really have to have a scan? I just hate the idea."

He regarded me with a puzzled look, "Why my dear? It's quite a normal procedure, purely a precautionary measure, nothing to concern yourself about. Anyway, we can discuss it in more detail prior to removing the eggs from your ovaries."

Over the next couple of days, at the very mention of removal of eggs, Simon would make some inane joke about omelettes, or scrambled eggs. I went to the I.V.F. clinic by myself. The removal of the eggs was quite straightforward. Simon had made quite a fuss, saying that he should accompany me. I made the excuse that he needed to be at work. At least if he wasn't there, I might get a chance to do something about the scan.

Three days later two embryos were transferred back into me. On this occasion Simon was adamant that he was going with me. "This is an 'us' thing Jen'," he said solemnly. The whole procedure was much easier than I had expected it to be. Far less traumatic than a visit to the dentist.

The one thing that eased my concern was the apparent confidence of the consultant regarding the odds of my becoming pregnant. "An excellent chance my dear, an excellent chance," he beamed. Little did he know that those odds might possibly be improved, by a certain Roman Catholic priest.

The I.V.F. scan had all been done so quickly, I had barely time to take it all in, but I was obviously relieved. Everything was now in place for me to have Simon's baby. And it was going to be Simon's.

A week later and I realised that my 'period' was late. I should have 'come on' yesterday. I bought a testing kit from the pharmacy, and as soon as I got home I used it. Blue! It was blue! Oh my god, I really was pregnant. I walked though into the lounge and opened the drinks cabinet. I reached for a bottle. Whiskey? Brandy? I'd no idea what it was... *No you stupid woman...you shouldn't drink when you're pregnant,* I muttered to myself. Pregnant! I started to laugh uncontrollably. I laughed until the tears began to run down my face. I went into the kitchen and put the kettle on. Ah, the good old cup of tea. That will do the trick. Should I tell Simon over dinner? Or should I wait until the doctor confirmed it? I decided to wait.

"Yes Mrs Coleridge, I can confirm that you are indeed pregnant. Congratulations." The consultant beamed at me, as I smiled and thanked him warmly. I suddenly felt relieved, and then I realised that I was genuinely pleased to be having a baby. Simon's baby! It had to be Simon's.

On the way home I purchased a bottle of champagne. I placed it in the middle of the dinner table. Simon arrived home, and went into the bathroom to freshen-up before dinner. I busied myself preparing the meal. Suddenly he wheeled himself into the kitchen, the bottle of champagne jammed between his legs. He looked quite serious. I looked at him in a non-committal sort of way, but I couldn't keep it up. A smile began to play over my lips. Simon could hardly contain himself. Holding the champagne aloft he quietly said, "Please tell me that this means what I think it does."

I just grinned widely and nodded.

He could hardly speak. "Oh Jenny luv, that's wonderful. Bloody wonderful. A baby! We're goin' to 'ave a baby. Come 'ere and give me a kiss."

I put my arms around him and kissed him warmly. This was going to be okay. Everything would be fine. From now on, it would be just Simon and me and the baby. No more thoughts about Colin. Who's Colin?

Laurie

33

They say that time flies when you're having fun. While over the next few weeks, that might have been true for me, I don't believe the same could be said for Harriet.

"Nine bloody months? Seems more like nine bloody years to me," she grumbled tetchily, one evening over dinner, and this was just three months into her pregnancy. "Just look at the state of me. I'm as big as a house-side already. Bloody men: you'd keep it in your pants if it was you that had to put up with this." She was rather large even at this relatively early stage.

"You look blooming," I cooed. "Perhaps it's twins," I added with a grin.

"Bugger off Laurence, it better not be," she countered, clearly not amused. Then with a worried look she asked, "Oh lord, you don't really think so, do you?"

From what Simon had told me in his daily reports – come to think of it, more like, hourly reports – Jenny was sailing through her first few weeks. "Chuffin' radiant old mate …chuffin' radiant!"

"Tell Simon from me – bollocks!" Harriet fumed, as we got into bed. "He's quite capable of taking himself to bloody training. You wipe his backside all bloody day. You're not going to do it in the evenings as well." True, I thought. It couldn't be denied. I was going to have to become more assertive with Simon. He had to realise that after working hours, my place was with Harriet.

"You would think that he would be happy to stay with his wife in the evening, instead of gadding about training, or whatever it is that he does," grumbled Harriet, pulling the duvet up to her chin.

"Bollocks! How nice. How ladylike," I said, grinning as I snuggled up beside my lovely gorgeous woman.

"Ladylike? Bloody ladylike? The last thing I feel is ladylike ...and I don't know what you think you're going to do with that 'thing', but you can forget it."

She pushed her hand none too gently, in the region of my groin. She said it with good humour though, and then added sweetly, "Go an' fetch me a bun or something, Laurence luv."

They also say, that time stands still for no man. Too bloody right! Things started to get a bit hectic.

"I've received a letter from the court. The trial starts on the 18th," announced Simon one morning over a cup of tea. He had a dig at me over that! "What no fuckin' coffee? F' Christ's sake, Laurie, I don't ask f' much," he growled bad-temperedly.

I was about to give him some of the same, but thought better of it. I simply said, "I'll bring some in tomorrow. So what about this court job then? Do y' want me to come with you, or should I stay here and take care of things?"

Simon looked suitably chastened. "Oh, I think I'll be okay. You keep things tickin' over here. From what I understand, it won't be a long job: just a couple of days. I understand the lad'll be pleadin' guilty" He paused for a few seconds, then said, "Sorry about jumping down y' throat over the coffee. It's just this business with the court case. I'll be glad when it's all over."

Simon however had a change of heart. "Jenny's just goin' t' go for the verdict on the last day. There's no sense in puttin' unnecessary strain on her. Seein' as we're a bit quiet at the moment, I thought perhaps you might go to court with me after all," he suggested rather pensively. "That's if you don't mind," he added quietly.

"Of course I'll go. You're my mate, and mates look out for each other, don't they?" I said, maybe a bit too effusively.

It really was a relief when the day of the court case finally arrived. The last few days at work, to say the least, had been a bit tense. What with Simon doing his version of pacing the floor in his wheelchair, and muttering, "I'll be soddin' glad when it's all over and done with."

The fact that business was rather slow only made

things worse.

"If I wasn't stuck in this bloody thing, perhaps I could get us more work," he grumbled. Also, his training regime had been put on the back burner. "I can't soddin' concentrate. I'll start again after the trial."

Even enquiries regarding Jenny's condition, or remarks about Harriet's ever increasing size, didn't seem to have the desired effect.   A cursory, "What?" had become a regular response. As we drove to the court he said for what seemed the hundredth time, "Christ I'll be bloody glad when it's all over."

Naturally we had speculated as to how the case would go. I, being rather ignorant in these matters, had been particularly curious as to what form the trial would take.

"Oh the whole 'bag o' mashin' old mate. Wigs and gowns. Just like on the telly," Simon said, rather smugly.

Indeed it was. It was also pretty obvious, that it was going to be short and sweet, if that's the right analogy, in such a serious case? One thing Simon did get wrong was his expectation of the defendant – the fifteen-year old lad, who was up before the court on the charge of 'causing injury by careless driving'. "I'll bet the little bastard's dressed t' the 'nines', in a fuckin' suit and tie, lookin' just like a fuckin' choirboy."

He wasn't. Clad in jeans and T-shirt, a less-caring little shit, it would be hard to imagine. He just sat there with a cocky smirk on his face throughout the entire proceedings. I felt like... What? Killing the little bastard!

I occasionally glanced at Simon to see how he was coping with everything. After all, it was his life, his disability, his and Jenny's future that these proceedings were all about, and about the future of a fifteen-year old lad, who hadn't enough self-control to stop himself from taking a car, and driving it such a way that he cripples someone for life.

The jury was sworn in. Rather a lengthy process. They looked your average mix – perhaps a couple more men than women – young, and not so young. One woman of Afro-Caribbean origin had a wonderful presence: big, buxom, and cheerful looking.

"They look okay," I whispered to Simon.

"Okay? How d' y' mean okay?" he asked grumpily. I just shrugged my shoulders. The lad was then asked if he pleaded guilty, or not guilty? He paused for a second or two, as though milking the moment.

"Guilty!" he eventually pronounced: still no hint of regret, still the arrogant smirk.

"If I could just get my hands on the little shit, I'd…" I spat out between clenched teeth. I took another sideways glance at Simon. He was showing no emotion. He just stared at the fifteen-year old boy.

No sooner had the jury taken their seats, than the judge announced, "I think this would be a suitable time to adjourn. We will break for lunch." He looked at his watch. "We will reconvene at one-thirty." Without further ado he rose and left the chamber: 'Left the chamber', just like on the telly.

Simon hardly touched his sandwich. He sipped his coffee. I ate my sandwich almost in silence. Simon continuously looked at his watch. Suddenly I found myself reaching out, and holding Simon's arm, I said with what I hoped was an encouraging smile, "Come on, it's twenty-five past. Let's go and get the little bastard."

I was pleased to see him smile back, even though it was a rather weak smile.

"All rise," instructed the court-usher. A hush fell, as the judge entered and took his seat. This was followed by loud coughing, and shuffling of feet. The first witness was called for the prosecution. This was the consultant who had been in charge of Simon's initial examination, and his programme of recovery. He spoke very concisely, and what he said would almost certainly have compelled any decent person to feel the utmost sympathy for Simon. Of course, Simon sitting there in his wheelchair only compounded this. Cross-examination bore no fruit for the defence.

Next to take the stand was the policeman who attended the accident. Although his evidence was brief, much was made of the fact that the young driver had not stopped at the scene of the accident. Nor had it been the first time he had taken a vehicle without the owner's consent.

Then the man who found Simon lying in the road took the stand. His evidence was particularly compelling. He stated that he feared Simon was dead, when he found him. He described the appalling injuries that Simon had suffered: again, no joy for the defence and the little bastard sat there, still smirking.

Simon just sat in his wheelchair, his face not giving a clue to how he was feeling. I knew only too well how I felt! I wanted to smash the evil little bastard. Suddenly, it was Simon who grabbed my arm. He squeezed gently and shook his head. He said nothing, but I'm sure he knew exactly what was going through my mind.

The schoolgirl was the next to give evidence. She barely looked twelve, never mind fourteen. Her school uniform and scrubbed face, free of any make-up, made sure of that. The prosecuting council made much of boy's influence over her, and of the fact that she was no longer seeing him. Everything she said simply compounded the boy's guilt.

"He doesn't stand a prayer," I whispered to Simon, behind my hand. It was obvious that the experience had been quite traumatic for the young girl, and the judge looked long and hard in a meaningful way at the defence council.

"No questions m' lud'," said the defence barrister, quietly.

I looked again at the young lad. Was the smirk now slightly less assured? Was he now looking a little less cocky? I glanced around the chamber. A woman, who I took to be his mother, wiped her eyes as she shed a silent tear.

At the point where the defence was expected to put their case, the boy's barrister asked to approach the bench. A brief discussion took place, and then the judge announced, "My learned colleague for the defence has informed me that he will not be calling any witnesses, but will sum up at the appropriate time."

Then glancing at his watch, he continued, "I feel this is a good time to halt the proceedings for today."

As Simon drove me home I tentatively asked, "Are you okay?"

He looked tired, just nodded, and said quietly, "Yes, I'll be fine."

"We could pop out later …for a swift one if you fancy it," I offered, rather stupidly thinking that a 'Stella' could be a panacea for Simon's state of mind.

"No thanks old mate, perhaps tomorrow. Hopefully, it should be all over by then." As we neared home Simon said, "Laurie. Thanks for comin'. See you in the mornin', eh?"

"Yes, see you in the morning. Goodnight Simon," I said, relieved to be home.

Harriet called, "Is that you Laurence?" as I entered the house. It really was good to be home. Good to hear Harriet's voice... Bloody great to know that I was going to be a dad, and one thing I was determined to make sure of, was that no child of mine would grow up to be a 'little shit' like the one in court today.

If the first day in court had been fairly predictable, then we were all in for a bit of a shock on the second.

Jenny had come along to support Simon on what we hoped would be the final day.

With hindsight I suppose Simon and I should have seen it coming. The prosecuting council summed up swiftly and succinctly. It was whilst the defence was attempting to make excuses for the 'nasty little shit', that Jenny suddenly rose to her feet and started yelling at the top of her voice.

I definitely heard, "If you don't stop bloody smirking …I'll wipe that grin from your bloody face …you evil little bastard." And something about, "Don't you care that you've ruined someone's life, you little swine?"

As the judge was hammering away with his gavel and calling for order, Jenny slumped back into her seat. Tears were streaming down her face. Simon, whose wheelchair was positioned just in front of Jenny, was trying to get to her even though it was virtually impossible.

I was trying to see if Jenny was alright, and at the same time trying to assure Simon that she was. Jenny, gradually regaining her composure, was trying calm Simon down.

The judge finally ceased banging his gavel, but naturally he had to make his little speech. "If there are any further unseemly outbursts, I shall clear the court."

Whether or not he realised Jenny's condition, he addressed the clerk and quietly said, "Get the young lady a glass of water."

Quite a palaver, but order was soon restored. I glanced across at the young lad, and I suddenly realised, that today the T-shirt had been replaced by a smart shirt and tie.

Also, I took no pleasure in noticing that the smirk had now been replaced by a far more serious and worried look.

The jury were out for less than two hours. GUILTY!

"Malcolm John Robinson, you have been found guilty of causing injury by careless driving. Throughout these proceedings you have shown no remorse for your actions, or for the tragic consequences of those actions. I shall also take into account your appalling record. Have you anything that you wish to say." The judge took a long meaningful look at the boy.

The lad simply looked at the floor and shook his head. The judge then continued in true judicial fashion, and gravely said, "I have no alternative but to give a custodial sentence and commit you to a youth detention centre for a period of at least five years. Take him down."

There was no cheering.

No great exultation.

I looked at the lad as he was led down the stairs to the cells, and to God knows what sort of future. Strangely, all the hate and anger were suddenly replaced by sadness.

I looked at Simon, and then at Jenny who had left her seat to put her arms around her husband.

I wasn't sure what was going through their minds. Then we all looked towards the boy's mother, who was being comforted by her elder son. She was dabbing a handkerchief to her eyes, but managing to maintain her dignity.

As we were leaving the court, she and Simon sought each other out.

They spoke simultaneously. "I'm so sorry Mr Coleridge. Mrs. Coleridge," the woman whispered.

"I'm sorry too," was all that Simon said.

The woman's older son was still supporting her, as he said, "I feel partly to blame. If I'd only hidden the keys, perhaps it wouldn't have happened. But then …the little sod would probably have hot-wired it anyway." With this he put his arm around his mother, and ushered her away.

While this was happening, I could sense Jenny inwardly struggling to keep control and Simon's relief that she did.

Simon and Jenny dropped me off at home, but declined my offer to come in for a cup of tea.

"No thanks old mate. I'll see you at work in the morning"

No point in making any suggestion of a 'celebratory drink' later on in *The Feathers*.

No celebration! No point!

Jenny

34

It wasn't so much a feeling of anti-climax after the trial, but a strange lack of satisfaction in the fact that justice had been done. I don't deny that I, personally, was glad that the boy was going to pay for his actions. Simon on the other hand, seemed loath even to talk about it. However, it had been decided that 'a night out' would do both of us good, so we arranged to go out for a meal with Laurence and Harriet.

Finding something nice to wear had become an issue. It wasn't so much a case of; does my bum look big, as does my *bump* look big in this? Simon glanced across the bedroom to where I was trying on my third choice of outfit, and with a smile said, "Sweetheart, you look wonderful."

I didn't feel wonderful. I really was starting to show quite a bit now, but when we entered the restaurant and I saw Harriet's condition, it was quite a shock. Considering that we had conceived within a short time of each other, she really was big. Naturally, I didn't say anything but Harriet, having noticed my reaction said, "I know ...horrendous isn't it. I feel like a bloody whale."

At least she was smiling as she said it.

We all simply made small-talk as we ate our food, and sipped our wine. "One glass won't hurt," Harriet and I insisted as 'the boys' reminded us of our maternal obligations.

Between mouthfuls Harriet and I discussed the pros and cons of breast-feeding. Much to the consternation of Simon, who reminded us that, "People are trying to eat here."

"I'll probably suffocate the poor little mite," Harriet said, looking down at her even larger than normal bosom.

"Any poor little mite of mine, will have to go looking for them," I said.

"I'll swap you any time Jenny," smiled Harriet.

No, thank you very much dear, I thought rather cattily, but of course I didn't say it. Simon and Laurence were in deep thoughtful conversation about a much more important issue – how would the 'REDS' do this season? Simon made his opinions clear. Laurence in the main just nodded in agreement. Simon also announced his intention of getting back into training.

"There's a novices' race in a few weeks that I'm going to enter."

Over dessert Laurence, to his credit, did manage to change the subject. "So, Simon, what about this fatherhood thing?" Simon looked askance at Laurence.

With a very sombre countenance Laurence reiterated, "Fatherhood! You know Simon …becoming a dad. Are you ready for it?" Harriet and I could see that Laurence was struggling to keep his face straight.

Very earnestly Simon eventually said, "Oh yes, of course. In fact I've already decided on a name for him. Kenny, Michael, Owen, Emlyn, Ian, Shankly Coleridge." I swear his face never changed as he spoke. Then as we all looked at him in horror, he burst out laughing.

"So it's going to be a boy is it?" I asked with a smile.

"Of course, what else?" Simon smiled back, and squeezed my hand.

The evening was just winding down nicely over coffee when, 'out of the blue', Simon said quietly, "I'm going to visit the lad." We all looked at him in shock. I was astounded.

"What?" I said slowly.

"The Robinson lad ...I'm going to see him." It was a statement and usually when Simon makes a statement, he sticks by it. Anyway, I decided this was not the time or place to discuss it.

I found sleep hard to come by that night. I lay deep in thought. I had hoped that after the trial, we would be able to put it behind us or at least be able to move on.

Now it seemed that Simon wasn't going to let that happen. Sometimes he could be so bloody selfish.

Bloody football!

Bloody training!

Our baby was going to be a boy!

Now he's going to open up a whole new can of worms, by visiting this lad in prison.

Whatever Simon bloody well wants!

What about what I want Simon? *What do I want?*

Do I want a boy or a girl?

Will I go back to work afterwards? NO! That's definite!

I shall be a proper mother.

I had managed to put Colin to back of my mind for the last few weeks. Now as I lay there, staring through the darkness at the ceiling, he was suddenly to the forefront of my thoughts. Colin, where are you now? Do you still think about me? I'm still thinking about you Colin. Big blond, gorgeous Colin. Big hard cock! I put a hand over my mouth to stifle a gasp, as Simon stirred in his sleep. A proper mother? Are you sure Jenny? These questions kept me awake for a long time.

Over breakfast Simon brought up the subject regarding his intention to enter his first wheelchair race.

"It's near Chester. Six weeks on Sunday. We could make a day of it if you like. That's if you feel up to it," he added quickly.

"Yes that would be nice. As you say, if I feel up to it," I said none too convincingly. I was struggling a bit with my feelings of guilt, about what I had been thinking of in bed last night.

"Are you okay?" asked Simon.

"Yes, fine. I'm just a bit worried about where you're going to do your training."

"Don't be worryin' about that luv', I'll be careful. I shall do it where it's quiet. Probably on the industrial-estate, or I might go over to Thurstaston Country Park."

We ate in silence for a few minutes. Then I remembered what Simon had said, about visiting the boy in prison. I knew that I had to approach the subject carefully.

"Simon …you know what you said about visiting that boy. Do you think it's such a good idea? I mean, won't it be difficult? Upsetting for you, I mean." I paused, not knowing what else to say.

Simon looked at me thoughtfully. "Yes luv', I've been giving it some thought. I might go and 'ave a word with his mother first, but my gut feeling is that I should go 'n' see 'im. It's just that I think …maybe the lad never really had much of a chance. Apparently, 'is dad ran off with another woman …so y' know..."

I decided to let the subject drop. Simon kissed me on the cheek and left for work. I sipped at the dregs of my tepid coffee, looked down at my swelling belly, patted it and said, "Right little one, time for us to be going too."

Laurie

35

The trial out of the way, both Simon and I, were able to concentrate our efforts on other things. Business began to pick up. We secured three or four small contracts that required bringing in a couple of agency electricians. I obviously felt easier in my mind when we had orders in place. You need security with a family on the way.

Simon also started bringing his racing wheelchair to work.

He had devised what he called a great training circuit, around the industrial estate. He dashed round it like a whirling dervish every lunchtime.

He was heartily cheered on by all the workers who sat around, eating their fish and chips, or burgers, alfresco. Not for us, any longer, such culinary delights. Oh no, now it was pasta or rice.

"What!" I'd protested. "It's you that's in training, not me. I want my chips."

"Ah, but you see old mate …you might not realise it

yet, but you do need to train. When you become a dad, you'll need all the energy you can find," Simon said with a grin.

The next month passed quite uneventfully. Simon had made no further mention of going to see the lad. Probably thought better of it, I mused.

Then one evening just before we 'shut up shop', he said out of the blue. "I went to see the lad's mother last night. We had a long chat, an' she agrees with me …about my going to see the lad. She'll need to set it up with the governor. I was wondering how you'd feel about going with me? I don't mean to actually go into see him. Just go over with me, and wait outside. He's in Risley, near Warrington."

I realised that this wasn't the usual confident Simon speaking. He sounded unsure of himself.

"Yes of course I will, if y' sure that's what y' want," I said, trying to reassure him.

It was arranged for the following week. We drove over after finishing early on the Friday afternoon. Neither of us had spoken more than a few words, throughout the entire journey. As we parked the car I asked him, "Are y' sure y' don't want me to come inside with y'?"

He just nodded his head, as he looked over towards the entrance of the custody centre. I helped him to get the wheelchair out of the car, and watched him as he went inside.

I was a little surprised how soon Simon returned. He was obviously angry and very upset. I didn't know what to say, so I stayed silent. I put the wheelchair back into the car. Still neither of us spoke. I couldn't bear the silence any longer and finally said, "Well?"

Simon gripped the steering wheel. I could see that he was seething. "The little bastard! The evil little bastard! D' y' know what he fuckin' said to me?" Without waiting for me to ask, he continued, "… *'Well fuck me, if it isn't the cripple',* that was the first thing he said. The *only* thing as it happens. One of the warders heard him, and carted 'im off before he could say anything else. Well fuck him! He can fuckin' rot as far as I'm concerned." Simon was close to tears.

Even as I said, "Yes you're right, let the little bastard rot," I realised it was the wrong thing to say. Simon wasn't just upset for himself.

I obviously wasn't thinking clearly, when I offered to drive back. "Laurence, the car's got *these*," he said patronisingly, as he patted the special hand controls. The journey home was even more subdued. Somehow I knew that it wasn't the end of the matter.

Thankfully, the next day being a Saturday, there was the joyous prospect of a day out with 'the lads' at Anfield ...Liverpool V Tottenham Hotspur ...Scousers versus Jolly Cockneys: and a surprisingly jolly lot they were too.

As we entered our favourite waterin'-hole for a pre-match pint, it was a relief to note that there wasn't a kilt in sight. Nor was there sight of a 'Pearly King', but there was certainly the sound of them. Talk about *The Ball ...m*ore like *The Old Vic'*, in 'Eastenders'. *Leave it* *aght, Fack orf, Shat it,* were just a few of the splendid examples of cockney dialect, which assailed our ears.

One of the 'Spur's' supporters, on seeing Simon's wheelchair, nudged his pal and said, "Oy, John, shift y' self. Let the gent cam froo wiv' 'is wheelchair." Magically, a passageway opened to the bar. The landlord of the pub had a wonderful look of horror on his face, as he recognized us.

"Oh, not you lot again, I thought I'd barred you."

"We come in peace mine host," said Simon, in placatory voice, at the same time holding both hands up.

Happily I can report, that there was no repeat of the mayhem that our previous visit had wrought. Indeed we enjoyed a very pleasant thirty minutes or so, in the company of some 'good lads' from the capital. The game itself was a bit of an anti-climax. A nil-nil draw.

"A right waste of soddin' money", was the general consensus as we made our way from the ground.

As we were about to part company, Ronnie said – *yes it was definitely Ronnie*, "A' you in *The Feathers* tonight Simon?" I inwardly cringed at the thought of Ronnie and the others, attempting to socialise with Simon and me if, as was a strong possibility, Harriet and Jenny were to accompany us to the pub, for the Saturday night Quiz.

Later that evening, it was every bit as bad as I'd feared.

"Question one. Who put Harriet in the club?" trumpeted Ronnie with a loud guffaw. Harriet gave him a look that could have killed, but he was far too thick skinned to notice.

As he started to speak again, Jenny quickly jumped in, "Don't even begin to ask question two," she spat icily. Even the insensitive Ronnie seemed to get the message. Without another word he slunk off to join the rest of 'the lads'.

"Bloody moron," I muttered grumpily.

We all sat quietly contemplating our drinks for a short while, then Simon came to the rescue. "Right, are we all going to Chester next Sunday then?" The two girls and I looked at each other, feigning puzzlement.

"Chester? What, to the zoo?" asked Harriet, with feigned innocence. "Don't you think it would make more sense to wait till the babies are born, and are old enough to enjoy the monkeys?" She, Jenny and I, were barely able to keep our faces straight. Not so, Simon.

"Oh very funny Harriet, very droll," he said. "No seriously …it would make a great day out. It's only a ten-kilometre race. I'll be finished for lunchtime. Then we could go into Chester or something. Don't forget you two, you'll be stuck in the house soon enough."

Even though he had said it 'tongue in cheek', both of the girls gave him a withering look. "I'll take that as a no then shall I?" said a rather chastened Simon.

36

The big day arrived. I knew that I had no choice in the matter.

"You'd better go with him, or you'll never hear the end of it," Harriet had said a couple of days earlier. "I imagine Jenny's going?" she added.

"I understand so."

"Well, if it looks like being a nice day, I suppose I could drag my heavily pregnant body, with its horrendously pendulous breasts along to cheer on he who must be obeyed." Harriet said it with good humour, but I knew that she was beginning to feel the effects of carrying our baby.

"Only if you really feel up to it Harriet. It's you that matters. Not him, or his bloody race."

As it turned out, it was to be a very eventful day. The sun shone, which of course was nice. Simon acquitted himself really very well, considering it was his first race. As a novice event, most of the competitors were also making their debuts. To be honest, if he hadn't had a number on his wheelchair, I doubt whether any of us would have recognized him. They all looked the same: skin-tight clothing and crash helmets. Simon has since told me that they are *racing* helmets, not crash helmets. The race was over a course set out in a country park. I think Simon said the race was a distance of about eight kilometres.

There was much preparation required. While the girls sat in quiet amusement, their faces feigning a suitable amount of interest, I busied myself getting Simon's racing wheelchair ready. Having climbed aboard, he made his way to the starting line, after Jenny had given him a 'good-luck' kiss. Harriet and I just settled for 'good luck'. Then suddenly they were 'off'.

Each time we thought we saw him approach, it was hearty shouts of, "Come on Simon," or, "Keep it going Simon...nearly there." Anyway, he finished in fourth place out of eighteen riders. This led to much backslapping, and words of congratulation.

"Well done luv," enthused Jenny.

"Yes well done Simon," added Harriet, and I. Naturally he was bubbling with excitement.

"Christ, it was bloody brilliant! Did you see me passing them? Christ you can't 'alf make these things shift," he said gleefully, slapping the carbon wheels of his racing wheelchair. You couldn't help but be caught up in his enthusiasm. It was good to see him so full of happiness. And yes, he did deserve it.

As we all felt that the weather was far too nice to be window-shopping in Chester city centre, it was agreed that a pub-lunch down by the river would be a much better option. Having found the ideal place we decided to eat outside. We found a table and ordered food and drinks. Harriet and Jenny were swapping some of their most intimate, and to be truthful, less savoury pregnancy experiences. Simon had for the moment, gone into a quiet reverie over his earlier marvellous effort. I sat quietly anticipating my meal. I had ordered gammon with egg and CHIPS!

Someone had left a newspaper on the bench. I picked it up, and started casually flipping through the pages. About midway through an article caught my eye. I turned back the page.

Whether or not I said anything, I'm not sure. Maybe I gasped. However, I was aware that they were all looking at me with puzzled expressions.

Without asking, Harriet took the paper from me and started looking at the article. To my horror she started to read it out loud. She read slowly and precisely:

CATHOLIC PRIEST RUNS OFF WITH DOCTOR'S WIFE.

Colin Johnston, a young catholic priest, has stunned his congregation in Sheffield by running off with local doctor's wife, Joan Babbage. She has left her husband of twenty-two years, and her two teenage children. The blond-haired priest apparently has something of a reputation. Being young and handsome, he had become increasingly popular with the ladies since his recent transfer from Bootle, near Liverpool. Dr Babbage says that he hopes it is just a 'mid-life crisis thing', and that his forty-three old wife will soon see the error of her ways."

Harriet slowly put down the paper. "So, what's so shocking about that Laurence? Transferred from Liverpool? Do you know him? Don't tell me you're a closet catholic," Harriet said, looking at me curiously.

As I stumbled over my words of denial, I was aware of Jenny's ashen face as she suddenly stood up from the table, and excused herself.

"I'm sorry I'll have to just nip to the toilet. I feel a bit sick."

Harriet got up with slightly more difficulty, took Jenny's hand and led her inside the pub.

I took a careful sideways glance at Simon.

Thank god he appeared totally unaware of Jenny's reaction to the newspaper's revelation, other than to say, "That's the first time she's done that. Can't be morning sickness in the afternoon …can it? Will you pop inside and see if everything's okay, please Laurence."

My god he called me Laurence! Mind you, it is Sunday.

Jenny was adamant that she was fine. "I suppose it's to be expected now," she said. Her colour had returned and she certainly looked alright.

Throughout the meal I couldn't look in her direction. I was worried that she would read something into my manner.

Simon and Harriet ate their food with gusto.

"Two t' feed!" announced Harriet.

"Looks like it could be three!" kidded Simon. Before Harriet could contradict this, Simon looked at me, then my plate, and said, "What's up old mate, not hungry?"

I'd hardly touched my meal. Not even the chips!

"No it's fine. I'm just a bit slow." I managed to eat most of the food, but didn't enjoy it at all. Jenny too, seemed to have lost her appetite. Thankfully the newspaper article seemed to be forgotten. By Simon and Harriet, that is!

As we walked over towards the car, I was acutely aware that Jenny had become very quiet. "Yes perhaps we'd better get off home. I must admit that I do feel a bit tired," she spoke to Simon, but looked at me rather oddly.

Tired? I thought. It's not tiredness lady. It's bloody guilt that troubling you.

Jenny

37

To say I was dumb struck is putting it mildly. When Harriet took the newspaper from Laurence, and started reading the article about Colin and the doctor's wife, I couldn't believe what I was hearing.

Why was Laurence drawn to that particular article?

Does he know something?

How could he?

My mind had been racing.

I did genuinely feel sick.

I don't know what I would have done if Harriet hadn't have been there.

The journey home from Chester seemed to take forever. The only person who didn't seem to notice anything untoward was Simon. Thankfully, he was still wrapped up in his race.

"Top three place next time ...that's my aim," he announced.

"Yes luv, of course," I said quietly, praying that he wouldn't ask me what I was so deep in thought about.

"You're quiet," said Simon, as we sat watching television later that evening. Well, Simon was watching television. I couldn't stop thinking about that had happened earlier that afternoon.

"I'm just tired," I lied. "I think I'll have a shower and an early night." I kissed him on the cheek, and walked through to the bedroom. I undressed and went into the shower cubicle. As the warm water cascaded over me, I glanced down at my 'bulge'. It had to be Simon's. Dear God it had to be! My mind was in turmoil.

Colin had said that he loved me. He had said that he had never met anyone like me. He had said that he was broken-hearted when I said we had to part. Now here he was running off with another woman. A forty-three year old woman! "You bastard Colin: *what a bastard!* How could you?" I cursed under my breath. The anger just spilled out of me. How could I have been so stupid, so bloody gullible? Suddenly, something that Simon would sometimes say, when he was angry with someone, came to me, "Tell him to, go forth and multiply." *Yes, Colin you do that ...you bastard,* I muttered angrily, as I grabbed a towel and roughly began to dry myself.

I lay there in bed, racking my brain. Cursing my stupidity, one second, worrying myself sick the next. What if Laurence did know something? But, how could he? Would he say anything to Simon? Dear god, it would kill him! When Simon came to bed, I pretended to be asleep. Could I find a way to put my mind at ease? Perhaps I could casually mention the newspaper article to Laurence, to see if there was any reaction. No, that would be madness. Just leave things alone.

It was a long time before I drifted off into an uneasy sleep.

Sometime later I awoke suddenly, shaking and sweating. Oh thank God! It had just been a dream – a horrible dream. A big black car, in a car park – dark, late at night: raining heavily, pouring down! Me, on the back seat of the car with my legs wide open and my clothes all torn: Laurence stripped from the waist down: his cock huge, and throbbing, his face a contorted mask of …what? Evil? Lust? And Simon and Colin banging on the car windows, screaming and shouting. 'Go on Laurence ...shag her. Go on. Go on, make 'er 'ave it.'

Simon said over breakfast, "Why don't you stay at home this morning? You look really shattered," "In fact, perhaps it's time you thought about finishing work altogether."

"No not just yet. Anyway I'm fine, really!" I said, trying to reassure him. I needed to get out of the house. I had to do something, to take my mind off Colin? No, I realised it wasn't Colin that was worrying me this time. It was my marriage. It was Simon, and our baby! Us as a family! I didn't want to lose that. *Please Laurence, if you do know something, please don't tell Simon.*

"Jenny. Jenny." Suddenly I realised that Simon was speaking. I looked up from my untouched toast.

"Sorry I was miles away," I stammered.

"I was just saying, I'm off to work. Are you sure

you're okay?"

I smiled weakly and said, "Yes luv, I'm fine. I'll see you this evening."

Thankfully the distraction of work did help, but later that evening, at home, the worries returned. So much so, that when the telephone rang later that evening, I nearly jumped out of my chair. I picked up the receiver. A woman's voice that sounded strangely familiar, said, "Could I speak to Mr Coleridge please." Probably a job for Simon and Laurence, I thought as I passed the phone to Simon.

He spoke in hushed tones, for some considerable time. Even though his comments were mostly, "Yes, or no," with the occasional, "Right, I see." I realised this wasn't a business call.

Eventually, he slowly put the telephone down. I looked at him curiously, as he wheeled his chair back across the room. "Who was that, some secret lady friend?" I said flippantly with a false smile.

He sat quietly for a moment. "No ...it was young Malcolm Robinson's mother. She wants me to go and see him again." He held his hand up as I began to protest. "No, hang on Jenny. Apparently his older brother has been talking to him. Trying to put him straight. His mother says he wants to see me. She says he needs to see me. It sounds as though he may've seen the light. I've told her that I'll think about it. I will go though. I'm just not sure when."

Laurie

38

My initial thought was, *You must be chuffin' crackers but you'll please y' self anyway,* but I settled for, "The little bastard could be just trying to set you up again you know. Why should he behave any differently now?"

Simon cut in, before I could vilify the 'little-shit' even further. "I'm doin' it for 'is mother, more than for 'im. Maybe he *has* changed y' know …maybe he's realised that 'e needs to get 'is act together. Anyway, I've decided that it's worth givin' it one more try."

To be truthful, I was quite relieved when Simon spoke about his decision to visit Malcolm Robinson again.

I had been more concerned that on arrival at work on that Monday morning, he might mention the newspaper article, and my particular show of interest in it, but thankfully not.

Of course, I should have known that next on the agenda would be, "Did you enjoy it yesterday? Good race wasn't it? Fourth! Not bad eh? I can't wait f' the next one." Good old Simon. Never fails! Me, me, me!

"Yes it was a good day out: nice weather, nice pub, good meal, and the girls seemed to have a good time. Pity Jenny felt a bit 'off it' towards the end," I said.

What the bloody hell am I doing? Askin' for trouble? I thought to myself.

"So come on then, are you going to tell me what that was all about yesterday?" Harriet asked over dinner that evening.

"What? Tell you about what?" I said, trying to look as innocent as possible.

"That newspaper article, the bit about the Catholic priest and the …what was it? Doctor's wife?" Harriet insisted.

"Oh that. Oh it was nothing really. Just the photo in the paper, for a second I thought I recognised him but I was mistaken," I lied.

I didn't like lying to Harriet.

I could have told her the truth.

So why didn't I? Loyalty to Simon? Yes of course.

Anyway, it was all-over between Jenny and that bastard, wasn't it? It just goes to show what a bastard that priest was. Still is!

He's split up another family now.

I had to change the subject. I told Harriet about Simon's decision to go over to the young offenders' institution again. I told her about his reasons, and about the fact that he had decided to go alone this time.

Harriet looked at me thoughtfully and said, "Well

you know Simon. He'll do things his way. Let's just hope he doesn't get hurt again."

Having washed the pots, I was just putting the last of them in the cupboard, when the phone rang. It was Simon. "Can I have a word with Harriet?" he said rather mysteriously. With a sigh and an effort Harriet dragged herself from the sofa, and with a puzzled look she took the receiver from me.

"Hello Simon." After listening for a moment or two she said, passing me the receiver, "Okay hang on, I'll put him back on,"

"Laurence," *usually a bad sign when he calls me Laurence,* "Old mate," *that's better,* "can you get out for an 'our? I need to talk to you." I would have asked if it could wait until the morning but he went on, "I won't keep you long. It is important. I'll pick you up a.s.a.p. Is that okay?" He did sound worried.

I looked across at Harriet and she just nodded and mouthed, "Yes, go."

As Simon's car reached the bottom of our road I asked, "Come on then, what's this all about?"

I was scared to death that it was something to do with Jenny and that bloody priest, but all he would say was, "Let's wait until we get t' the pub."

He drove straight past *The Feathers*. A few minutes later we pulled onto the car park of another pub.

A pub that we normally just drove past.

There were only two or three other cars parked. "This should do," said Simon, quietly.

Having got Simon's wheelchair positioned in a quiet

corner of the lounge, I went to the bar and ordered his 'half of Stella', and a half of bitter for myself. I sat down at the table rather apprehensively. I looked Simon directly in the eyes.

After several seconds he said, "I'm sorry about the mystery …and all the dramatics. T' be 'onest, I feel a bit stupid now."

He took a drink from his glass. "It's just that I felt the need t' ask you something." I tensed. *Here we go* I thought.

Then feeling slightly apprehensive I said, "Go on then, what's the problem?" Another long pause ensued.

"Laurie old mate …do you think that I've adapted pretty well? I mean to life, in this wheelchair?"

The relief was enormous but of course, I should have known. The mystery wasn't about Jenny, or anybody else. It was about Simon.

"Adapted to it? Of course you have. Like a bloody good'n. Why …what's brought this on?"

"Oh, I don't know. I suddenly found myself wondering …about how I would cope with a child and about how I would manage, as it grows up." This was a new Simon.

He looked vulnerable.

In all the years that I had known him, I had never seen him quite like this. I put down my glass, reached over and squeezed his arm.

"Simon, you'll make a great dad. Honestly, a great dad. And with Jenny to keep y'..." My words almost choked me.

"What? What were you goin' t' say?" he asked.

I cleared my throat in embarrassment. "I was about to say, with Jenny there to keep y' feet on the ground."

To my great relief he roared with laughter, then said, "D' you know Laurie, the strange thing is …sometimes I forget what it was even like, before I finished up in this thing."

He picked up his glass, drank the dregs and then said, "Right old mate, if you're ready, I'll get you back to that lovely wife of yours. And thanks. Just talking t' you has made me feel much better."

I packed Simon's wheelchair into the car and he started the engine. There was a slightly uncomfortable silence as we headed back home. I was relieved when Simon broke it, but somewhat taken aback when he said, "I've been meaning to tell you something f'r a while now. It reminded me when you were standing at the bar. It's not just the girls that's gettin' a belly. What do you weigh now?" I hadn't a clue, and said so. "Time you got your trainers out old mate. You're gettin' fat. Just because I'm not runnin', doesn't mean you can't."

"Eh, y' cheeky git, I am eating for two you know," I retorted with a grin.

Harriet was in bed when I got home. I climbed into bed carefully, trying not to disturb her. "Come on then, what was that all about?" she whispered in the darkness.

"Oh nothing much. He just wanted to tell me that I was getting fat."

"What!" she said incredulously.

I told her everything that Simon had said. She

listened in silence, and with understanding. A few moments passed, then she kissed me on the cheek and said, "He's right about one thing though. You are getting a bit chubby."

And, he was right about something else. Harriet *is* lovely!

The next morning as I finished the last of my sausage, egg and tomatoes, I asked her, "Were you serious last night? Do you really think I am gettin' fat?"

Harriet looked down at her swollen belly and said, "Well sweetheart, as someone who is something of an expert, I have to say, that you're not quite the svelte hard-muscled Adonis that thrilled me, the first time I laid eyes on you. In other words …yes, a little, and I've got an excuse. You haven't!"

Right! I thought. I'll dig my old trainers out. I'll show you!

I expressed my resolve to Simon later that day. "The first thing I'll do when I get in tonight is to check my weight. Then I'll dig out my joggin' gear." I saw Simon's raised eyebrows, and quickly continued, "Yes, yes alright, runnin' gear. Fat, eh! I'll bloody well show you."

Simon nodded in encouragement. "Pleased to 'ear it old mate. You'll need to be fit when you're playin' football with our two lads. Oh, and talkin' about lads, will you be able to manage without me on Thursday afternoon? I'm goin' over to see young Malcolm Robinson again."

Nearly twelve and a half stones! Bloody 'ell! I'm usually about eleven and a bit. I went into the bedroom and began to rummage around in my cupboard. Eventually I found a tatty tracksuit, and rather smelly pair of trainers. *Right, I'll get started: tomorrow!* I muttered to myself. Just then Harriet called to inform me that dinner was ready.

I was feeling pleasantly hungry, and looking forward to a good hot meal as I sat down at the table. Harriet placed my plate in front of me. Salad? Even though she smiled as she did it, her expression dared me to grumble.

"Right! Lovely: *salad,* just the job," I said returning her smile weakly.

Thursday afternoon found me wondering how Simon's visit to Risley was going. On Friday morning I got the answer.

"Much better old mate. I couldn't believe the change. I don't know who has said what, to 'im, but he's like a different kid. All that chuffin' cockiness was gone. He was so quiet and then, when he apologised – I mean really apologised – I'm sure 'e meant it. Then he did the weirdest thing. He went to his locker, and brought out these fluffy dice. D' you remember them? I hadn't seen any f' years. Apparently the lad found 'em in an old shoebox. Some of 'is dad's old stuff. Did I tell you …'is dad 'ad run off with another woman?"

I just shook my head, as Simon hesitated, before going on. "Anyway, these dice …they're not the really big ones, just small ones. He said that he sticks them on the interior mirror, when he nicks a car ...for good luck, so as he doesn't get caught by the 'busies'. Not that they actually did much good on the day when..."

Simon faltered for a second, and cleared his throat. "Anyway, then he said that he wanted me to have them, as 'e wasn't goin' t' need 'em anymore. He said I should put them on my racing wheelchair when I race. He called them his talisman. That surprised me a bit.

"Perhaps I'm being a bit unkind to the lad, but I didn't think he'd know what a talisman is. An' I must admit, just f' a second, I felt like tellin' 'im to stick 'em up 'is arse. They didn't stop 'im runnin' in to me, and putting me in a friggin' wheelchair did they? But anyway, I didn't. I just thanked 'im an' put them in my pocket. Then we talked about him, and his future. I didn't say it at the time but I'm thinkin' about offerin' 'im a job here when 'e gets out."

I can't deny that I was shocked. "Christ Simon, as you've just said, this is the lad who put you in that wheelchair."

It was almost as though he didn't hear me.

"An' it turns out that we 'ave something in common, young Malcolm and me. Music: I know, it's weird, I mean, I know bugger all about today's stuff. What is it? Is 'Rap' still in? 'R & B'? 'Hip-Hop'? Christ knows! Anyway, apparently he heard a C-D of his brother's, with 'T-Rex' on it; and he thinks it's great. Well ...I was well into Marc Bolan, an' 'T-Rex', when I was younger. Suddenly, he says, eh I've got an idea. When you're racin', why don't you 'ave your own tune? Like boxers do when they're goin' into the ring. Then he gets a bit carried away. He says that perhaps I should paint my racin' wheelchair white, an' call it 'White Swan' an' play, 'Ride a White Swan', on my ghetto blaster every time before I race. Chuffin' mad or what?"

He paused long enough to switch the kettle on, then said, "I don't think I'll bother with the paint job, but I might just play the music."

39

After a pretty uneventful weekend, the following Monday morning brought news of a most shocking event.

I had opened up the warehouse as I normally did, at about eight-thirty. I would expect Simon to arrive shortly after.

It was after ten o'clock when he came in. He looked dreadful. It was obvious that something had deeply upset him. Just for a moment I feared that it might be something to do with Jenny and the baby.

Slowly he gathered himself, and then he told me. "It's the young lad, Malcolm Robinson. He's dead!"

For a moment I struggled to take it in. "What? Dead? How?" Was all I could say.

"He's committed suicide. They found him in the showers." Simon sat slumped in his chair. "Why, f' Christ's sake, why? He seemed fine when I left 'im on Friday, but do you know the worst thing? I think he'd already decided to do it before I went to see 'im. That's why 'e gave me those fluffy dice; 'e knew he wasn't goin' to need them anymore."

I put the kettle on, as one does in the event of such news. I was lost for words. I handed Simon a mug of coffee, and waited for him to continue.

He'd taken a telephone call from the governor at Risley, at about eight o'clock this morning. They had found the lad on Sunday evening. Apparently he'd cut his wrists with a piece of sharpened metal.

What do you say? What can you say?

Eventually, I did speak.

"You should have stayed at home Simon. You look awful. How is Jenny?" Then I suddenly had a mental picture of the boy's mother. "Christ, his mother must be devastated." This brought Simon back from a state of deep thought.

"I shall have to go an' see her," he said, with a deep sigh. After a moment or two, I quietly repeated my question regarding Jenny.

"She's okay. It was Jenny who finally made me come in. She said it was better than just sittin' in the house. She's right of course." I could see that he was struggling to get a grip on his emotions. Then he quietly said, "Come on Laurie, we've work to do. We'd better get stuck in."

And stuck-in we got. Even so, I found it impossible to put the tragedy out of my mind. We closed up earlier than usual. As we walked to our cars, I suddenly felt the need to make sure he got home safely. I made a feeble excuse to follow him. "I haven't seen Jenny for a day or two. I won't stop long," I said. I'm sure Simon knew that at that moment, my main concern was him.

"I am okay y' know." But he knew that I would go with him anyway.

"He'll be alright now," Jenny assured me.

Simon was occupying himself with washing and changing for dinner. "But, thank you for seeing him home. And thanks again Laurence, for everything." She came over to where I was standing, and gently kissed me on the cheek. Now what was that all about? I wondered.

The next few weeks passed, with only the funeral of Malcolm Robinson to inject anything into an otherwise mundane period. I don't mean that to sound as cold as it perhaps does. After some thought Simon decided that he would go to the funeral, but only to stay in the background, and make sure that he didn't intrude on the family's private grief.

While Simon was attending the funeral, I found that I had no choice but to reappraise my feelings about the lad.

He was only fifteen after all, and apparently he had come to realise how his actions had affected the lives of others. At least that's what Simon believed.

Anyway, who was I to stand in judgement?

What did I know about the life of young Malcolm Robinson?

Christ what a waste!

I did actually start 'jogging' again. Yes okay, I know, *running*. Three times a week I followed Simon in his racing wheelchair, around his training circuit on the trading estate. Much to the amusement of the rest of the workers, taking their alfresco lunch breaks. Ribald shouts of, "Get goin' old cock, or he'll fuckin' knock y' down." Or along the lines of, "Watch y' lunch-boxes lads, 'ere comes Linford Christie."

I checked my weight after several sessions, and wasn't exactly comforted by the fact that I had only lost about four pounds.

Bloody wonderful! Looking in the mirror, I couldn't see a scrap of difference.

Still…early days, I thought.

Simon had entered his second race. It was taking place in Nottingham.

Before he could ask me, I made it clear that I would not be able to accompany him to any events, until sometime after Harriet had given birth.

"Of course old mate. Quite right! No, obviously you should be with her. It won't be long now will it?"

"Less than a month," I replied.

"Christ Laurie just think …you an' me …dads! I can 'ardly believe it."

I had to admit, now that it was so close, I was beginning to experience even more mixed feelings.

Worries about the actual birth.

Worries about whether I would make a good father.

Of course, I knew that Harriet would be a wonderful mother. And of course, I was very excited.

Will it be a boy or a girl?

Harriet had recently had a scan.

Just to make sure everything was okay but we both

agreed that we didn't want to know the baby's sex until it was born.

Well it won't be long now before we find out.

Jenny

40

The shock of the young boy's death, hung over Simon for some considerable time.

Initially the affect was awful.

He would sit in total silence, obviously deeply upset.

There were times in bed when I knew he was awake, thinking about it. I would do my best to comfort him.

Gradually he appeared to come to terms with things but when the day of the funeral arrived, naturally he became very agitated.

Because the boy had committed suicide, there had to be a post mortem, and of course this prolonged things. I did offer to accompany Simon to the funeral, even though I can't deny my emotions were somewhat different to his.

Of course it was a tragedy.

A young life wasted.

Heaven knows how his mother was coping? But this was still the person who had crippled my husband, and robbed us of a normal life.

Nor will I deny that I was relieved, when Simon, having thanked me for my support, suggested that, due to my rather advanced condition, I should stay at home.

I had by now taken up my option of maternity leave as I had begun to feel rather tired, working at the pharmacy. The staff had wished me well, and presented me with a lovely card, and several gifts for the baby.

It was a couple of weeks, before I began to sense the old Simon, returning to his usual self. "This race in Nottingham at the weekend luv: I'll make it the last one until after the baby's born. Are you sure you're alright about me goin'? I can give it a miss, if you'd rather."

I assured him that I'd be fine. The baby wasn't due for six weeks yet. Little was I to know just how much we were to regret this particular decision.

Saturday arrived.

Simon had set off a couple of hours earlier on his journey to Nottingham. I had just finished my lunch, and was about to sit down and put my feet up, when I suddenly felt the most awful pain in my stomach. It was so severe that I almost sank to my knees. I was also extremely frightened. "Dear God …not another miscarriage," I begged.

Naturally, being alone added to my plight.

Somehow I got myself partially seated on the sofa.

I made an effort to calm myself. The initial pain lessened until it became more like a dull ache. I knew that I must get help. My mobile phone was in my handbag, which was on the floor beside the sofa. Slowly I reached down. I took out the phone and called the hospital.

I had no idea what time it was. Only that it must be later in the evening. I was in a hospital bed, and Simon was holding my hand: holding it a little too tightly.

"Right, Mr and Mrs Coleridge, first, let me put your minds at rest." The doctor's voice sounded rather hazy, yet quite reassuring. "There has been no major trauma. The tests we have carried out show that. However we are going to keep Mrs. Coleridge in for a day or two under observation."

Before he could say anything more I asked nervously, "I haven't miscarried then?"

The doctor smiled warmly, and said, "Goodness gracious no. I'm sure that what occurred was caused simply by fatigue. A good night's sleep is what you need young lady. I will leave you in capable hands, and I will see you in the morning. Good night." With this he left the room.

"I'm so sorry luv. Christ I wish I'd never gone. I should 'ave known." Simon was still squeezing my hand.

I was so relieved by what the doctor had told us that any recriminations were far from my mind. "What time is it?" I asked.

"Just after eight," said Simon glancing at his watch. "Look sweetheart, I'll make myself scarce. Then you can try to get some sleep. I'll go an' see one of the nurses to ask if there's a room where I can stay for the night."

He couldn't reach to kiss my face from his wheelchair, so he kissed my hand instead. I started to protest.

"No, you go home, and get some sleep. I'll be fine."

"I've heard that once already today luv," he said, "and anyway, I don't want to go home. I'm goin' to be with you all the time now until you've had our baby. Now, not another word. Try to get some sleep."

As Simon started towards the door I said, "How did your race go?" He just smiled...

"Oh that! I had just started when a marshal waved me to stop. That's when I found out about you bein' in hospital. I just chucked everything into the car, and drove back like a bat out of hell. That's why I've still got this lot on. I'll get my bag, and find somewhere to change." I hadn't realised that he was still in his racing clothes – his sexy Lycra skin suit. Well that's what Simon calls it.

Two days later I was back home feeling much better, and much relieved.

Another two days later, and I managed to convince Simon that it would be better for both of us, if he was to go into work.

"Don't forget Harriet is due to have her baby soon. You'll need to sort things out with Laurence."

Simon looked very sceptical, but eventually agreed.

"Okay, I'll go in for a couple of hours or so but you must promise me that you'll phone at the slightest sign of a problem."

That evening over dinner, Simon explained the arrangements that he and Laurence had made to cover the business commitments, for the next few weeks. "I phoned a chap I know in the trade, Tommy Morrison. He's out of work at the moment and he's glad of the chance to earn a few quid. I've known him a long time, an' I feel pretty sure I can trust 'im. An' we've still got the two lads from the agency. Between us, me and Laurie will keep an eye on things. We'll muddle through the best we can. The main thing is you 'n' Harriet an' the babies."

At times I still found myself hardly able to believe that we were actually going to have a baby. A child of our own: Simon and I.

Yes Simon's child.

Not bloody Colin's!

Why do I keep doing this to myself? I wondered.

Happily over the next couple of weeks or so, there were no further scares. Simon was admittedly finding it difficult spending so much time at home, but regardless of whatever assurances I gave him to the contrary, he insisted that his place was with me.

I did however persuade him to pop into work, or do a training stint occasionally.

"Go and see Laurence. Find out how Harriet is. She's almost due now. Go on, get from under my feet for a bit," I chided him.

Laurie

41

The end of Harriet's pregnancy was nigh. I had been on the proverbial starting blocks for the last few days. Every time Harriet moved in what I construed as an odd way, or any time she made an odd sound, I would leap to attention. I was like a coiled spring. My every instinct, razor sharp.

"Laurence. Laurence wake up!" A voice somewhere in the distance was calling me. "Laurence for God's sake, wake up." Suddenly I *was* awake. Wide-awake! I shot bolt upright in bed.

"What? What is it?"

"Laurence just get out of bed calmly. Go to the telephone, phone the hospital for an ambulance, put on some clothes and then help me downstairs." Harriet spoke the words quietly and precisely, as though she was concerned that she might send me into a state of panic, or reduce me to jelly. I jumped out of bed, went to the phone, and made the call as calmly as I could. I came back into the bedroom and reached for my trousers. My trousers weren't where I had left them.

"My trousers! I can't find my trousers!"

"They're over the chair …there, where you left them, where you said you would easily find them. Now Laurence, calm down and get dressed. I'll do the panicking for both of us."

I can hardly remember the journey to hospital, or Harriet's grand entrance. However, I do remember the hours that I sat waiting and worrying.

Having got myself the first of several cups of bitter coffee from the dispenser, eventually I thought to look at my watch.

Twenty past three.

We had been here about …what, about an hour? That meant Harriet went into labour at about half past two-ish?

"Dear god please let everything be alright," I said quietly to myself. My mind turned to thoughts of Jenny and Simon. Until I had asked Simon how he had got on in his race at Nottingham, I had no idea about Jenny being rushed to hospital. Even though it was an obvious relief that there seemed to be no serious problem, it was never the less a worry. Of course I didn't mention any of this to Harriet. I glanced at my watch. Ten minutes to four.

A chap who had been sitting quietly across from me suddenly said, "Nearly as bad as taking the car for its M.O.T. in't it?" He opened another packet of cigarettes, and offered me one. I smiled my thanks, but declined. I asked him if he wanted coffee, but he too declined saying that he thought the coffee tasted worse than the fags. I took another look at my watch. Bloody hell! Five past four.

I must have been catnapping in the chair. Suddenly I was aware of a gentle voice. "Mr Breakspeare." A young nurse roused me. "...Mr Breakspeare, would you like to follow me. Your wife's given birth."

"Given birth? What do you mean, given birth? She can't have given birth already! I'm supposed to be with her. I said that I'd be with her." My mind was in a whirl, as I dutifully followed the young woman along the corridor.

"In here Mr Breakspeare ...and many congratulations."

I entered the room and crossed the floor to Harriet's side. She lay there looking absolutely shattered, but she smiled the most wonderfully radiant smile that I had ever seen and she was holding a baby! Holding a baby to her breast: I could hear the soft sound of it sucking hungrily.

"Hello luv, meet your daughter," Harriet greeted me. I opened my mouth but nothing came out.

My mouth was so dry but my eyes were moist, with tears of joy. I gently put my arms around Harriet and kissed her cheek. I looked at that tiny child, and couldn't comprehend that she was mine. My daughter! That tiny little thing was our daughter. "You look like the cat that's got the cream," said Harriet softly.

"Oh it's much better than that luv. Much better! Are you alright? You look whacked out. But gorgeous!" I quickly added.

"You might look whacked out if you'd been through what I've just been through," she said with a tired smile. Then she looked at our daughter and said, "I think it was worth it though, don't you?"

I was lost for words. It was just amazing to see them both …and to know that that they were my family.

"Aren't you going to ask what she weighs?" said Harriet. I just nodded inanely. "Almost nine pounds!" she announced with great pride.

"Blimey," I exclaimed.

Before I could say anything else, Harriet grinned and said, "Don't you dare make any crack about, like mother, like daughter." Just then the young nurse entered the room.

She smiled warmly and said, "Right Mr Breakspeare, it's time we let Mrs Breakspeare get some rest."

"Right …yes of course," I said. "I'll be right there. Could I just have another moment or two?" As the nurse left the room I took hold of Harriet's hand and said, "Did you hear what she called you? Mrs Breakspeare! It sounds good to me. What do you think?" I smiled at her, and left the room before she could answer.

I returned to the waiting area with yet another cup of coffee, and sat there deep in thought.

Mrs Breakspeare?

Did I just propose?

I suppose I did. Well, why not?

Will she accept? Married?

Me an' Harriet.

I knew then, that that was exactly what I wanted. The final brick would be in place. My happiness would be complete. Please Harriet, please say yes.

Names? During the weeks prior to the birth, we had discussed possible names for our forthcoming child. "If it's a boy, possibly Steven, or Peter," said Harriet.

"What about Simon?" I said, mischievously.

Harriet gave me a disdainful look, and just said, "No. And definitely not, Connor, Darren or Damien," she added, adamantly. Amongst my no, no's, for some inexplicable reason I mentioned Colin! "Why, what's wrong with Colin? I quite like Colin," said Harriet. She then added, "If it's a girl, perhaps, Emma or Jemma, or Sarah …or what about Laura? Laura! A bit like Laurie. Yes that sounds nice."

Harriet had a talent for getting her own way with that sort of thing. Anyway, unless it was a name that I really disliked, I would do my best to agree.

As I sat there in the waiting area I finished my coffee, and began to wonder what I should do now.

I glanced at my watch.

Just after nine-thirty.

Do I stay, or would it be alright if I go home for an hour or two, to snatch a bit of sleep?

To tell the truth, I was feeling pretty tired myself. After all, it had been a very stressful night. We men feel it too you know!

Just at that moment, the young nurse that I'd seen earlier, walked towards me. As she was wearing a topcoat, I assumed she had finished her shift and was going home. As she smiled a farewell, I sought her advice as to whether I should stay or not.

"Mrs Breakspeare and your little girl are fast asleep. Everything is fine. The best thing you can do is get off home and get some rest. You're going to need it," she said with a smile. Then just as she reached the exit she turned and said, "Oh by the way, I think your choice of name is lovely."

I must have looked strangely bemused, because she smiled and said, "Laura! Don't tell me you've forgotten already?"

"Your first was it? I can usually tell," asked the taxi driver, as he drove me home.

Naturally I told him all about it.

My daughter's name.

Her weight.

How absolutely gorgeous she was.

How brilliant I felt.

How I had asked Harriet to marry me.

Even though he was almost certainly bored to tears, because he had heard it all so many times before, he didn't let it show, bless him. He thanked me for the couple of quid tip that I gave him. How could I not feel generous?

First thing I did when I got home was put the kettle on. A decent cup of tea was my first consideration. Then I relaxed on the sofa and enjoyed the moment. Laura? Yes …I like the sound off that. Mrs Breakspeare? I mused. I liked the sound of that even more.

The time was getting on for eleven o'clock. I was past feeling tired. I had got my second wind, so I discounted any thoughts of going to bed. So, what to do now? I wondered. I ought t' pop down to work, just to check on things, and of course I have to tell Simon and Jenny the news. Not over the phone though, I want to see their faces when I tell them. I slipped my jacket back on, and then picked up the phone, and rang the maternity unit.

"Yes Mr Breakspeare, your wife and baby are fine... No, I'm sure that it will be quite alright if you can't get to see them for a couple of hours... Yes that's fine Mr Breakspeare, I'll pass your message on to Mrs Breakspeare."

I had a mental picture of a rather harassed hospital receptionist saying to herself, "Bloody men, they're more trouble than the mothers."

I called in at the warehouse, to have a quick chat with Tommy, the chap who was keeping an eye on things. Thankfully he had no problems to report. After briefly walking around trying to give the impression of someone who was on the ball, I told him my earth shattering good news. Heartiest congratulations ensued, followed by an assurance that neither Simon nor I needed to rush back.

The company was in safe hands.

That afternoon I drove over to Simon's.

Jenny answered the door. "Hello Laurence …come on in."

I followed her though into the lounge.

"I'll call Simon. He's just doing some accounts." Jenny busied herself making tea or coffee, and biscuits.

As I followed her into the kitchen, I was aware of the fact that she was now heavily pregnant, so I said, "Why don't you go an' sit down. I can do this."

She smiled at me and replied, "Thank you Laurence, that's very sweet, but honestly there's no need. I'm fine. Anyway, I'd rather keep moving. No need to fuss." She shooed me back to the lounge, and I heard her call to Simon. Moments later he entered the lounge.

"Afternoon Laurie my old mate, how's tricks?" Before I could tell him how marvellous tricks were, he asked, "Have you been down to the warehouse this morning? I 'aven't. I've been a bit busy with the old ledger. Bloody V.A.T. an' stuff."

I put his mind at rest, and waited my moment.

Jenny brought the drinks through, and sat down opposite me in an armchair. I couldn't help but notice how tired she looked. Seeing her like that even made me feel guilty. How different she looked from that night when... What? When we might have had sex...

"How is Harriet?" she asked suddenly, almost stealing my thunder.

"Well she is rather tired," I said casually, "but I suppose that's what giving birth to a baby does."

For a second or two neither of them seemed to comprehend. Then the penny dropped. Jenny struggled from her seat, and Simon almost fell out of his wheelchair as he manoeuvred it around the furniture.

"You old bugger! Why didn't you say? She's had the baby? You're a dad?" he gasped. I was overwhelmed in a cacophony of backslapping, and congratulations. All the anticipated questions ensued.

"I think it's probably going to be Laura. Almost nine pounds! Yes she's beautiful. Lots of hair, and chubby cheeks. Yes they're both fine. I'm going back to the hospital as soon as I leave here."

Simon wheeled his chair into the kitchen. I heard the sound of bottles rattling. He returned carrying a large bottle of champagne.

He gestured towards a cabinet and said, "Be a good chap, and pass some glasses would you please Laurence?"

As we sipped at our drinks I had, naturally, to recount most of the details again, mainly for Jenny's benefit. Eventually after glancing at my watch several times, I finally made my excuses, and prepared to leave. Just before I did I turned to Simon and said, "By the way Simon ...have you ever been anyone's best-man?"

"Best-man? No. Why?" Then, as he answered, he began to grin widely. Jenny also started to smile broadly in anticipation.

"Well, I've sort of asked Harriet to marry me. Fingers crossed, she'll say yes. So hopefully I'm going to need a best man."

42

A couple of days later whilst working in the warehouse, I took a telephone call from the hospital. It was Harriet. "Hi, it's me. Can you come and collect us?" I was busy putting an order together, but I instantly put my pen down.

I shouted a quick, "See you later," and dashed out to the car.

I was like a child at Christmas, as I drove quickly to the hospital. If anyone had spotted the inane grin on my face, they could have been forgiven for thinking that I was crackers!

Future wife – fingers crossed and daughter safely, and tenderly, seated in the car, I transported my precious cargo sedately home. I actually carried our daughter from the car and into the house. "Put the kettle on luv. It'll be nice to have a proper cup of tea," said Harriet with a sigh of contentment.

I gently placed our little girl in her mother's arms, and went into the kitchen. When I came back moments later, Harriet had put her into the carrycot, which she had placed on the sofa beside herself. They were both quietly sleeping. I sat opposite them, a cup of tea in my hands, looked at them and thanked God.

I was woken from my reverie by a sudden banshee-like wailing. "What? What's the matter?" I said, feeling rather worried.

"She wants her tea, don't you sweetheart," cooed Harriet as she unbuttoned her blouse.

Later that evening we took our baby daughter upstairs, and tenderly placed her in the cot, which was in the specially prepared bedroom, complete with a baby alarm system. As I switched it on, seeing the concern on my face, Harriet smiled sympathetically. "She will be alright you know."

But for all her assurances, all the time we were talking, I had one ear to the door and we did have a lot to talk about. "We can't keep on calling her 'our little girl', or 'our baby'," said Harriet. So we each considered various names, and then agreed that it *was* to be Laura. There was of course one other important issue, that hadn't been far from the forefront of my mind, since I first mentioned it. Marriage!

"It can wait, if you're too tired," I suggested.

"No, I'm fine. So, do I take it that that was a proposal the other day?" Harriet asked, in a disapproving tone, and yet, with a hint of a smile.

I tried to appear suitably abashed, and then rather dramatically going down on one knee in time-honoured fashion, trying hard to keep my face straight, I said, "Dearest Harriet, would you please make me the happiest of men, and accept my hand in marriage?"

The expression on her face was a vision to behold.

"Are you sure your name isn't Shakespeare? After a speech like that I think you might just be related."

For the next hour we talked it over. Thankfully it became evident that Harriet was just as keen as I was to get married. But whereas I laid down no pre-conditions, Harriet made several. "I would rather have a quiet wedding: even possibly at a registry office or at a hotel or something, not in a church Laurence."

"Oh …why's that then?" I asked.

"Well, I've always thought it rather hypocritical, getting married in church, if like me you're not really religious, and perhaps just Jenny and Simon there. What do you think?"

Then she fell silent for a moment or two as I said, "What about our parents?"

All through our time together, there had been little mention of our parents. Harriet's mum and dad were separated. My mother and father never married. He disappeared soon after she became pregnant. I've never seen him. Strange to think, that I wouldn't know my own father even if I saw him.

Harriet visited her mum quite often at her home in Widnes. Her father lived somewhere in Runcorn. She hadn't seen him for about three years. "I haven't a clue whether he's with anybody or not," she said sadly.

I found myself suddenly feeling rather guilty regarding my own mother. Throughout the bad times with my ex-wife, I had often used mum's shoulder to cry on but after that bloody slapper Molly had buggered off with her guitar playin' twat, I gradually stopped seeing mum. Now I feel ashamed, and full of remorse. That is going to change. After all, she's a grandmother now ...and she has a right to know.

We continued to discuss our wedding plans, and the christening of Laura. Because Jenny and Simon were such close friends, they were pivotal to those plans. We decided to wait to get married, until after Jenny had her baby. Then when things were settled, we could all get together and have a chat, about our wedding and about christenings.

"I wonder, do you think that they might fancy a double christening?" Harriet said. "Would you fancy the idea?" she added quickly.

I thought about it for a few seconds. "Do you know luv, I think that's a smashin' idea – except of course, you did say that you weren't religious, and christenings do take place in church."

Harriet sighed and paused, "Yes I know, but I think it's something that you have t' let a child make its own mind up about, when it's old enough. At least if the child's been christened you know that you've done your bit to give it a proper start. Do you know what I mean?" I nodded that I did.

Then Harriet stretched her arms aloft, and signalled her desire for bed with a yawn. So a pleasantly tired mum and dad slowly climbed the stairs.

Tired wasn't actually the word that sprang to mind. More like, knackered! And yet, I didn't sleep much that night. I passed the time listening to Harriet's gentle breathing, and getting out of bed every half-hour or so, to go into our baby's room to check that all was well. And then of course, just as I was drifting off to sleep, our daughter decided that she was hungry.

How can such a tiny thing make such a tremendous amount of noise?

I wearily brought Laura through to our bed.

Her half-asleep mother was propped up by a pillow, with her milk-laden breasts exposed to give sustenance to our lovely, but very noisy little girl.

Jenny

43

Laurence was naturally bursting for us to see their baby. We agreed that it would be best if they came over to us, due to my advanced condition. Only two weeks to go now thank the lord. We had decided that a 'Chinese' would be a good idea.

"Save you havin' to prepare anythin' luv," was Simon's considerate opinion.

Even though I had done my best throughout my pregnancy to take care of my appearance, I suddenly felt very drab and frumpy, when I saw Harriet.

She looked wonderful! She had obviously made an effort. Of course her radiance was accentuated by the fact that the last time I saw her, she had been as big as a whale.

Laurence spent much of the evening grinning like the proverbial Cheshire Cat, and fussing over the baby, who was absolutely gorgeous. Simon insisted on getting the camcorder out. "For posterity," he said. Simon and I naturally had to hold baby Laura for a few moments. After we had enjoyed a leisurely meal, Laurence announced that he would clear the table, and wash the pots. "Second nature to me now," he said with a smile. Simon offered to 'dry'.

While the 'boys' were busy in the kitchen, Harriet and I chatted about babies. She did her best to put my mind at ease regarding my own impending delivery and of course, once again, we discussed the pros and cons of breast-feeding.

"One girl at the pharmacy told me hers had finished up like spaniel's ear-holes but another said that her husband said hers looked even better afterwards." I said, trying my best to sound positive.

As though on cue, the baby began to cry.

"She must have heard us," said Harriet as she picked up the tiny bundle from its carrycot. "Will it be alright if I feed her while Simon's out of the room?" I just nodded in agreement. I have to admit, there was a strange curiosity within me, and it wasn't just about the breast-feeding procedure.

I suddenly realised, that I actually wanted to see if Harriet's breasts really were that large. My god they were enormous! And the way the child suckled on them! I can't deny some feelings of envy.

These feelings had been with me throughout the evening. I envied Harriet the fact that she had had her baby.

I still had to go through it all.

I envied the way she looked.

Absolutely marvellous, just days after giving birth! I doubted very much that I would look anything like as good. But as I struggled not to stare at those huge breasts I rather cattily thought, that's one thing I don't envy you.

Or, I should say, two things.

I don't know whether Simon considered his timing just right or not but he came back into the lounge just as Harriet was moving baby Laura from one breast to the other. With his usual diplomacy he said loudly, "By god, she's got something there to get stuck into."

"Simon, don't be so crude," I scolded him.

He just sat there grinning, as he countered. "Oh come on Jen' I've seen a pair of boobs before. Anyway it is rather fascinating to watch such a little mite enjoying itself so much."

I think Harriet was relieved that Laurence had gone to the toilet, and had missed Simon's bawdy frankness.

I was starting to feel tired, and had reached the stage where I was willing them to go when Simon cheerfully said, "What about this wedding then?"

Laurence looked taken aback.

Harriet looked surprised.

I glared at Simon as if to say, big-mouth! "What? 'ave I said something wrong? Oh bloody 'ell, you 'ave asked 'er 'aven't you?"

There was an awkward silence for a few moments, then Harriet smiled at Simon and said, "Yes Simon, Laurence has asked me …and I'm happy to say that I have accepted."

Any tension that there had been was instantly replaced by smiles and words of congratulation. Harriet explained that they had decided to wait for a few weeks until things were a little more settled.

Smiling at me, she said, "I know that Laurence has asked Simon to be his best man. I was hoping that you might consider being my...well not bridesmaid, but perhaps matron of honour." I said that I would be delighted.

Harriet realising how tired I had become, insisted that it was, time they went. "We'll talk more about it, later, in a few weeks' time. Laurence luv, will you get my coat please?"

In bed that night bad memories returned to trouble me. How could I have been so stupid? So selfish! Me an adulteress!

What a fool I had been, believing everything that Colin had told me. I bet I wasn't the first woman that he been with. Now the conniving sod had run off with another woman. And Laurence! I can't believe that I had tried to seduce Laurence. He's a lovely bloke, but I never fancied him. And yet, I stood naked before him, Simon's best friend and partner. But no more: from now on I would be the perfect wife and mother.

Later that week Simon drove me to the hospital for another scan.

"Just precautionary Mrs Coleridge," the doctor said, attempting to assure me, but a few hours later, things had changed. I could see by the concerned faces of the doctor and nurse that something was wrong.

Quietly spoken words did nothing to allay my fear.

Eventually the doctor turned to Simon and me. He spoke slowly and precisely.

"Mrs Coleridge, I am going to admit you immediately to the maternity ward. There has been a change in the baby's position. I have reached the conclusion that a normal birth could be somewhat difficult. Therefore I have to recommend a caesarean section be performed."

Even though his manner had been totally professional and calming, I was still utterly stunned.

I just looked at him and then at Simon. Simon also had a look of shock on his face.

For a few seconds nobody said a word.

Finally the doctor placed his hand gently on my arm and said, "There is absolutely nothing to be concerned about my dear. It is a routine procedure. We carry out caesarean procedures nearly every day. The main thing is your welfare, and the safe delivery of your child."

Twenty minutes later I was in a hospital bed. And I was frightened!

It didn't matter what Simon, or the doctor, or the nurse, or anyone said, I was frightened.

What would a caesarean entail? …Would I be at risk any more than with a normal birth? Would the baby be okay? …And would I be scarred: horribly scarred?"

All these thoughts, and more, ran through my mind …worrying me: frightening me.

"I'm going to take you down to theatre now Jenny," the hospital orderly gave me a warm smile. I could see that Simon was doing his best to be brave. He knew that now was the time that he would have to let go of my hand.

I smiled reassuringly and kissed his cheek. "It will

all be over soon…and then we'll have our baby." I was fighting to hold the tears at bay and just about managed to say, "Love you," as the bed was pushed from the ward.

Through a seemingly endless mist I gradually regained consciousness.

Who were these people?

Where was I?

What was happening?

"Wake up Jenny. Wake up dear."

A hazy female voice entered my head.

Then, slowly, I did wake up.

I looked to one side of the bed to see my Simon sitting in a wheelchair. Why is he in a wheelchair? I wondered. But then of course, I remembered.

"Simon. Are you alright?"

"Am I alright? It's you that's got to be alright you daft thing," he said, smiling. As he spoke these strange words, my thoughts gradually became clearer. I was having a baby. But something felt strange about my body. About my insides! I suddenly felt panic.

"The baby! What's happened to the baby?" I gasped.

The nurse was holding my hand tightly. "Your baby is fine Jenny. Everything is fine. Just stay calm dear. Let me adjust your pillows for you, and then I'll leave you for a little while. Your husband wants to be the one to give you the news." She gave us both a warm smile as she left.

Simon positioned his chair as close to the bed as possible. He took my hand and with a beaming smile he said, "Congratulations Mrs Coleridge, you have produced a wonderful son and heir." A boy! I could hardly take it in.

I just looked at my husband and smiled weakly. "Where is he? Where's our baby?" Suddenly the panic returned.

"He's fine. Don't worry luv. I've seen him and he's going to be fine." The words, 'going to be fine', made me worry even more.

Simon quick to see this, added, "He's fine Jenny. He's in the delivery room. They've just put him in an incubator for a while."

He spoke quietly and slowly in an attempt to calm me. "Apparently he's just a bit tired. The doctor said that they were just making sure that he was okay – just giving him a little support for a while."

None of this made me feel any better.

In fact my concern for my baby got worse.

I must have become sufficiently agitated for Simon to call for a nurse.

As she handed me a tablet and glass of water, I was only vaguely aware of her words, "This will help you to sleep for a while Mrs Coleridge."

When I awoke I was aware that it was night-time, or at the very least, evening.

Simon was dozing in his chair. I pressed the alarm button. After a couple of minutes, a rather officious ward sister appeared at my bedside. "Ah, Mrs Coleridge, back with us I see."

At the sound of her voice Simon jumped in his chair. Rubbing his eyes he said, "Hello luv. I was just 'avin' five minutes. Right, I think it's high time you saw your son …don't you?"

He looked apprehensively towards the rather intimidating sister, and said, "That's if that's alright?"

Intimidating or not, the sister smiled and simply said, "Of course."

I was gently helped into a wheelchair, and Simon and I were ushered along the corridor to see our son. Being in the wheelchair it suddenly hit me. This is what it's like for Simon almost all of the time.

"Come on luv, I'll race you," he grinned. We entered a room full sound, the sound of babies crying. Not all of them, just those who were hungry, or in need of having their nappies changed. Simon pushed his chair quickly into position. "Well here he is, Mrs Coleridge …meet your son."

I looked at the small form in the incubator.

Could that tiny little bundle be our baby? It looked so little. And because he was wrapped up all I could see were his tiny fingers and chubby face.

He was so still.

Momentarily I wondered whether he was actually breathing. I looked at Simon. He was grinning from ear to ear. Tears began to well in my eyes. Simon was quickly by my side.

"Eh come on now luv, this is supposed to be a happy time. We're a family now. You, me, and our little boy."

A little boy! I wiped my eyes, smiled and said, "Yes and we shall have to put our thinking caps on, and come up with a name for him." We spent a few more moments looking at that tiny, little 'thing', before going back to the ward.

It was my mixed emotions that puzzled me. As I looked into the incubator, I found it difficult to come to terms that the baby lying there had come from inside me but, even so, I was so disappointed when I was told that I wouldn't be able to hold him for a little while yet.

Back in bed, I suddenly realised how tired Simon looked. "It's time you went home and got some sleep Simon. Will you be alright on your own?" I asked him tenderly.

"Don't worry about me. I'll be fine. You get some rest …and I'll see you in the morning." He began preparing to leave. All of a sudden I was aware of the fact that I hadn't asked that time old question, "What did he weigh?"

"Six pounds, three ounces," Simon smiled proudly. "I think the three ounces make up his 'willy'." Typical Simon!

Then, as he began to push his chair towards the door, he turned and said, "Tell you what is a bit strange though. I know you couldn't see him properly because he was so wrapped up …his hair is really blond!"

Laurie

44

Only a few days after the birth of our daughter, Harriet was quite adamant that I should return to work. I somewhat reluctantly agreed. Like any other father I believed my little girl to be best in the world, and of course I wanted to spend every moment with her, but as Harriet reminded me, Daddy had to earn some pennies.

We had put Laura to bed, and were just about to relax in front of the telly, when there was a loud knocking at the front door. I dashed to open it before some dozy sod woke our baby.

Simon sat there – in his wheelchair – with a grin as wide as the Mersey tunnel.

He was in a highly excited state.

Just as he was about to burst into words I put my finger to my lips, and 'shushed' him and pointed upstairs. Then as quietly as possible I manoeuvred his wheelchair into the lounge.

It was pretty obvious what he was about to say, but Harriet just said, "Go on then, tell us."

"I've just left Jenny at the hospital. I'm pleased to announce, that I'm the proud father of a bouncing baby boy." The sheer joy in his face was an absolute delight.

We sat listening to Simon's account of the events of the last few hours and, bless him, he didn't miss a single detail. Because he was driving, we just had the one glass of champagne. Just as well really. That was just about all that was in the bottle.

It was almost eleven o'clock before he had left and Harriet and I lay in bed chatting quietly. We reiterated our plans for the wedding and the christening.

As she kissed me 'goodnight' Harriet said, "I'm so happy Laurence. Sometimes I get scared because I'm so happy – scared that something will spoil it all. I love you and our little girl so much."

I kissed her gently on the cheek, and reassured her that nothing was going to spoil anything for us. Little did I know what was on the horizon.

Simon phoned me at the warehouse the next morning, just checking! I put his mind at rest and told him to concentrate on Jenny and his son. I busied myself with paperwork and checking up on jobs being carried out by the two lads from the agency. At lunchtime I shut up shop, and then made an executive decision. Well two decisions actually. Should I start jogging again? Will it be a chip-butty or salad sandwich for lunch? Decision one: yes I will start jogging again, tomorrow! Decision two: chip-butty today, salad tomorrow!

At home that evening, Harriet finished feeding Laura and then gently placed her in her cot. I had done the pots and had switched on the T.V. to watch the 'news'. Harriet sat beside me on the sofa and snuggled up. That's when it happened! In truth I was not paying that much attention to the television, until I heard Harriet gasp. Then I heard the newsreader's voice,

"Dr Babbage and Father Colin Johnston have both been fatally wounded. A shotgun has been recovered at the scene. Dr Babbage left a note, saying that he could not condemn his two teenage sons to a life without their mother. It is believed that his forty-three year old wife was having an affair with the thirty-two year old catholic priest. The cottage in Derbyshire is now cordoned off, whilst the police make further investigations. An inquest will take place within the next few days. And now, the weather."

It was a few seconds later when Harriet suddenly said, "That's the same case that you read about in the newspaper …at the pub by the river …when we all went to Chester."

She paused for a second, a puzzled look on her face. Then she went on, "The priest who was shot was called Colin. Strange, that you're so adamant about not liking Colin as a possible name if we'd had a boy."

I tried to bluff it out.

"Don't be silly. It's just a coincidence."

Harriet knows me too well.

"Come on Laurence. I can tell you're trying to keep something from me." She looked me straight in the eyes.

I couldn't do the same.

Should I break my oath of silence to Jenny?

Or should I be deceitful to the woman I wished to

marry?

It really was no contest. So I told Harriet everything. Well, nearly everything. About how I'd seen Jenny: with this blond haired man, how I'd traced him and warned him off. How I'd confronted Jenny.

To say that Harriet was gob-smacked is putting it mildly.

She was too shocked to speak, so I quickly continued. "Harriet …Simon knows nothing about this. God knows what it would do to him if he found out. It would almost certainly finish them as a couple. Please don't say anything Harriet. Jenny swears it was just a moment of madness …and I believe her. I'm begging you. I honestly don't think Simon could cope."

Harriet sat quietly saying nothing for several minutes. Then she asked me a number of pertinent questions, and finally agreed to say nothing to Simon.

"Or to Jenny," I begged.

"Alright Laurence, I won't say anything, but I must say that my impression of Jenny has been badly affected. How could she do such a thing, after everything that's happened to Simon? I'm not sure I still fancy the idea of a double christening now."

Harriet was very quiet for the rest of that evening.

She was obviously very shocked by what I had told her. Heaven only knows how much worse that shock would have been, had I told her about Jenny drunken attempt to seduce me.

Deception or not, that was something that I simply couldn't risk telling her.

Neither of us slept well that night.

The next morning the car wouldn't start. Flat battery? *Fuck knows*, I thought grumpily. I climbed out and tried my trusted old habit of a swift kick to one of the tyres. It had often worked with the old Focus.

No joy!

Fortunately a neighbour came to the rescue with a set of jump-leads. "I'll give you a jump," he offered. *Oh, no you fuckin' won't,* I mused under my breath. Bloody 'ell, that's twice I'd used the F-word in less than a couple of minutes. Not like me at all. Not a good example for a new dad!

I hadn't been at work many minutes, when Simon banged on the roller-door. "Mornin' old mate. How's tricks? I'm not stoppin', just called to 'ave a word with Tommy. We'll 'ave to let 'im go now that you're back at the 'elm. Is that the kettle I c'n 'ear boilin'? ...I'm gaggin' f'r a drink."

"I'll bet y' haven't had any breakfast this mornin', have y'?" I asked.

"No, I'll get something at the hospital. Ask Tommy to come in will y'. Sooner I get this over with the better."

Tommy took his impending departure with good grace. The extra hundred quid that Simon bunged him doubtless eased the blow.

Simon left for the hospital with my orders to offer Jenny, mine and Harriet's heartiest congratulations. "Tell her we'll be up to see her this evening."

Lunchtime arrived and, as I had vowed, it was to be four laps of the trading estate.

I was aware of the odd isolated shout of encouragement or jeer of derision, although I jogged largely unobserved, as it wasn't the sort of weather to tempt many to sit outdoors to eat their fish and chips.

Lucky sods, I could just eat some, I thought, as I gasped for breath but I knew that if I wanted to lose weight, and get fit …and run the HILL all the way to the top, I had no choice other than to 'bite the bullet'. After all, a man has to do what a man has to do!

Quite suddenly after only two laps, I gasped, "Ah, sod it …that *will* have t' do." I slowed to a stop outside our warehouse. "I'll do the other two tomorrow."

I went inside to enjoy my salad sandwich.

That evening, Harriet and I drove to the hospital to see Jenny and their new arrival. Simon was cradling his son in his arms, as we entered the private ward. His grin was possibly even wider than before.

Harriet and I kissed Jenny on the cheek, and made all the customary sounds of congratulation. I could sense that this was a real effort for Harriet. My revelation of the previous night was still troubling her deeply. Then we both turned our attention to the baby.

Our immediate reaction was not exactly what a new mum and dad might expect.

The only thing that I could see was this shock of extremely blond hair.

The significance of this hit me like a hammer! I must have gasped or gulped or something: Simon looked surprised. As I had my back to Jenny I couldn't see her face.

Later, Harriet told me that she was sure that Jenny drained of colour. Harriet hid her reaction much better than I did. Before Simon could speak I quickly gathered my wits, and threw my arms around him. I did everything but kiss him.

"Oh Simon …Jenny, he's gorgeous. Look Harriet, isn't he just absolutely gorgeous." Harriet looked at me as though to say, *steady on, don't go over the top.*

Her arms reached towards Simon as she instinctively said, "Can I hold him for a few moments." Simon reluctantly allowed Harriet to ease the baby from his lap, and to her maternal bosom.

The small bundle had been surprisingly quiet for about half an hour. Then he let rip! "He wants his tea," said Jenny, reaching out for the tiny bundle of noise.

"Now it's up to you. You can stay, or whatever. I'm breast-feeding him, you see."

Before either Harriet or I could say anything to the contrary, Simon chimed up, "Of course they'll stay. It's not as though Laurie 'as never seen a pair of boobs before. Is it old mate? Just ask 'im about Corfu."

I could not look in the direction of Jenny. I just looked at the floor as I thought, *Simon, if only you knew how many times I fantasised over Jenny's breasts.*

If he knew that not only had I seen them, but that I'd seen everything else as well.

Seen her totally naked! God help me if he, or Harriet, ever found out.

I also knew that eventually I would be drawn to look at Jenny feeding her child. Would her breasts still be the beautiful shape that I seen and lusted over? In a strange way it was a relief that I couldn't actually see them. One was still concealed within her 'nightie'. The other was completely covered by the shimmering blond head of her son.

Jenny

45

Time passes so quickly. Our son Daniel is nearly five weeks old: Daniel Alexander to be precise, after much debate, and admittedly a few cross words – I wasn't having our son named after any footballer (even if he might one day play for Liverpool F.C) – Simon and I finally reached an agreement. Alexander is Simon's dad's name. He has been very supportive since Simon's accident. On at least two occasions he has sent financial help so I suggested that it would be a nice gesture to name our son after him.

Daniel has put on almost two pounds. He is absolutely wonderful and now sleeping through until about seven each morning. I had to put him on the bottle a few days ago. My milk dried up and, truth be told, I don't miss the sore nipples ...and thank goodness, his hair is going darker. When I first saw how blond he was I nearly died. I was dreading Laurence seeing him.

Thankfully he didn't say anything, although I do

wonder whether he has told Harriet about my affair with Colin.

She has seemed a little distant since Daniel's birth. This was compounded when she asked me if I would be too disappointed, if she decided not to have a maid of honour after all.

Thankfully, as I said, Daniel's hair is definitely getting darker. Apparently this happens quite often so, hopefully, my indiscretion will be allowed to fade into the mists of time.

Of course the news of Colin's death was a terrible shock. I knew nothing of it until a couple of days after leaving the hospital. Thank goodness Simon was out when I saw it on the television.

When the newsreader made the announcement, I remember shouting 'Oh my God', out loud. The report went on to say that, apparently, Dr Babbage had traced his wife Joan, and the Roman Catholic priest Father Colin Johnston, to a cottage in Derbyshire. The doctor had first shot the priest in the back of the head, wounding him fatally as he tried to escape. He had then turned the gun on himself.

At the inquest, the coroner ruled that Dr Babbage had killed Father Johnston, while the balance of his mind was disturbed, and had then committed suicide.

Naturally my immediate reaction was one of utter disbelief. For several days afterwards I found myself creating a mental image. I could see Colin from behind. He was running. I could see the back of his head with that mane of wonderful blond hair, but it isn't just blond, it's also streaked with bright crimson as the blood spurts out.

It is only with the passing of time that I have realised that, in a strange and rather cold way, Colin's death released me from any lingering attraction towards him. That makes me seem such heartless bitch, I know!

I am now doing something that I haven't done for months. I'm standing naked in front of the full-length mirror in our bedroom and I have to say that I'm quite pleased with what I see. I was really worried about any scarring after the caesarean birth, but it's already healing up nicely. My belly is reasonably flat, and my legs – which I've always been rather proud of – look as good as ever, and my breasts? ...well, considering what they've been through this last few weeks, they don't look too bad at all. Perhaps a few little stretch marks, but all in all Jenny old girl, you look pretty good for a wife and mother.

I'm actually in the process of getting ready for Harriet and Laurence's wedding. They are due to get married in about two hours time.

It's just going to be a quiet Registry office 'do'!

I must say I'm a bit surprised. I would have thought that Harriet would have wanted the 'Full Monty': the white dress and all the trimmings but apparently not.

Now what to wear? It looks as though the weather is going to be fine, so what's it to be, trouser suit or mini skirt?

Better make it the trouser suit – mustn't go flashing my legs, and upstaging the bride.

Simon has bought a new suit. It's the first time I've seen him in a suit for ages.

He says it will come in handy for the christening as well. Oh yes, and something amazing happened a few nights ago. We decided to have an early night.

Right from the time that I'd conceived, we had shown no inclination to try to have what you might call, real sex. Since the accident I had harboured strong doubts about full sex in the future.

Well hopefully not anymore!

At first we just started kissing.

Then it became rather more passionate.

Simon was very insistent that I help him take his pyjamas off, and that I should take everything off as well. Then he was all over me like a rash. I reciprocated …and do you know what? He got an erection! I mean a proper erection. Well what's a girl to do?

We had the best sex since the accident.

I know …Colin!

But, I do have to try to forget about Colin.

Colin was a mistake: a shocking mistake.

Well anyway, things are looking up now.

No more mistakes!

My god, look at the time!

Simon, who is nursing Daniel until the babysitter arrives, has just shouted, "Look sharp, or we'll be late." Just a bit of 'lippie' and we'll be off.

Laurie

46

Well there's no doubt about it. The last few months, to say the least, have been very eventful.

Talk about ups and downs.

I am now a married man.

I'm also the proud father of our daughter Laura.

She's almost six months old now. She's absolutely gorgeous. The poor little soul is already teething, and don't we just know it!

Is there going to be a happy ending to our story? I honestly don't know. God willing, it won't end for a long time yet.

As for Harriet and me, I'm as confident as it is possible to be that we'll have a long and happy marriage. No doubt there'll be times when we have to work at it – and work at it we will, for the sake of Laura, and any other children that we may have.

We do intend to have a least one more.

I pray that they will be blessed with long life and

happiness

As long as Jenny only takes her knickers off for Simon, then I'm sure they will be happy too.

A couple of days ago it was my birthday. Thirty-bloody-eight!

Harriet bought me a pair of really good running shoes. I'm trying them out right now.

Yes, right now!

I'm out running our old six-mile circuit.

Not joggin', but runnin', as Simon has occasionally reminded me. So I hope you'll understand if I get a bit breathless now and again.

Harriet also bought me a St. Christopher, which she has insisted that I wear whenever I go out running.

She has also instructed me that I mustn't go running in the dark.

Nor must I run on the lane where Simon had his accident.

Simon has got his talisman: his fluffy-dice. Now I've got mine. I can just feel the St. Christopher moving against my chest with each stride and, nowadays, I actually quite enjoy running, in that masochistic way that we sportsmen do.

The wedding went really well. Just a quiet 'do' as Harriet had wished for. There were just the four of us. Harriet and me, Jenny and Simon. We hummed 'n' ah'd whether or not to take Laura, but finally decided against it and asked a neighbour to baby sit.

I thought a registry office service would be rather

formal, but not a bit of it. The chap that carried it out was smashing. He put us all at ease.

Then we went for a meal at our favourite Italian restaurant. I ordered chicken pasta al a crème with chips.

Simon chimed up, "Eh old mate, no chips f' you. Don't forget, you're in trainin'." Harriet bless her, quickly intervened on my behalf, "Now, now Simon, if my husband wants chips on his wedding day, then chips he shall have."

Champagne was declined, so it was white wine for the 'ladies', and Italian lager for Simon and me. "Three quid f'r 'alf a pint ...a' bet the bloody Mafia own this place," grumbled Simon.

We were all pleasantly replete by about five o'clock, so we went back to Jenny and Simon's for coffee and liqueurs. It was then that Simon came up with his big surprise.

"Me and Jenny 'ave been talkin' Laurence ...and we both agree that it's time we offered you a partnership in the business."

I know that both Harriet and I sat there totally stunned. However, before either of us could say a word Simon carried on. "I can see it's a bit of a surprise, but please Laurence, we both really want you to accept. You've been brilliant right from start with the company, but particularly since my accident and please let me add, this is not a weddin' present. It's purely on merit. It's no more than you deserve old mate."

I started to protest, but Simon was having none of it.

Well ...how could I refuse?

After all, he *had* called me Laurence. Nor can I deny a certain smug satisfaction, when I look at the new sign above the warehouse:

COLERIDGE & BREAKSPEARE Electrical Specialists.

That night Harriet and I celebrated with what I can only describe as fantastic sex.

You'll have to excuse me for a few seconds while I get my breath back a bit.

I'm just over halfway now.

It's the prospect of the HILL that is my main concern, but just like Sylvester Stalone running up those steps in the film 'Rocky'(or was it ' Rocky 2'?) – I'm determined to do it this time.

Simon says that he'll be waiting at the top.

One stipulation to the partnership that Simon made was that I get a new car. "Something more in keeping with the company image old mate," he said.

Not easy for someone on my salary and with my commitments. "I'll sort it. Call it a wedding present," said Simon. So now I'm the proud owner of a nearly-new 'Mondeo'. It's lovely ...and I haven't had to kick-start it once!

Oh, and I mustn't forget, Simon had his first wheelchair-race win.

We all went over to Manchester to watch him. He beat fourteen other riders. Naturally he was over the moon. "Must 'ave been the fluffy-dice," he said with a wry smile.

If the wedding was slightly low key, then the double christening most definitely wasn't. After the usual formality of the church proceedings we all went to *The Feathers* for a buffet, which the landlady Melanie put on free of charge. "It's the least I can do f' you two lovely lads, after all the custom you've given me over the years," she said, demonstrating her best pose, as she flashed her cavernous cleavage for the benefit of Simon and myself.

It really was a memorable day.

In church, Laura really exercised her lungs. She screamed her displeasure the whole time the vicar held her over the font.

Daniel, on the other hand, hardly made a sound.

One of the nicest things about the day was seeing our parents again.

Simon's mum 'n' dad came over from France. It was the first time they'd seen their grandchild.

Jenny's parents made the relatively short journey from Southport.

My mum behaved just like you would expect any grandma' to do. Naturally her granddaughter Laura simply just had to be the star of the show and mum and I 'ave promised that we will start seeing each other on a regular basis.

It was particularly nice seeing Harriet's parents together. Apparently her dad had contacted her mother and offered a lift. Harriet and I learned later that neither of them were in a relationship, and had agreed to meet up again. "Nothing definite mind," said her mum, when she got Harriet to one side, but you never know.

I'm not far from the HILL now ...about another five minutes.

Whew! It's bloody hard-going, but I know I'm goin' better than I've ever done before. I've lost nearly two stones in weight. I'm nearly down to ten and a half stones now.

Just got to keep it going ...it's just that bloody hill!

Sod the bloody hill. I'll worry about it when I get there ...*about a mile and a half to go.*

Where was I? Oh yes, the christening. The buffet that Melanie put on was excellent. Naturally 'the lads' made sure that they didn't go unnoticed. The usual lascivious comments regarding Melanie's vital statistics abounded.

Ronnie and Tony had been pre-warned by me, via Harriet, about making any spurious mention of names such as Juliet, Portia or any other Shakespearian female characters.

She needn't have worried in the least.

The warning left them looking utterly bemused.

All in all it was a smashing day.

The HILL is fast approaching. BEEP, BEEEP – there goes Simon, blowing his horn.

Nothing new then, I think with a forced smile.

He's waving encouragement, and shouting, "Come on you old bastard, dig in ...keep it going."

Now that is a novelty!

Simon giving encouragement to someone other than himself but, to be fair to him, if anything positive has come out of his accident, it's the way he has ...what?

Grown up, I suppose. He's said as much himself. "D' y' know Laurie old mate, in some ways, the accident has made me look at life differently. I think in some strange way it 'as been the makin' of me. Oh f' sure I sometimes wish I wasn't stuck in this thing, but generally speaking I feel more content than ever: a gorgeous wife, a lovely son, good friends and a budding racing career. Who knows, maybe I'll make it to the Paraplegic Games one day: all in all, not a bad life. What more could a man ask for?"

What more indeed Simon.

Yes, there's no doubt about it. The last few months had shaped the lives of Jenny and Simon, and Harriet and me.

I've just hit the bottom of the HILL so I hope you'll bear with me for a few minutes.

Whew! This is so bloody hard but I know I'm goin' to do it.

Agh! Christ, nearly there.

Keep goin' y' old sod.

Just keep chuffin' goin'.

Simon is parked at the top. I can see his hand waving. He's shouting.

I can't hear what, but he's shouting.

Jesus Christ I can hardly breathe ...*almost bloody there*.

Slap, slap go my new running shoes.

Smooth running!

I must remember to throw my arms in the air, just like Sylvester Stallone did at the top of all those steps.

My bloody lungs are bursting!

But I'm grinning because I'm going to beat the HILL!

Arms going up...

...NOW!

THE END
Maybe not!

ACKNOWLEDGEMENTS

Brian Clarke, author of " Whose Life is it Anyway ? ", for his gift of inspiration some thirty years ago; the lovely and very helpful ladies at Rotherham Central Library. (I'm afraid I don't know their names.); to Norman Roddis. (Chairman of the Rotherham Wheelchair Users Group); to Kim Landsell, LLB (Hons), for legal advice.

Thank you to Bromakin wheelchairs. Thank you to Cyclone wheelchairs. Thank you to the British Sports Foundation. A big thank you to Denise Harding at Creating Excellence for her patience. Another thank you to wheelchair racer extraordinaire Dame Tanni Grey-Thompson. Thanks also to the staff at Rotherham General Hospital Maternity Unit. Last, but not least, many thanks to Gaile and Mai at UPP for their invaluable help and patience.